John Laycock, like the lothario Peter Holmes, is a proud Yorkshireman. But that is where the similarity ends. John, for all his working life, was an electrical engineer, his only professional writing being that of technical specifications and letters (the things we used as written communications before the advent of e-mails and texts). John is a family man with four children and two grandsons. His first novel, *The White Storks*, was self-published in e-form and is available on Amazon. *The Lothario* is his first novel to be published in print.

John Laycock

THE LOTHARIO

A Man on the Make

AUSTIN MACAULEY PUBLISHERS™

LONDON * CAMBRIDGE * NEW YORK * SHARJAH

A CIP catalogue record for this title is available from the British Library.

ISBN 9781788239141 (Paperback)
ISBN 9781398419230 (ePub e-book)

www.austinmacauley.com

First Published (2021)
Austin Macauley Publishers Ltd.
25 Canada Square
Canary Wharf
London
E14 5LQ

Thanks to my wife, Dorothy, for her support (I shall always wear it) and patience, particularly when I go missing for hours either writing or watching sports on TV.

Everybody possesses imagination, but not everyone uses it.

An 'andsome young man from t'White Rose,
T'London 'e ups 'n 'e goes,
'E learns all about sex,
'N 'ow much money it mex,
So 'e travels 'n reaps what 'e sows.

Chapter 1

He lay on his Desert Island beach re-reading his favourite book, Ian Fleming's *Moonraker,* and listening to his favourite record, Derek and the Dominoes' 'Layla'.

His favourite object, his travel kettle, was secreted in his hotel room awaiting service.

It wasn't really a desert island beach, but it was a beach, not just any beach, but his favourite beach in the whole world, and he'd visited a good few.

The fine golden sand ran for 200 yards in both directions from where he lay under an umbrella on a comfortable sun lounger.

The beach ran the length of a small, almost circular cove the entrance of which was protected by a sand bar which did a fine job of eliminating the intrusion of large waves.

He removed his headphones for the sound of Clapton's strident guitar riff to be replaced by the gentle lapping of the sea on the gradual gradient of the beach.

He reached for the Pina Colada that sat waiting on the table at his right hand.

It wasn't just any Pina Colada, it was the best ever Pina Colada, prepared with the perfect blend of pineapple juice, cream of coconut, Mount Gay Rum (the most essential ingredient) and crushed ice by William, the seasoned bartender of the Beach Hut Bar.

The appearance of the Pina Colada told him the time was past midday as William had been requested to make the delivery immediately after he'd sounded the bell advising Happy Hour had begun as it did daily at noon.

Condensation had already formed on the outside of the glass as he lifted it and sipped through the articulated straw. It was up to William's usual high standard.

The beach was a public beach but it was the domain of the Palm Court Beach Hotel whose staff kept it in pristine condition.

The Palm Court Beach Hotel was and is a family-run hotel which sits between the beach and the south coast main highway in Hastings, Barbados.

He was a regular visitor.

He'd been there five days.

Five days of perfect weather, clear blue skies and a daily temperature as high as 28°C with low humidity.

He'd managed to enhance his tan without burning, he looked fit and well, and that he was.

It was a Wednesday and there was a race meeting at the Garrison Savanah, home of the Barbados Turf Club.

It was in close proximity to the hotel.

It had become a ritual, if his visit coincided with a meeting, then it was a must for him to attend.

He made to leave, noisily he drew the last of the Pina colada from the glass, stowed his book, tablet, earphones and towel in his beach bag and strolled toward the hotel access stairs adjacent to the beach bar veranda.

He kicked the hot sand with his toes in an attempt to avoid the searing heat burning the soles of his feet, it didn't work, he strode on.

He cut a handsome figure, a tanned and honed body, broad shoulders and narrow hips.

The amply filled "Budgie smuggler" Speedo swimming trunks presented another attraction for the fairer sex, which most did not fail to notice.

Of the several people on and around the beach, only one pair of Prada sunglasses covered eyes followed him.

The eyes were blue, set in a round fair-skinned face, not pretty, not beautiful, but neither plain nor ugly, nondescript is what best described her, she lounged in a wicker chair on the beach bar veranda wearing a flowered one-piece swimsuit, a matching large brimmed hat and beach sandals. Her figure was, as generous advertising would describe, full, not fat or portly, but full, she sighed as he disappeared from sight.

The man that had just left the beach, the man that she'd just lusted after, was Peter (Pete) Holmes, although at that moment in time, she didn't know that.

Pete Holmes had entered Barbados on his genuine British passport but would leave using one of the other two fraudulent ones that he had bought at some considerable expense.

His genuine passport listed him as being born on 22nd July 1980, a 35-year-old, in Leeds, Yorkshire, although no one would ever guess with his sanitized accent. The coloured photograph did not do his rugged, handsome features justice but he regarded this as an asset. He welcomed anonymity rather than fame, except with his amours.

Back in his room, Pete put his travel kettle to work before taking a shower.

His timing was perfect, he emerged as the water came to the boil, he quickly threw a tea bag into his travel mug and made a brew. He drank it black as he dressed in jeans and white open-necked linen shirt. Now he was ready for an afternoon of racing.

He stood on his balcony overlooking the beach, he spotted William bustling around. He was serving a cocktail to a youngish woman in a flowered swimsuit. He couldn't see her face for the large hat she was wearing.

It was difficult to assess whether or not she warranted further attention, he thought clinically.

He'd showered and dressed quicker than anticipated, there was plenty of time before the first race scheduled for 1:30 pm. It was only a short distance from the hotel to the racecourse, he strolled nonchalantly on the intermittent pavement.

The Garrison Savanah Racecourse takes its name from the fort, the real Garrison Savanah that guarded the entrance to Bridgetown Bay in the days of yore. The racecourse covers an area behind this edifice.

Pete paid the $10 Barbados entry fee which gained him admittance into the terraced stand, generally occupied by the vociferous locals. He always enjoyed the banter and the sheer exuberance of the local race day crowd.

The third race, a race for Maiden Two-Year-Olds finished. yet again Pete proved he was hopeless as a tipster, again the Tote used his money to pay out others.

Before each race he'd put the Tote tickets in different pockets, this ploy had not worked, he was still winless. A different venue may do the trick, he paid an additional $10 and relocated to the "Nobs" Stand.

Now he was surrounded by the higher echelon of Barbados society, the horse owners, the moneyed set and the celebrities although he recognised none.

Race No. 4, this would be it. This would be his crowning moment, this would be when he broke the Tote bank. He analysed carefully the form of the ten runners and randomly, as per usual, selected two numbers he had not used in the previous three races, very scientific. He visited the Tote, $10 on the nose of No. 3, and a $10 Forecast No. 3 and No. 7, he returned to "Nobs" stand.

The starting gates opened and the ten runners broke evenly as they began the 1,170m, 6-furlong journey to the winning line.

No. 3 hit the front early, nearly always a bad sign in Pete's eyes, the rest were hot on its heels.

Before he knew it, they were all round the last bend and in the winning straight. Now he was looking at them full-on, four were in a line, it was difficult to tell which was leading, the commentator said it was still No. 3, followed by No. 1, No. 9 and No. 7.

He didn't normally get excited but on this occasion he did, "Come on No. 3, come on No. 7," he repeated excitedly.

They crossed the line together, he'd no idea of the result, and a letter P was posted, a photograph.

It seemed like half an hour but it was probably only minutes before the result was announced, No. 3, followed by No. 7, followed by No. 9, he'd won. "Bloody hell," he wheezed to himself.

Ten minutes later he was in the queue at the payout window to collect his winnings, a completely new experience for him.

Immediately in front of him stood a statuesque young woman, she must have stood almost 6 feet tall as he was looking directly into the blonde wayward hair. Her height was enhanced by the white 4" stiletto heels she wore making her long shapely legs look even longer.

She wore short, white, figure-hugging shorts defining her narrow waist that showed bare between the tight-fitting tied white shirt.

Pete admired the view.

She moved forward and presented her winning ticket, Pete moved to close the gap between them.

With her cash in hand she turned sharply, catching Pete unaware and bumping into him. She made to apologise, but her words stopped short.

"Shit," shouted Pete, he couldn't help the expletive, the pain was instant and excruciating. She'd trod on his foot, her stiletto heel had penetrated through the synthetic material of his training shoe and sliced the side of his right foot.

"Oh sorry, I'm very sorry," she apologised profusely as Pete hopped on his left foot clenching his teeth and avoiding further sounds of pain or additional cursing.

"Sorry, very sorry," she repeated.

Pete tentatively put his damaged foot to the floor, it still hurt like hell. He looked at the young woman in the face for the first time, even through the pain, he appreciated the view. She was young, early twenties he estimated, an oval face with fine features. It was her beautiful blue eyes that drew his attention, he was speechless. Maybe it was the pain that had him lost for words for it was not something that afflicted him normally.

"I'm okay," he stammered.

"Do you think a visit to the First Aid Post is called for?" she ventured.

"Not until I've collected my winnings," he replied. She smiled gracefully.

The medic carefully removed his ruined shoe along with his torn sock and exposed the still bleeding gash, she winced at the sight. Pete sat with an air of indifference suppressing the desire to scream.

The medic dressed the wound and with care managed to refit the shoe.

Pete thanked him profusely and put a generous donation in the charity box that sat on the corner of the office desk, the young woman did like-wise.

He hobbled back to the stand, tentatively placing his foot at every step. She held his arm lightly, he liked that, it felt good.

Safely back in the stand he found himself surrounded by friends and acquaintances of the young woman.

"I'm Penelope, Penelope Bradford Jones but for Christ sake call me Penny, Penelope is so ostentatious," she said with a perfect BBC accent.

"Listen everybody, this is…" and she waited for Pete to fill in the void.

"Jim," he lied. He lied naturally and instinctively; it was a kind of inherent precautionary protective instinct that he had acquired over the years.

"You don't live here, I'd know you if you did. For my sins I seem to know everyone, well everyone that's worth knowing, on this island."

"Thanks for the compliment," he replied, "Your right, I'm a tourist on holiday, stopping at the Hilton," he lied again nodding in the direction of the multi-storey building that protruded above the general skyline in the direction of the fort.

"You're English?" she assumed.

"Of course, and you?" he returned.

"Most certainly, but I escape here as often as possible."

She stood close to him, now eye to eye. He detected the fragrance, he recognised it as Fantasia de Fleurs by Creed, A favourite of royalty and the American rich.

"I am so sorry," she reiterated, "I was so busy counting my winnings I –"

"Enough," he said more sharply than he'd intended. "It was just one of those things," he placated. He wanted to say 'shit happens' but refrained.

"I know but –" he interrupted again. "It happened, now forget it, try and win another race but be careful when collecting your winnings," he jibed.

"Okay," she said raising her hands in supplication.

The runners of the next race appeared, she studied them with what appeared to be a knowledgeable eye. She consulted her race card and marked one of them with an asterisk.

"Would you like me to take a bet for you?" she asked.

"Very kind," he replied.

The 'scientific' approach had been successful once, he tried again. This time he selected horse numbers 4 and 5, for no apparent reason other than they followed 'No. 3' and came before 'No. 6'.

He gave her a $20 Barbados bill. "You're not paying for my bet," he asserted.

"I was going to," she responded.

"Yes, I thought so but no."

She left.

He adjusted the position of his right foot so that it rested on the back of the seat in front. It was painful, he grimaced as he set it to down.

She returned and handed him his betting slip. "Best of luck," she said.

Pete (alias Jim) sat unmoved as Penny and her friends followed the progress of the horses to the winning post, she was jubilant, he was not.

"Take care," he said sarcastically as once again she left to go to the Tote office.

She was waving a fistful of Barbados dollars in the air as she shrieked her arrival back in the stand; she waved them teasingly under his nose.

"My treat for dinner, Mr Jim," she said.

"If you say so, thank you," he returned.

"Least I can do," and added, "Is it any better?"

"I'll live."

"I feel awful."

"Don't," he stressed. "A free dinner, it will be free won't it? It will be fine, thank you."

"Of course, with all the trimmings," she said, and he thought he detected a cheeky grin. "8 for 8:30 okay?" she continued. "The Cliff, do you know it?"

"Of course," he lied yet again. He made a mental note to Google 'The Cliff' on his return to the Palm Court, not the Hilton.

The pain in his foot was not easing, he thought it was time to make his exit.

"Until tonight," he said as he rose unsteadily to his feet.

"Don't be late," she said and to his surprise, planted a kiss tenderly on his cheek. "Take care," she added.

Even though the distance back to the Palm Court was short, he took one of the waiting taxis.

He was pleased to reach the sanctuary of his room and took up residence on the balcony with his injured foot at rest on the drinks table. He surveyed his favourite scene. It was bereft of humanity; a few crabs grazed the empty beach. He was comfortable and at ease. He dropped asleep thinking, "A successful afternoon, a win on the horses and a date. Who knows what the evening will bring?"

He was totally oblivious to the woman on a balcony one higher and 20 yards to one side from where he slept, it was the same woman that had been wearing the flowered swimsuit sat on the Beach Bar veranda earlier. She eyed him again. "Mmmmm," she muted.

Chapter 2

He showered awkwardly, his dressed foot protruding from the shower cubicle avoiding the cascading droplets. He laughed at his own predicament.

The foot wasn't as painful as it had been but it was still sore and a full shoe was a definite no. He wore a pair of leather sandals with the strap of the right hand one looser than normal.

The sandals didn't exactly complement the beige slacks and cream shirt he'd selected for the evening soirée, but they would have to do.

He looked at himself in the full-length mirror. *I'll* do, he thought. 'Best not to go over the top,' he'd found, by experience that the rich cared less about their appearance than he did, or was it they didn't care what people thought of their appearance? The sandals had to stay.

He booted up his tablet and Googled 'The Cliff'.

"Fine restaurant literally perched on the Cliff overlooking the Caribbean Sea on the elite West Coast", Salubrious. *Very nice,* he thought, but he wouldn't have expected anything less.

When he said 'The Cliff', the taxi driver's eyes lit up. *Anyone going there is good for a big fat tip,* he thought, little did he know that it was a Yorkshire man that he carried, not known for their generosity.

Pete did carry the normal Yorkshire traits but on this occasion he more than adequately recompensed the driver. "Shall I come back for you?" he asked hopefully.

"No thanks," replied Pete.

The bar was full but Penny stood out like a sundew melon in a box of baking apples. The tight white shorts had been replaced by a slightly longer version and the tied white blouse by a lemon one. The offending white stilettoes had gone, now she wore a similar lemon pair.

She was perched, as only a tall long-legged blonde beauty can, on a high stool at the bar. She had a tall glass containing a peach-coloured liquid topped with an assortment of fruit, on the bar beside her.

The moment she saw Pete, or Jim as he had introduced himself to her she wriggled off the stool and scampered across the room to greet him with a continental kiss.

"What's your poison?" she asked when she'd dragged him back to her perch. He still limped a little but this was more for effect than necessity.

"I'll have the same as you if you please, whatever it is."

"Another Mai Tai please Robin," she called to the barmen. "Make that two," she added.

"Cheers," she said lifting her glass to his. "Here's to brand new foot," she giggled. He smiled with her as the glasses clinked.

"Are you hungry?" she asked.

"Most certainly," he replied. "Pain makes you exceedingly hungry, you know."

She ignored the barb with a wistful glare. "What do you fancy?" she asked.

"One thing at a time," he replied.

She noted the innuendo but made no comment; just another wistful glare.

The Maître d'hôtel appeared from nowhere. "Would you like to order now, or take your table, it's ready when you are?" he asked.

Penny looked at Pete (Jim) questioningly.

He put the ball back in her court, "It's your show, you decide," he prompted.

"Okay, we'll take the table now, I'm getting hungry, winning money on horses must have an effect on my appetite," Penny smirked. They passed through the body of the dining room, the décor. and furnishings were in keeping with the architecture of the building, traditional colonial with a chic touch.

Their table was outside on one of the several balconies overlooking a small bay with rocks at each end and a fine sand beach in its centre.

The stray light from the overhead lanterns illuminated the crashing waves as they collided with the shore.

It was a romantic setting, *Was that intentional?*

The Maître d' left them with the menus.

Pete (Jim) searched for something he could afford, remembered it was Penny's treat and ignored the exorbitant prices. Now he knew why he'd never been to The Cliff before.

He chose a Spicy Thai style beef salad and Mahi Mahi with Baked potato cake, wilted greens and baby onions.

Penny's selection also had an Eastern influence, Moo Shu pancakes and Seared Tuna with crushed new potatoes and saffron/caper sauce, sounded interesting.

"We'll have a bottle of Finca Valpiedra please, George," Penny added making it even more obvious she was a regular visitor to The Cliff.

Looking around Pete (Jim) spotted at least three faces he recognised as well-known British entertainers.

"Tell me about yourself?" she asked.

He'd been anticipating this question and fended it by returning, "No, I'm sure you don't want to hear my boring story, tell me about yourself you appear to be well known around these parts."

No more ado, she accepted the invitation, "Mummy and Daddy are divorced, been divorced a long time now. Daddy's an American, some kind of financier, investor, that sort of thing. I don't see much of him but he pays the bills."

The waiter delivered and poured the wine, she took a sip and continued, "Mummy lives in Kensington, you know it?"

"Only that it's in London," he replied.

"Mummy's a bitch," she almost snarled.

Pete (Jim) refrained comment and attempted to remain impassive.

"Daddy gave the house here in Barbados to Mummy as part of the divorce settlement. I use it more than her, definitely not at the same time. We don't really see eye to eye."

Pete (Jim) savoured the wine, it was good. With the glass to his lips he again avoided any sign of surprise. It's not often a daughter refers to her mother as a bitch, the obvious dislike was blatantly apparent.

The wine was extremely palatable, the bottle was nigh empty.

"Another bottle," she indicated to a passing waiter. "Of course, madam," he replied and hastened back of house.

As the waiter corked the new bottle, Penny's story regressed to her childhood.

It became apparent that her parents' marriage had never been a happy one. She'd spent most of her early and teenage years away at various Boarding schools spending her holidays at either one parent or the other, but never with both. A loveless childhood.

The Swiss Finishing School had moulded her into the fine young woman that sat with him now, although they would not be her words.

She was obviously wealthy, probably in her own right but she didn't appear egotistical or obnoxious. She was good company and of course, easy on the eye.

"Enough about me, what of you?"

He was prepared for this eventuality. He moved unnoticed into fantasy mode and gave her a cock and bull story of Jim's background. To be fair, it wasn't too far removed from his real-life story but the names and places were fresh out of his imaginative mind.

He'd often thought of putting this imagination to good use at some time in the future, write a book maybe. Somebody, and unusual for him, he couldn't remember who said, "Everybody has a book in them." Who knows, he could have one too.

The first courses arrived but the conversation continued, albeit interrupted for food.

Pete (Jim) manoeuvred the conversation away from himself and onto other things, as is the norm, flitting from one subject to another, digressing and backtracking constantly.

The starters were replaced by the main courses. Pete (Jim's) Mahi Mahi, Dolphinfish to the uninitiated and Penny's Tuna were presented as works of culinary art. It seemed a shame to destroy the picture but they did.

The consumption of the wine had slowed somewhat. It was sipped rather than quaffed. It was a fine selection and deserved savouring; it accompanied the fish well. Penny apparently was something of a connoisseur.

The waiter removed the empty plates and returned with the sweet trolley, not just any sweet trolley but the sweet trolley from confectionery heaven. Everything apart from the fresh fruit shouted calories.

No physical exercise today and probably none tomorrow, thought Pete (Jim). *But what the hell.* He chose mango cheesecake to which the waiter added cream. He vowed that the following day he would eat in moderation, a definite maybe.

How did Penny retain her figure if she ate here or places of similar ilk on a regular basis? "She must work out," he concluded.

They both concluded the feast with black coffee and retired to the bar, where, without asking, she ordered two brandies, two Remy Martin XO's. *Her education into the finer things in life must have been pretty complete.* Pete (Jim) knew this to be not just a fine brandy but a very expensive one. *God knows what the price was in this fine establishment.* It was definitely a sipping and savouring drink, definitely a drink to be treated with respect.

Through the meal and onwards at the bar, their conversation never wavered. She'd been great company, a great host Pete (Jim) had enjoyed every minute.

"I guess I'd better make my way back to my hotel, thanks for the freebie," said Pete (Jim).

"I'll drive you back, my car's out front."

"No you won't, I can take a cab and anyway what about the wine and the brandy?"

"I'm fine," she insisted. "The police here don't bother us. Only if we wrap a car round a tree then they mind, damaging the environment is a serious crime, drinking not so."

"Okay, if you insist."

It was no great surprise to Pete (Jim) that her car was a sports car. A white, the colour of preference in Barbados, BMW soft-top. No more than a couple of months old in pristine condition.

The instant his seat belt clicked home, she pressed hard on the accelerator pressing him back into the black leather seat. The wheels spun, gravel clattered the chassis, the tyres gripped, and the BMW raced forward.

She slid to a stop at the highway but instead of turning right toward Bridgetown and his hotel, she swung gracefully to the left.

She accelerated smoothly through the gears before signalling right and applying the brakes.

The secondary road had a perfect asphalt surface and deviated only slightly from a straight line.

She handled the car like a female Lewis Hamilton caressing the wheel gently as she sped through the several chicanes.

She decelerated to turn sharp left into a brick-paved drive.

The drive was no more than 50 yards long and terminated outside a large single storey white stucco finished house with a dark, possibly red-tiled roof.

The portico was illuminated by two carriage lanterns, one on each side of the large stained-glass panelled door.

In the moonlight it appeared as a grandiose hacienda set in a tropical garden.

"We've arrived," she said as she clambered out of the BMW.

"It doesn't look a bit like the Hilton to me," he said with a smile.

"I thought you might like a nightcap."

"Good idea," he replied as he rose to his feet unsteadily, exaggerating discomfort.

"You still in pain?" she asked, concerned.

"It's okay," he replied nonchalantly and limped slightly exaggerating the injury which in truth was nothing more than a dull ache.

The door opened on to a huge open plan area. The entrance area being defined with its perimeter bordered by the clever use of statuettes, ornamental pottery and tall spreading plants.

Beyond stretched the reception area, itself larger than the ground floor area of an average British detached house.

To the right was the dining area housing an enormous mahogany table surrounded by ten carver chairs.

The complete décor, furnishings and artwork had been either the work of a professional interior designer or a very talented amateur.

He suspected the latter which was confirmed when she said, "You like? All my own work," Pete nodded in appreciation.

She continued, "It's Mummy's house but she let me have a free hand with the décor. She just paid the bill."

"Very nice," he understated as he surveyed the opulent surroundings.

"That drink," she said disappearing behind the permanent, well-stocked bar.

"What's your poison?" she asked.

"Surprise me," he replied.

The clink of ice on glass could be heard as she prepared whatever concoction she had in mind.

She emerged with two tall glasses filled with a dark liquid topped with a slice of lemon and lime.

He sipped it tentatively, "What's in it?" he asked.

"Do you like it?" she retorted.

He took another sip. It had a warming kick, the taste he couldn't place but it was very palatable. "Okay, give, what's in this witches brew?"

"I don't know if it's got a name, I just mix it, good isn't it?"

"It is, but do tell, what the devil's in here?" he imbibed another small nip.

She finally gave the recipe. "Not much," she said. "Jim Bean, Coca Cola, a twist of lemon, oh! And a little tequila."

"Mmmmm, good," he drank deeper.

"Park your bottom," she invited.

He sat in the middle of a white leather settee that was large enough to accommodate six. She joined him sitting at one end crossing her long, tanned legs such that one stilettoed foot was pointing skyward.

"It's better than the Hilton," he said, indicating the room.

"Glad you like it."

"Music?" she suggested.

"Why not."

Again she disappeared behind the bar, the dulcet tones of Michael Bublé filled the room from concealed speakers.

"Do you dance?" she asked.

"Only when invited."

"Consider yourself invited."

She stood tall, gyrating her rounded hips to the rhythm of the music. He rose to join her.

He moved in close, took her right hand gently in his left and placed his right hand on her bare back, her skin was as soft as it looked.

Pete (Jim) was no dancer but a slow smooch with a very attractive young lady was well within his capabilities. She hummed the tune in his ear as gradually the space between them decreased.

He could feel his manhood rising, *could she?*

She made no attempt to pull away, on the contrary she moved even closer, she must have detected his bulge.

His right hand climbed her back under the short shirt and to her shoulders, he moved her closer, her nipples pressed to his chest.

She flicked her loose hair to one side and her face touched his.

The lobe of his ear was nibbled, her tongue explored the rest, his penis was reaching full extension, *she must be aware of it.*

She let go of his hand and arched her back. She was in full contact with his erection and yes, she knew it.

She undid the buttons of his shirt and peeled it from his shoulders.

Pete (Jim) untied the knot in her shirt and likewise removed it. Her breasts were round and firm and the nipples pink and hard as his hands found them, she mewed quietly.

Her arms went around his neck. She kissed him fiercely on the lips her tongue seeking his.

Both his hands slid down her back and into her shorts. He cupped her derriere and drew her flat stomach close to his.

Slowly he eased the shorts over hips and let them drop to the floor.

She reciprocated by unzipping his fly and removing both his trousers and boxer shorts. He stepped out of the crumpled heap and kicked off his sandals, the damaged foot a memory.

Naked they embraced, his erection pressing hard against her lithe body. The kissing stopped, they found the leather settee, it's coolness went unnoticed as she lay with her legs wide for him to enter her naked slit.

Without haste he manoeuvred his stiff member into her receptive cunt, she moaned as he moved slowly in and out with the slightest of lateral movement. Her feet, still with shoes were high above his head.

Pete (Jim), a very experienced lover of many years recognised that Penny was no novice. She had not learned this at finishing school.

He varied the rhythm, slow and easy, a little faster, slow again. She orgasmed loudly, he continued varying the pace. She orgasmed again and this time so did he.

They lay still, her legs relaxed on to his calves. His erection subsided inside her.

"Wow!" she exclaimed, "That was good."

"I agree," he replied.

"Can we do it again?" she asked.

"If you insist," said Pete (Jim).

Carefully, they disentangled and rose from the settee.

She led him by the hand through one of the many doors.

It was her bedroom, very girlie in various shades of pink with white furniture. The bed was either king or queen-sized with only white cotton sheet covering.

She peeled it back, climbed on to the bed and drew him with her. She lay on her side propped on her right arm and gazed into his eyes as he lay beside her.

"I could get to like you," she said.

Pete (Jim) had been here before. It was easy to get drawn into a relationship that was doomed from the start. He knew it, he wasn't sure that she did.

'Enjoy it while it lasted,' was his motto.

"And me you," he replied.

She snuggled close, her left hand finding his groin and what lay dormant there.

Her touch was soft as she stroked the sleeping monster awake. She liked what she held; he was well endowed, intact, unadulterated as nature had intended.

He fondled her breasts and moved downward to her groin. His fingers parted her welcoming lips, she was moist as he found her love spot. He rubbed, she squirmed, she squeezed, he stirred, they coupled together again. This time she fucked him.

As she came wildly, so did he. They collapsed into sleep.

Chapter 3

Maybe she stirred, maybe it was that which woke him.

She, *"what did they call her? Oh yes, Penny,"* laid with her head buried in the silk pillow. Her blonde hair in disarray covered her face. Her left arm was across his and her leg rested across his hip and groin.

Only a little light filtered through the slight chink in the curtains. His eyes caught the movement of something, it was a large spider traversing the ceiling, *"How do they do that walk upside down?"* he pondered.

What a night, he thought as he gazed at the recumbent naked body beside him.

"I'm a lucky bastard. I sometimes wonder how I do it, another fine fuck, another conquest, it keeps happening. Let's hope for a few years yet."

This thought set him thinking of how his infatuation with the fairer sex begun.

"What would I be? Ten, maybe 11, Jenny, Jenny something, Brownlea, Brownridge, something like that. A party just before Christmas. I remember, she grabbed me under the mistletoe, kissed me hard on the lips.

"It was the first time anybody other than family had kissed me and then not often on the lips.

"I remember it clearly. The sensation, not a tingle, a strange feeling hard to explain but it felt good.

"I kissed her back, I held her lightly.

"It was good, I liked it and I think she did too. Ten, 11-year-olds kissing.

"That was the start. Thinking back, I'm sure that was the start.

"Sexual enlightenment came gradually after that. Am I different to most men? I think not, luckier maybe but different, no."

He'd had no formal sexual education. If there was such a thing, of course. He'd learnt in the classroom the basics of the anatomical parts and the facts about reproduction but that's not the same as learning first hand.

From that first kiss under the mistletoe, it had been a natural progression to a hand in a girl's shirt at 13/14, under the bra at 15 and on to the nether regions.

Yes, strictly speaking to the letter of the law, he and his partners had participated underage but at the time that never entered his head. One or two of his partners were not amenable to his advances, they soon disappeared from the scene to be replaced by ones more amenable. His appetite developed through his teenage years and remained today and hopefully for a few years to come.

Penny's arm moved but she remained fast asleep.

His watch was on the bedside table, he didn't remember taking it off.

It was six o'clock.

Time to go.

He carefully extricated himself ensuring her arm and leg were disturbed little. She slept on.

One by one he recovered his clothes and shoes from where they lay strewn across the floor of both the bedroom and reception room.

He dressed quickly and quietly, and left the house.

As he walked, free of the limp, down the drive, the sun was rising, he looked back at the fine house and manicured gardens.

"Thank you, Penny," he whispered. "Have a nice day, have a good life."

It had been a good evening, a good night. A fine meal and an excellent fuck, make that several fucks.

His disappearance was well in keeping with an old adage he'd heard a long time ago from one of the lads, a right Jack the lad he was. "Find 'em, feel 'em, fuck 'em and leave 'em," he used to say, Pete complied wherever possible.

"Thank you, Penelope Bradford Jones," he waved.

It was a short walk back to Highway 1, the main west coast arterial road. There was no one at the bus stop, not surprising in the Sandy Lane area. Only the itinerant workers used the buses here, the residents would either drive or have their chauffeurs drive their Bentleys, Jaguars, or the like.

It was still early but he didn't have to wait too long, a blue bus rattled to a stop. He paid the $1.50 Barbados fare and took a seat among the early Bridgetown workers.

He was still tired; no great surprise. A combination of the bus's movement and the constant reggae music had him nodding fitfully.

The bus emptied and refilled at the bus station; he could barely keep his eyes open.

Thankfully, he was awake as the bus approached the Palm Court hotel. He alighted immediately outside the hotel entrance gate fortunately, had sleep had overtaken him he would have finished up in Oistins, miles away and then had to travel all the way back.

In his room, he undressed almost as quickly as the previous night but this time unaided. He laid naked on the bed and slept.

It was the chambermaid that woke him as she knocked and entered expecting to find an empty room.

"Whoops," she screamed as she did an about-turn and ran through the door. The sight of a completely naked man approaching her didn't frighten her; startled her, yes and amused her, definitely. She'd have a conversation piece for days and no doubt just like a fisherman's story, Pete's penis would be bigger each time of telling.

"Sorry," he shouted, but she was gone.

Chapter 4

The cold of the shower ensured he was fully awake, gradually it warmed and eventually it became hot. He lingered a while enjoying the refreshing sharp droplets tingling on his now dark skin.

He emerged, he made to shave inspecting his juvenile beard in the mirror. His chin and cheeks were dark with two days of growth, already he was sporting 'designer stubble'. *"What the hell,"* he said to himself. *"I'm on holiday,"* and dispensed with the shaving kit.

He donned a sweatshirt and shorts and looked for his Nike trainers. *"Damn,"* he recalled he'd dumped them. He remembered the damage inflicted to them and who by and the ensuing events, but now he needed some new ones.

With his sandals, 'Jesus wellies' as his old dad called them, on his feet he made his way along the dilapidated pavement alongside the Southern Highway toward St Lawrence Gap A walk of about 20 minutes took him to a branch of Cave Sheppard, the store of choice of wealthy residents of Barbados.

The choice here was not the same as Foot Locker or stores of similar ilk in the UK but he acquired a perfectly adequate pair. A brand he didn't recognise at an exorbitant $150 Barbados.

He added some trainer socks to his purchase, put them on together with the new shoes and carrying the now redundant sandals jogged eastward.

When he reached Hastings Beach, a distance of a mile or so. He crossed the road, passed through the small complex of gift shops, bars and restaurants to the timber walkway that followed the beach and rocks back to the Palm Court Beach Hotel.

William must have seen him coming, as a freshly made Pina Colada was waiting on the bar as he leapt the two steps on to the veranda.

"Cheers," he gasped. "Can I have a glass of water, please?"

He downed the water in one gulp.

"I guess you were thirsty," a female voice said from behind him.

He turned. It was the woman that had been wearing the large hat the previous day.

The large hat had gone, she wore a pink visor. Her brown hair tumbling above, she had large round dark eyes set in a round pretty face.

She sat in a beach chair; her legs stretched out with her feet sat on another chair.

"I certainly was," he replied and replaced the empty water glass with the Pina Colada. "Salute," he doffed his drink in her direction.

"Skol," she returned tendering her near-empty glass.

"Can I buy you a refill?" he offered.

"Thank you, kind sir, a martini please, a dry martini."

"No problem. William!"

William had heard the exchange and was already on the move.

A tall glass, plenty of ice, a slice of lemon and a generous pouring of extra dry vermouth from the dark green martini bottle.

Pete took the glass from the bar and carried it to her table.

"May I join you?"

Unbeknown to Pete she'd been hankering for this moment for several days. *So far so good,* she thought.

She introduced herself, "I'm Jude."

"Hey, Jude," he said and quickly added, "sorry that was awful, as if you've never heard that before."

"Once or twice," she replied, "I've got used to it, have you a name?" she asked, although she already knew it, having wheedled it from William.

"Pete Holmes, at your service, ma'am," he bowed in mock reverence.

She took her feet from the chair and Pete sat.

"How do you like it here, Jude?" he asked, indicating the surroundings with a sweep of his arm.

"Beautiful," she replied, "Paradise, you happy here?" she added.

"Love it, my second home," as soon as he'd said it, he wished he hadn't, too much information. The less people knew about his real self the better, too late, just be careful in future.

"Where's home?" he enquired.

"Faversham, Kent, the Garden of England."

"The land of hops and apples," he ventured.

"You've got it," she said, "And you, where's home for you?"

"Oh, here, there, there, here, nowhere for long."

"You must be wealthy," she probed.

"Not really, I make a buck here and there, this and that, enough to get by okay."

"Well spending time here, you must be doing more than okay."

"Mmmmm," he muted, neither confirming nor denying.

"Have you ventured far around the island?" he asked.

"I've been as far as Bridgetown that way," she pointed west, "And the Gap that way," pointing in the opposite direction.

"That's not enough, you should go further. It's a beautiful island."

"I should, are you going to take me?" she certainly wasn't slow at coming forward.

"It could be arranged."

"Do you have a car?" she asked.

"No, I'll do better than that. I'll go with you on a conducted tour with the best tour guide on the island."

"Sounds good and who is this feller?"

"Ted, of Ted's Tours. He's one of the family members that owns this hotel, he's a gas, you'll love him and what he doesn't know about Barbados is not worth knowing and he's a laugh."

"Sounds good, when will this happen? Tomorrow I hope, I go home Saturday."

"Yeah, it will have to, I'm away on Saturday as well," giving, he hoped, the impression he was going back to the UK. He'd lie if she pressed.

"Let's see what we can do."

"William," he called, "May I use your house phone?"

"That's settled, 8:30 in the morning. Hotel reception, Ted's Tour," said Pete returning to the chair adjacent to Jude.

Pete was no Einstein but then he didn't need to be to know that Jude was interested in him and not just for his intellect, his instincts were telling him so but there was trepidation there as well. It was best to tread careful.

"That's tomorrow sorted, what about tonight?" Pete ventured.

"Do we have a date?" she sounded surprised.

"If you'll allow me to escort you to dinner, M'Lady?" he confirmed.

"Fine and where are you taking me?" she asked.

"What about McDonald's?" he replied. "No, only joking. There's no McDonald's here anyway. About the only place in the world they didn't take off. The Barbadians are chicken eaters, not into burgers."

"Okay, not McDonalds, how about KFC?"

"No, I think we can do a little better than that, so no jeans. That okay?"

"Fine," she said. "Gives me a chance to air clothes that haven't been out of the wardrobe yet."

Happy hour had been and gone. Pete had finished his third Pina colada, Jude had matched him with martinis. "I'd better make this my last for this afternoon or I'll be too pissed to take you out tonight," Pete said pushing his chair back, "See you at 7:30. Is that good for you?" he asked.

"Brill, Reception 7:30," she replied, sipping the diminishing contents of her glass.

Pete looked from his balcony. She was still sat where he'd left her and her glass was full.

Chapter 5

Showered and shaved *(that felt better),* Pete investigated his wardrobe. *I must remember to send some to laundry before the tour tomorrow,* he thought.

He selected white trousers, they could be laundered in the morning together with a crisp white cotton shirt that he'd already earmarked.

White underwear, white socks and white leather shoes completed the evening's attire.

Pete was somewhat surprised when he set eyes on Jude.

Two reasons. Firstly, her stature – she'd always been sat when he'd seen her, on the beach bar veranda. She was short, no more than 5'3" was his estimate. Even with heeled shoes he still towered over her.

Secondly was her appearance. Gone was the unruly hair replaced by a sleek controlled coiffure that could have been out of Vidal Sassoon's salon.

With the clever use of makeup, her eyes looked brighter, her lips fuller and her face narrower. She was much prettier than she'd appeared earlier.

Her clothes were in excellent taste hiding the fullness of her figure.

Her top was turquoise, a chiffon-like material with a neckline that revealed enough cleavage to be of interest. It was loose-fitting, worn over trousers coloured a complimentary green. The cuffs sitting comfortably on pale green shoes with a modest heel.

She looked delightful, a different person to the one he'd invited to dinner. He already knew he would enjoy being her escort for the evening.

"You look wonderful," he said and he meant it. He didn't always when he complimented a woman but on this occasion he did.

It was good that they were both punctual. The taxi Pete had ordered was waiting outside.

The restaurant was not quite so salubrious as the previous night's venue, The Cliff, but nevertheless the Aqua, Pete's choice, was select and again had a beach view, but this time in the less autocratic area on the Barbados South Coast.

Pete was a regular visitor here and was instantly recognised by the headwaiter. Pete lived well on his ill-gotten gains. He always chose comfortable not necessarily expensive hotels and he ate in the better restaurants. This happened to be one of his favourites, maybe he was biased, it was, after all, located on his holiday island of preference and he'd visited many.

They were shown to a table in an alcove, the tables overlooking the sea already being occupied.

Jude's drink of choice, a dry martini, arrived together with Pete's Banks's beer.

Pete clinked his bottle against Jude's glass. "Cheers again," he said.

"Where did we get to this afternoon?" opened Pete. "You're Jude from Faversham, Kent, Garden of England but that's all I know so far, tell me more."

"If you insist," she began, "Jude Bignell, 35 years old, spinster of the parish of Faversham. A beautician in my own little business," she added.

Beautician, Pete thought. *That answers the transformation, she's good.*

"What more can I tell you?" she asked.

"Dare I ask, is there a man in your life?"

"You at moment," she winked cheekily.

"Fine," retorted Pete. "Anybody back home?" he pressed.

"Sometimes," she was playing him at his own game, he noted.

"Footloose and fancy free," he commented, remembering one of his dad's sayings.

"Yeah that about sums it up," she nodded.

The waiter arrived and proffered two open menus, he left them to contemplate their selection.

"You've obviously eaten here before, what do you suggest?"

"That depends. Meat, fish, vegetarian, what's your preference?"

"Not vegetarian, meat or fish, don't mind."

"It's all good here but maybe lobster, that's good or perhaps the veal."

A few minutes passed as they both considered the extensive choice.

The waiter returned, selections made. Caesar salad and the lobster.

"Seafood bisque and veal," they advised him.

"It's your turn now," said Jude.

"You don't want to know about me," he tried to divert the query.

"Oh yes I do," she insisted.

It was time, yet again, for his imagination to kick in.

"Okay, potted history of Peter Holmes coming up."

"Born and bred Harrogate, North Yorkshire," he lied.

"You don't sound like a Yorkshire man," she interrupted.

"Ah! The effects of university and living and working in London," which happened to be the truth.

He had indeed attended university, Kings College, London where he'd acquired a first in French and French history. He omitted to tell her that and the fact that afterwards his working life had begun as a freelance interpreter with much of his time aiding and abetting commercial enterprises in and around the metropolis.

"Ever been to Yorkshire?" he asked.

"No, I'd like to sometime."

This, he was pleased to hear. He couldn't be contradicted if he erred in his description of the area, its history or the so-called places of interest.

He was in the middle of a diatribe about Yorkshire and North Yorkshire in particular when the starters arrived.

Eating is not always conducive to talking, they ate in relative silence.

With an empty plate and soup bowl redundant on the Egyptian cotton covered tablecloth, Pete continued his narrative on God's own county.

"You might have the orchards and the Oust houses, but we have the Moors and the Dales some of the most rugged and beautiful country-sides in the world."

"Whoa there, we have beautiful countryside in Kent as well," she said, protective of her birthplace.

Pete had by devious means managed to distract her away from his personal history. He pushed forward on this tack, "I suppose you take advantage of your close proximity to Dover and nip across to France for your cheap booze?"

A handsome lobster accompanied by a minimal quantity of vegetables was set in front of Jude.

She was about to reply to his question but stopped, "How do I attack this?" she pondered.

"With great difficulty," he joked and attracted the attention of the waiter.

"Help us out here will you please? Undress this lobster for the lady."

"No problem, sir." He removed the plate from in front of Jude. Took it to a nearby workstation, deftly removed the lobster's shell, snapped off the claws, cracked them and returned it back to Jude in a ready-to-eat form, it had taken only seconds.

The food, Jude confirmed was as good, if not better than Pete had described it. There was very little left on either plate when the waiter returned sometime later.

Jude picked up the conversation from where they'd left it. "We go across to Calais now and again before Christmas and maybe June, top up with wine and beers but they're not as cheap as they used to be. There's a place just on the Belgian border affectionately known as Tobacco Road, cheap cigarettes and booze, sometimes we go there but who wants cigs nowadays."

"True," Pete interjected. "You don't smoke I take it?"

"Never, never appealed, bad for the skin especially in later life, you?"

"No, tried it once when I was 14, made me sick, never again."

The conversation meandered through everyday events with trivia thrown in for good measure.

The sweet trolley arrived. Another decision made difficult by the sweet sensations on offer.

Pete appeared very calorie-conscious when he went for a fresh fruit salad without cream, Jude thought, *What the hell,* and chose the chocolate gateau smothered in whipped vanilla cream.

Coffee and brandy, a bog standard VSOP for Pete, not quite of the same ilk as the previous night but good and a damn sight cheaper and a Tia Maria to accompany Jude's Blue Mountain exotic coffee.

The conversation never faltered. Pete was a natural conversationalist who retained a library of useful and trivial facts. Jude was good company, a good listener with a good turn of phrase herself.

It had been a good meal and a good evening and it wasn't over yet. Pete called for the bill.

"How much is my half?" asked Jude.

"Let me see now," replied Pete, appeared to be doing some mental calculations and continued, "You had that I had, that was yours, that was mine, yeah that adds up to exactly," he paused. "Zero."

"Thank you but please let me pay my half."

"Not likely, I invited you, remember?" Pete insisted.

"If you insist," she said. "But I owe you," there was a glint in her eye.

Pete paid with plastic and asked for a cab.

Chapter 6

"Would you like to go on to a club or something?" he asked.

"I'm not really into clubs," she replied. "A drink maybe, what about the pub opposite the hotel?"

"So be it," Pete instructed the driver who was disappointed his clients were only travelling a short distance.

The generous tip compensated him for a more expensive fare, it went directly into his pocket, not the company coffers.

The pub was nigh on empty, only a black guy propping the bar and a young mixed-race couple canoodling in a dark corner.

Two dry martinis, two beers and quite a lot of small talk later Jude suggested he walk her home.

The sky was clear with few clouds and an almost full moon, "A couple more nights and I turn into a werewolf," said Pete gazing skyward.

"That would be interesting," replied Jude, "All that hair and don't werewolves have a huge sexual appetite?"

"You don't have to be a werewolf to have a good appetite," Pete provoked.

She had her arm looped in his. She stopped, looked into his face. "I see," she said.

Jude's room was in a separate but identical block to Pete's, on the same 1st floor. The access was by a timber-covered staircase at the car park side of the hotel. The other side being the beach side, all rooms with a sea view.

They reached her door, "I'd invite you in but I have a rule and I never break it, not on the first date."

Pete knew exactly what she was saying but there was a suggestion that maybe things might be different on a second meeting.

"Until tomorrow then," he stooped to kiss her cheek. She turned her head, their lips met. She was on her toes, pressed against him. He felt himself stiffen, she felt it too. Reluctantly, she moved away.

She sighed. "See you in reception," unlocked her door, waved a 'bye' and was gone.

As Pete turned tail making for his own room. Jude was leant with her back to the door. "Wow," she mouthed.

Pete read no more than two pages of the escapades of James Bond before his eyes told him 'enough'. He put the book down and was almost instantly asleep.

Meanwhile, Jude could not find sleep. She was fantasising about Pete and pleasuring herself. She orgasmed with a shudder, it was good but not the same as a good fuck and she believed that Pete would be a willing and good, nay, terrific partner. *"Tomorrow,"* she hoped.

Chapter 7

There were ten other people as well as Pete and Jude waiting in and around the reception area for Ted's Tour bus to arrive.

It was another beautiful Barbados day. There were still a few puffy white clouds about but they lounged in a perfect blue sky. The temperature was already around 20°C but promised for a very hot day.

Ted jumped from his green and yellow bus, 'Ted's Tours' blazoned along the side. He was a tall, slim man. White Barbadian, early forties perhaps with a pleasant smiling face.

All Ted's customers, including Pete and Jude, wore similar garb, shorts, tee-shirts and loafers were the order of the day.

"All aboard the Skylark, Ted's magical mystery Tour is about to start for your pleasure," Ted called.

Ted, in his inimitable fashion, greeted everyone with a handshake as they boarded the bus determining their first name and place of origin as they passed. He'd remember the faces and names throughout the tour, he had an amazing memory in similar vein to Pete.

Ted didn't drive, he left that to a local. Ted introduced him as JoJo, this allowed Ted to stand at the front, microphone in hand and give a running commentary.

Pete had made this tour three times and each time the route had varied only slightly but the spiel and the nonsense jokes remained the same with the possible addition of the odd one or two new stories that he'd acquired from customers.

Ted was soon in full flow, facts, figures, anecdotes came like machine gun fire. Bridgetown was negotiated. Two enormous cruise ships came into view towering over the local buildings. Pete was reminded that his cruise and *'back to work'* day was nigh.

They passed the Kensington Oval, the World-famous Barbados and West Indian Cricket Ground and joined the West Coast Highway. Pete had a feeling of déjà vu as they passed The Cliff restaurant.

All along this coast were the villas and houses of the rich and famous, many of them becoming the buff of Ted's stories.

The bus stopped at a ramshackle cabin of a house perched on the clifftop overlooking the beach, "This is on the market," Ted said. "Anybody guess for how much?" he asked.

Several ridiculous figures were suggested.

"All wrong, would you believe 3 million US?"

The whole busload audibly gasped.

"Return here in a couple of years' time and you'll see a mansion in its place, it won't be mine. Any of you interested?"

A mixture of 'no', 'not bloody likely' and similar, resounded.

The first stop for a walk around was on the outskirts of Holetown.

Ted leapt off the bus and lowered the access door to the luggage compartment. As each person stepped off the bus, they were greeted with 'Fruit or Rum Punch'.

Jude chose the rum version, Pete the fruit. They drank them quickly before exploring the few shops of Holetown.

The punch was still on offer on their return. Pete declined the cup offered; he was happy with the cold water he'd bought. Jude accepted the alcoholic version and carried it back on to the bus. Before Ted took the microphone again, it had gone. *This lady can put away the booze,* noted Pete.

The beaches and marinas of the millionaire's playground, the west coast, were left behind as they reached their next stop, Speightstown. Once again punch became available.

The bus climbed the fertile hillsides and into the Barbados Wildlife Reserve. Ted commented on everything from fauna to farming and property to people before coming to a stop at a high spot from where almost all of the east coast of Barbados as far as the lighthouse on the southernmost tip could be seen.

Here there were several stalls of local handicrafts. Jude flitted from one to the other, sipping from the fresh cup of rum punch served from Ted's luggage compartment brew. Pete chatted with Ted.

Jude returned with a coral bracelet to be greeted with another rum punch which she didn't refuse.

Sunbury Plantation House was next on the itinerary. A tour of the house was followed by lunch. Simple local fare, rice and peas with jerk chicken and fresh fruit salad accompanied with the inimitable punch which was refused by Pete but not by Jude.

Back down to sea level and along the rugged east coast where the breakers of the Atlantic crashed to the shore, through Bathsheba, passed the Andromeda Botanical Gardens they travelled on to the Southern tip via the Airport, Sam Lord's Castle and Oistins. Ted's commentary incessant.

At the last stop, a church, Jude demolished another two rum punches whilst the rest of the tour walked the grounds and the church interior, she showed no ill effects of the booze.

The homeward leg was on the Southern Highway. "I know where we are," said Jude as they passed Lawrence Gap, a few minutes later they were back at the starting point. The car park of the Palm Court Beach Hotel.

Jude took Pete's hand as they alighted the bus, she led him toward her block. Pete did not resist.

She unlocked her door and led him in. The room was identical to his, simply furnished with a double bed, two bedside tables, wardrobe and dressing table.

She stopped at the foot of the bed, climbed on to it and knelt in front of him. The height of the bed assisting in her being face to face with Pete. Her arms went around his neck and she kissed him, her tongue explored his. He reciprocated.

She peeled his tee-shirt over his head and unbuckled his belt. She removed her own tee-shirt followed quickly by her white bra, her breasts were large and firm with deep red areolas and pink erect nipples.

She held and kissed him again with more ferocity. Her eyes showed the excitement she was obviously feeling. Pete was more controlled, fervour would follow, that he knew he'd been here before, many times.

She slid off the bed and removed her shorts and panties, her pubic hair were cut short and shaped to her bikini line, probably the result of an appointment in her own beauty parlour.

She rubbed herself with both hands before concentrating on removing Pete's shorts. She cupped her hands into the waistband of both his Bermuda shorts and his boxers. She pulled downward but they held on his erection. Her hands went to find it and she squeezed gently. "Very nice, all for me?" she whispered.

Retaining hold with her left hand she manipulated both shorts to the floor.

Pete stepped out of them and kicked off his new trainers.

Jude stooped to remove her own shoes; she did not rise immediately. She knelt and took Pete's hard and large member into her mouth. It wasn't the first time she'd pleasured a man in this fashion, her tongue roamed along the full extent, she took it deeply. Pete enjoyed with a muted moan.

She moved backwards until her bottom was level with the end of the bed, she had momentarily let go of his penis. She found it again and drew him toward her, she guided him into her moist and receptive vagina. Pete's feet were firmly planted on the floor, his penis deep inside Jude. He thrust gently with no great force, she moaned and opened her legs further. He thrust again only a little harder, her feet rose to Pete's waist and above. "Oh yes," she moaned.

Pete was enjoying equally as much as she. He increased the rhythm and she moaned in appreciation louder, it didn't seem possible but he went deeper inside her. She was ecstatic, he ejaculated in one last spasmodic thrust.

He withdrew as he became flaccid. Jude repositioned so her head rested on a pillow, "Come and join me," she said. He acquiesced and lay beside her.

She turned toward him pressing her adequate breasts into his hairless chest.

Her face came to his, she kissed him lightly on the cheek and located his ear, she nibbled and licked. It was a sensitive area of Pete's as she soon learned.

His penis reacted to the attention being paid to his ear and began to rise.

Jude felt it and again she reached to hold it. She manipulated it gently. It's girth too great for her to close her hand. "Jesus," she said to herself.

She released her gentle grip and led his hand to her slit. He probed gently with two fingers. Finding her erect clitoris was easy, he stroked it, she shuddered, he stroked it some more. She reacted by masturbating him smoothly and efficiently. Pete was enjoying but his appetite was for more.

He rolled her on to her back, she didn't resist. On the contrary, she aided and abetted. He towered over her; his penis was inside her again. Her hands were on his buttocks, she assisted each thrust.

He paused with his penis still inside her, he rose to his knees, both his hands found her breasts. He rolled her nipples between his fingers, the moan returned. From the kneeling position, he thrust in and out. "More," she demanded, he increased pace. "More, you bastard," she yelled. Pete returned to the missionary position and gave everything he'd got, faster, deeper. "Oh yes, oh yes," she cried as Pete orgasmed loudly and she did too.

Exhausted, his full weight was on her. She did not move; she lay panting under him. Partially recovered, he rolled from her and lay silently staring at the ceiling looking at nothing in particular. She did the same.

Pete closed his eyes but he didn't sleep. Jude edged closer, she lay her head on his chest. Her hand was looking for his genitals, he stirred and without the word 'no', inched his body away. She followed, he needed recovery time, it seemed she did not.

Disappointment showed clearly on her face when Pete rose from the bed. "Promise we'll do this again later but there's some business I must attend to." It was a lie, but he genuinely needed some real rest and recovery time.

"It's 5:30 now, see you in the bar at 7:30. I'll take you to Oistens for the Friday night fish fry, ever been?"

"No," she answered simply from her reposed position, still wishing he'd return for more, not later but now.

He dressed and left. "Shit," she said slapping the pillow. "Be patient, girl," she told herself. *Later, there's all night, something to look forward to. Who cares about a bloody fish fry?* Oh, what the hell," she curled into the foetus position and soon she slept.

Pete returned to his own room via reception where he collected his laundry.

He showered and packed the majority of his belongings ready for the morning.

He was now refreshed and no longer tired. Attired only in the hotel bath towel he sat on his balcony and caught up with James Bond and his encounters with Hugo Drax and his henchman henchwoman Krebs.

Chapter 8

The sun lowered and finally disappeared. The balcony light attracted a myriad of insects, time to take refuge inside. The mosquitoes loved him, he needed spray.

In just his boxer shorts, he liberally applied Jungle Formula spray around his calves and ankles, his arms and around his neck. The smell was obnoxious and nauseating but necessary to avoid the bites of the unseen little bastards.

He dressed in jeans, a cotton shirt, socks and the new trainers and made for the bar. Jude was already there with a martini in her hand. "A beer," he requested from the new barman, one that he hadn't seen before.

"Another?" he directed in Jude's direction.

"Please."

The bottle and the glass were soon empty. "Ready to go?" asked Pete.

"You're the boss," she replied.

"Taxi or would you like to try the cheap local bus service?"

"Let's go local," she replied.

Less than a minute later, an eight-seater people carrier with ten people on board stopped for them, they squeezed in, a couple of locals moved to let them sit. It was impossible for them to communicate as the music, reggae of course prevented it. Pete passed the fare through various hands to the driver.

The bus stopped several times on their way to Oistens. People got off, people got on. It was stretched to the limits when they arrived.

The deafening noise of the bus music was immediately replaced by the music from the fish fry loudspeakers.

Pete spoke into Jude's ear from a distance of about three inches, "The kitchens you see," pointing at the small brick-built buildings surrounded by plastic tables and chairs almost all fully occupied. "Are permanent leasable kitchens built for the cricket world cup, before that they were timber shacks."

"I see," she shouted.

"Trouble was, they didn't get finished in time. Opened the year after, big inquiry, big money changing hands in high places, so the rumour has it."

"Oh," she nodded as if she couldn't care less.

"The stalls selling whatever will be gone by Sunday but they'll be back again next Friday."

They wandered aimlessly through the stalls picking up a couple of bottles of Banks beer on the way.

A band was setting up their equipment on the big stage as the DJ continued to play beat music heavily influenced by reggae. People, not all young, danced and jived. Pete and Jude, bottles in hand joined in.

"You ready to eat?" he yelled in her ear.

She nodded.

Each kitchen/restaurant had a different menu, fish of various species, the occasional chicken, and jerk beef on offer. Standard accompaniments were rice and peas, the most common; potatoes fries or jacket and okra.

Pete and Jude debated the relative merits of several places and plumped for one with clean chequered linen tablecloths whose menu amongst other things included grilled tuna steaks and king prawns.

They took the two remaining seats on offer, ordered the tuna lightly cooked, the prawns with garlic butter and a couple of banks to replace the empties they had discarded in a rubbish bin or trashcan as it was labelled.

They shared the two dishes that arrived freshly cooked twenty minutes later by which time two more beers were required.

The incessant reggae beat permeated through the numerous food outlets to the periphery where they dined. The beat was pulsating and hypnotic, Jude swayed continually in unison with the rhythm.

Their meal, including the drinks, cost a fraction of what he'd paid at the Aqua the previous night and compared with The Cliff it was a pittance.

Again they meandered between the local handicrafts' stalls stopping only for Jude to buy an inexpensive local stone pendant.

Together they gyrated in front of the stage now occupied by a live band reproducing the songs of Bob Marley, UB40, Beanie Man and the like.

Jude hung from Pete's neck, she whispered in his ear, "Take me home."

The queue at the bus stop was 50 yards long and three or four deep.

There was no one at the taxi rank where a line of cabs awaited fares, no contest they jumped in the first cab in line.

The inescapable reggae, albeit in a muted form, filled the confines of the taxi. Jude snuggled into Pete, he put an arm around her shoulder, drew her closer and slipped his hand down the top of her summer dress.

The driver could see this clearly through his rear-view, he smiled. *Lucky bastard,* he thought.

"Wait for it, my man," she whispered as her nipple came to attention. She silently wished the driver would put his foot down, he did not. She urgently wanted more than a soft hand on a welcoming breast, *"Please hurry,"* she willed the driver silently.

To Jude, the time it took for Pete to pay the driver seemed an age, her nipple was tingling, and her vagina was wet moist.

She climbed the stairs two at a time and raced along the external timber walkway to her room. Pete was a stride behind.

She dropped her dress to the floor, apart from the new pendant. She was totally naked, she'd travelled to Oistens and back without underwear.

She almost removed the buttons from Pete's cotton shirt as she tore it open and stripped it from his bronzed body.

He removed his own jeans and boxers and stood with his proud erection touching Jude's navel.

Sex precluded foreplay, the soft mattress of the Palm Court bed cushioning their syncopated erotic movement.

Jude was nymphatic and tireless, Pete was obliging but even his extensive energy dissipated into exhaustion.

He slept only to be brought back for further sexual action by the wandering hands of Jude. The fact that the sun's first rays were permeating the flimsy curtains was of no consequence. She was awake and in need of further gratification.

Pete's penis was willing as was his libido but his testicles were spent, and his orgasm was semen-less.

Jude, on the other hand, was insatiable, Pete had done his best but had it been enough. He could do no more, he was spent.

"Time to go," he said, "It's 8 o'clock, you'll need to be away soon for your flight, mine's a little later," it was a lie of course. He would be going in the opposite direction on a cruise ship but she didn't need to know that.

He dressed; she lay spread across the bed hoping he would return but not to be.

"I'll see you off," he promised as he exited.

Chapter 9

Jude's airport taxi arrived on time; her luggage was loaded.

She passed him a slip of paper. "My mobile number, ring me."

"I will," he lied. "Have you got your phone handy?" he asked.

She removed it from her handbag, Pete manipulated his phone. "Add this to your contacts," he read off a number. It was a genuine number, not his own present number. It was one from a previous phone that no longer existed. There would be no further contact, of that he was sure.

"Au revoir," she said kissing him amorously on the lips, "Until next time. You will ring, won't you?"

"Of course," he lied.

She waved through the rear window of the taxi and he from the hotel steps.

Another liaison had been and gone.

Pete was a seasoned traveller, an experienced packer of luggage. He'd learnt by trial and error the best ways of folding and stowing every article of clothing and personal effects, invariably his shirts and trousers and in particular his dinner jacket came out of the case as they went in, pristine.

As he packed he reflected on the previous week's holiday. He could hardly call it relaxing, his fitness regime had been reduced to tatters He'd hardly relaxed and he'd read very little but then, on the other hand, sexually it had been most successful.

There had been the French lady at Lawrence Gap, never did get her name but ooh là là, then Lady Penelope, she of the free meal and the excellent night of carnal bliss and finally Jude, the rather demanding Palm Court resident, it had been a good week.

He laughed to himself when the thought, *a bus man's holiday,* came to mind.

Now it was back to business, sex was how he made his living, sort of.

His old dad had told him, "Never mix business with pleasure."

But pleasure was his business and the business gave him pleasure. *How's that for a philosophical thought?* he mused.

His formal and leisure shirts, his trousers, dress shirts, jackets and dinner jacket were folded in neatly surrounded by shoes, socks and underwear. His douche bag and travelling clothes he parked on the bed.

The tingling arrows of shower refreshed his tired body. He was ready for a new day, a new adventure and hopefully financial reward.

He shaved, careful to avoid a facial nick and the consequential appearance of an unsightly minuscule scab or, worse still, a plaster.

He vainly admired himself in the mirror. *Not bad,* he thought. *Now for the finishing touch.*

Out of his bag, he produced a bottle of professional liquid silver grey hair dye. With a practised hand, he applied it to the hair at his temples, above his ears and in the nape of his neck. He brushed it in carefully using a stiff-bristled artist's fan brush from which he'd removed some of the hair. The end product gave him a more mature appearance, temporarily ageing him a few years.

The dye and its application had been introduced to Pete by one of his circle of London friends, a make-up artist by profession. He'd also shown him how to use facial makeup but Pete declined to go that far.

He had found that the mature women of 50+ were more amenable to a man of 45 and over than they were to a younger man. The term 'toyboy' was an abhorrence to most, he'd had success before using this ploy.

He dressed in freshly laundered sports shirt, dress shorts and his new trainers.

He was almost ready to go but first he needed to organise his travel documentation.

He delved into the douche bag and withdrew a battered leather A3 size document case. He checked his boarding card, recommended check-in was 13:00 – 14:00, plenty of time. He then produced three passports, all deep red, all UK citizenship. He opened them.

The genuine Peter Holmes passport, the one he'd entered Barbados on and used there was put to one side.

He opened the other two simultaneously, he held them, and his eyes darted from one to the other.

The same portrait photograph appeared on all three. This was the only detail that was the same.

The passport in his left hand was in the name of Jolliff Benjamin, Passport No. 477202325. British citizen. Date of birth: 13 Jul/Juil 80. Sex M, and Place of birth: Oxford. Date of issue: 08 Oct 08 and an expiry date of 08 Oct 18.

The one in his other hand contained the name Goodwin James, No. 467312541, a birth date of 18 Jul 80, Sex M, Born in Bury St Edmonds with an issue date of 10 Sept 09, expiring 10 Sept 19.

Pete weighed the two, for the next two weeks or so he would be Benjamin, Ben, Jolliff, the name that would appear on the cruise manifest.

These two passports were, of course, forgeries. Extremely good forgeries, made by a master, tried and tested through many security checks.

Pete had never in his life associated with the criminal fraternity but an old friend of his had.

Daniel, Pete's best mate from university knew everybody worth knowing including the forger who had made the passports for Pete.

They hadn't come cheap but already to date they had paid for themselves several times over in giving Pete anonymity allowing him to disappear at will.

The genuine Peter Holmes passport together with the James Goodwin one he placed back in the document case and returned them to the douche bag. The Ben

Jolliff passport together with the cruise check-in documentation were conveniently placed in his man bag.

He dressed casually in a cool cotton shirt and linen trousers. A breast pocket housed his bankcards, the Peter Holmes one for use whilst he was still in Barbados and the Ben Jolliff one for use on board the cruise ship.

He settled his hotel bill and asked them to call him a taxi.

With his large case of clothes and carry-on bag of sundry items stowed in the boot, off they set for Bridgetown for a short stop for shopping.

The taxi stood with his engine idling while Pete (not yet Ben) leapt out and visited the large Cave Shepherd store.

He bought new underwear, socks, a couple of shirts and ties, two tee-shirts and three polo shirts. He used his Peter Holmes debit card for the last time for two weeks or so. He re-joined the taxi.

He alighted the taxi at the Cruise Terminal and immediately his one large case was whisked away by the waiting porters.

He paid the cab driver, generously tipped him and the porters and trundled his wheeled carry-on into the terminal.

The Bridgetown terminal was much the same as all the others he'd embarked from. It would appear that in principle they were all large sheds, in some cases re-invented warehouses, others new but all vast spaces.

Even the most reluctant inexperienced traveller would find it difficult to take a wrong turning. The numerous cruise personnel were everywhere aiding passenger progress.

Already he was in working mode, if being a professional womanizer could be called work, yes. Pete made his living from womanizing, ergo he deemed it work.

He'd gradually permeated to his present professional status from a natural inclination and circumstances.

His eyes scanned the preferential passenger zone as this would be the area through which his next 'client' would be processed. No one appeared to fit the required profile.

As his carry-on passed through the x-ray machine, he entered the security loop. The alarm sounded, no problem, it had happened to him before. The simple body search that followed was as he knew it would be fruit-less.

Processing through check-in was quick and painless.

Minutes later he was having the obligatory photograph taken prior to boarding. On the way he had spotted one or two single female travellers but none that showed promise.

His cabin or stateroom as the cruise line preferred to call it, was a clone of others he had occupied on other ships. Nothing ostentatious, a normal double, bathroom, bedroom with small lounge area and balcony, his home for the next two weeks.

He sat on the balcony and watched more passengers as they followed the same route as he had a few minutes earlier along the pier, his potential 'client' search continued.

As he sat, he recovered his Samsung notebook from his carry on, booted it up and connected to the ship's Wi-Fi which he'd ordered and paid for in advance.

He was still on the balcony as the boarding walkways were removed, boarding was complete.

Five minutes had not passed when there was a knock at the door. It did not surprise him to find no one there, there was however a white envelope in his message rack as he knew there would be.

He recovered it and opened it in the sanctuary of his cabin, it was a passenger manifest of the larger suites.

Each passenger's details were there. Stateroom No., sex, marital status, age and photograph, but no financial details, their personality was for him to determine.

One by one he carefully read them and set them to memory.

He'd been blessed with a photographic memory which had helped through school, university and now.

He asterisked several possible 'clients' as he preferred to call them, 'mark' or 'target' sounded crude and inappropriate. He then e-mailed their details to a US address.

For a substantial fee, the e-mail recipient, a resident of New Jersey by the name of Emmanuel (Manny) Strauss would find out everything there was to know about them including their financial status, and what's more, he'd do it in a couple of hours. Pete (Ben) didn't ask how. Manny, over the years, had accumulated a network of 'operatives' in all walks of life and in all sorts of positions, banks, police, multi-national corporations, everywhere even onboard cruise ships, hence the appearance of the envelope.

An acknowledgement came by return, he only had to wait a couple of hours for the information to be forthcoming.

Time for a wander around the ship to acquaint himself with the layout and of course survey the potential.

Pete (Ben) had travelled on several cruise ships of several different lines and in general terms they were all very much the same.

His cabin was on the port side, the left-hand side for landlubbers, the right-hand side being the starboard side. Even though he'd a good memory, Pete always had to think through the 'POSH' acronym: Port Out, Starboard Home, last viewing of Portsmouth on the voyage out and the first view on the return. Dearer cabins for the upper classes, hence POSH people.

If he could, he tried to get a cabin at the front or prow as it should be called, not 'sharp end', as Pete's dad called it and on this occasion he'd succeeded. It was A222 and it was on deck level 12.

Sailors must be suspicious people as there never seemed to be a level 13, therefore two levels above him was level 15, Lido Deck. He didn't wait for one of the bank of four local lifts, they were busy with the movement of luggage and newly boarded passengers. He bounded up the four flights of stairs.

Lido deck had some passenger accommodation but the majority of this level was taken up by pools, sun lounging areas and the buffet restaurant.

Already many of the sunbeds were occupied. Pete (Ben) assessed the sojourners, none of his shortlist were to be seen but there were some very attractive mature ladies who appeared to be without escorts.

The buffet restaurant was very well attended, there was barely a spare seat to be found, nevertheless he used the mandatory hand sanitizer and entered the food area. What to choose was a problem, there were two different soups, at least 12 hot dishes, cold meats, cheese, salads, fruits and pastries and more, so easy to go berserk and 'sod the diet'. He managed to compromise: a soup and a roll and a small salad.

A couple were just leaving a table next to the window, he commandeered it. The waiter swiftly removed the couple's debris and offered him a drink, he peered out onto the loading jetty at the ant-like people below. There were several solo female travellers to be seen, would one of them be his new client? He'd fixed on one when his coffee arrived, she looked the part, maybe she was the one.

Pete (Ben) made his way back to A222 taking a devious route, down in the aft lift to level 5, along the Promenade Deck and through Photo Gallery. the Charleston Club Entertainments Bar, the Atrium Open Staircase area passing the shops, and on via the Ramblas Bar to the lifts to the rear of the Theatre. He strolled nonchalantly appraising the many passengers as they too surveyed their new surroundings.

One of the theatre lifts took him up to level 12 for the short walk down the narrow corridor to his stateroom.

In the relatively short time it had taken him to lunch, his luggage had been delivered.

Andre, the Filipino Stateroom steward, had covered the queen-sized bed with a protective sheet and lifted his large suitcase and carry-on bag on to it. Pete (Ben) set about unpacking, not one of his favourite jobs but if he didn't do it, who would?

Everything was in its rightful place, and he was in the process of stashing his personal documents including the real and bogus passports in the safe when the blip of his tablet advised him of an incoming message.

Manny Strauss prided himself on his service, if he said it would take two hours, then two hours it would be. Pete (Ben) had sent his request 1 hour 58 minutes before. The e-mail read, 'Info as requested, fee as usual, pay into usual account asap, regards M.' There were four attachments.

One by one, Pete (Ben) opened the attachments and casually read the contents. He didn't have a portable printer to make hard copies but that was of no consequence. Once read, their details were filed in his memory banks.

Each CV was complete with a recent photograph, marital and personal details and most importantly, financial status.

He visualised each one in turn studying every detail.

He discounted two, both for the same reason, their financial status.

From a financial point of view the remaining two, both had merit. Both were widows who had been left extremely comfortable by their husband, husbands in one case.

From their photographs and physical descriptions, they both appeared easy on the eye and even their ages were similar. One being 55 and the other 56.

It was their families, their offspring or the lack of them which was the deciding factor.

The 55-year-old, Margaret Cellino, had a daughter aged 35, married to a CEO in the oil business, and a 33-year-old lawyer son.

The 56-year-old, Helen Schmidt, had no family. She was widowed, and her only son had been killed in a motoring accident.

Should things not go well, a family member lawyer would be best avoided, not that anything would go wrong if he played his hand correctly but that single fact guided Pete (Ben) away from Margaret Cellino.

Decision made, his new client would be Helen Schmidt presently residing in Stateroom No. L106, a Mini-suite located on Lido Deck, Level 15.

Pete (Ben) sent a short reply, 'Thanks Manny. Funds on their way, P.'

The account was paid electronically within the next few minutes.

This sum, this overhead expense was entered into the accounts ledger for the Helen Schmidt Project stored within his grey matter. Another benefit of having a computer-like memory, no paperwork.

Chapter 10

Pete (Ben) consulted the small fold-up plan of the ship that had been given to him as part of the boarding documents. L106 was two levels directly above him on the equivalent port corridor, it was the very front stateroom with a balcony overlooking the prow.

He went to look, there was no one about, not even a steward. That was good, a few seconds and he'd found out what he wanted to know.

A notice on the corridor wall reminded the residents of their Muster Station location in the event of an emergency, hers was the Theatre, Level 7 the same as his.

He returned to his cabin to hear the expected announcement that the Emergency Procedures Muster was imminent and that without exception, all passengers should make their way to their allocated Muster Station. This was his first opportunity to cast his eyes over the unsuspecting Ms Helen Schmidt.

He collected his life jacket and made his way to the Theatre, he logged in with the Muster Captain and took a seat at the very back from where he could see both circle entrance doors. He thought it highly unlikely Ms Schmidt would enter the Theatre at the lower level.

He was right, the majority of the seats were taken when Helen Schmidt made an appearance. She was obviously an experienced cruiser and new that proceedings would start at exactly 4:30 as announced. She timed her arrival accordingly.

Pete (Ben) recognised her instantly from the photographs provided by the anonymous ship's postman and Manny, none of them did her justice.

She might be 56 years old but she looked younger, no more than 50. She was not particularly tall, maybe 5'7" or 5'8" but carried herself very straight, very erect. He couldn't see her feet but suspected she wore medium height heels.

She wore a dark dress, navy or perhaps black, fitted shift dress with a scalloped neckline and a hem that finished just above her knee.

Over the dress she wore a red bolero jacket with three-quarter sleeves.

Even from where he sat, he could tell that her clothes were from a boutique collection, she looked an elegant lady.

He was no expert on hairstyles, but he liked what he saw. It was not short, slightly longer than her heart-shaped face and it was fair with even lighter highlights.

The close-up photographs showed her to be a handsome woman and his distant appraisal confirmed this to be correct. He looked forward to their first encounter, which he still had to contrive.

She took a vacant seat at the end of a row just as the Instructions and Procedures in the 'unlikely' event of an emergency began. Pete (Ben) found himself studying Helen Schmidt rather than listening to the information that could save his life.

He lost sight of her as the mandatory wearing of the life jackets took place but picked her back up again as she joined the mass exodus of the Theatre. He tried to get closer but there were too many people in between, she was gone.

Back in his stateroom Pete (Ben) leant on the balcony rail as first Bridgetown disappeared then Barbados and the sun, twilight turned to darkness as he pondered on how to introduce himself to Helen Schmidt.

This, he had found, was the moment of either success or instant failure. First impressions were vitally important.

In his mind's eye, he focused on the details of Helen Schmidt's Cruise account as provided by Mr Anonymous, she had selected Freedom Dining which, in effect meant that she would dine in the Stromboli Dining Room, albeit at a time of her choice which was obviously unknown to him.

She could, of course, choose to dine at one of the Speciality Restaurants or the Lido Deck Buffet, or even the Burger Bar but he thought all these were unlikely. His intuition said the Stromboli and he had a good record in this department.

He considered the information that Manny had sent. Helen Schmidt lived in waterfront property in Shelter Island, Long Island, New York State.

She'd travelled from there the previous day flying from Macarthur Airport (Islip) with American Airlines via Philadelphia and Miami and arriving very late at the Sandy Lane Hotel on the Barbados west coast for an overnight stay. How did he do it? *So much information in less than two hours, thank you Manny, you're a miracle worker,* he thought.

With this information, Pete (Ben) surmised that she would be a little tired. The journey had entailed two flight changes and a total journey time of over 15 hours, although she didn't look it, on the contrary, she looked radiant.

Maybe after unpacking she'd have a short siesta; if so, she wasn't likely to dine before 7 o'clock maybe even later, the dining room, after all, was open until 9:30.

That was his best guess. His plan was to follow immediately behind her into the dining room and hopefully join the same table.

He showered, shaved again and changed into casual clothes choosing carefully from his extensive wardrobe.

Nothing too ostentatious but then he didn't have anything too outlandish. He chose pale grey trousers and an open-necked, short-sleeved black cotton shirt, both black and white seem to enhance a tan and a tan gives an impression of health, which in his case was absolutely true.

It was 6:45. He left A222 and made his way to the Red Lion bar.

Pete (Ben) knew Helen Schmidt must pass the Red Lion bar in order to reach the Stromboli restaurant therefore he positioned himself such that he could see her approaching. He ordered a coke and sat alert and ready to move quickly the moment she appeared.

One coke led to another, time passed and so did a large number of diners but no Helen Schmidt.

He looked at his watch for the umpteenth time, it was almost 9 O'clock. He was on the point of giving up, it would seem his assumption was wrong. He stood to leave then stopped abruptly. Helen Schmidt was strolling unhurriedly immediately behind a group of six would be diners.

Pete (Ben) waited until she passed and dropped in behind her.

She'd changed into a different outfit. Now she wore a white tailored linen jacket and trousers with an open neck, buttoned through her pink shirt, her shoes were also white being of the open-toed cork wedge heeled type. She carried a small pink clutch bag and she looked radiant.

The moment she reached the dining room receptionist, Pete (Ben) was by her side.

She saw him out of the corner of her eye and was distracted from her initial intention of addressing the receptionist. She turned and their eyes met. There were no bells or flying hearts or little cupids with bows and arrows, it was simply a meeting of two strangers. "Good evening," said Pete (Ben).

"Oh! Hello," she replied.

"Table for two?" asked the receptionist.

"I don't mind sharing," replied Helen Schmidt.

"If you will follow me, please," said the receptionist with a clipped accent. *Another Filipino,* thought Pete (Ben).

Pete (Ben) followed in Helen's wake as the receptionist led them through the maze of tables to a table for six which was already occupied by two couples.

A waiter attended Helen's chair as she sat and then did the same for Pete (Ben).

As is the norm, introductions were offered.

"Jed," said the vastly overweight man with the round face and thinning red hair wearing a gaudy Hawaiian shirt. Pete (Ben) thought he looked like the hick country Sherriff from the Live and Let Die Bond movie.

"This is my wife, Dora," he added nodding in the direction of the small, mouse-like woman to his left and sat next to Pete (Ben).

"Hi there, I'm Jane," said the pouting blonde with the extremely low-cut dress in a theatrical seductive voice. *Yes, of course you are,* thought Pete (Ben).

"And I'm Geoffrey," offered the small bald man sat between Jane and Jed, the two of them making him look positively minute. *Is he her husband or sugar daddy?* mused Pete (Ben).

"Pleased to meet you all," said Helen. "Helen, Helen Schmidt."

"And I'm Ben," lied Pete.

"Where are you guys from?" asked Jed.

"Oh, we're not together," replied Helen. "We've only just met, just now."

"Oh, I thought…" Jed began.

"No matter," interjected Helen. "In answer to your question, I'm from New York State."

"We're from New York, aren't we, Dora? Whereabouts are you?" Dora nodded obligingly.

"A little place called Shelter Island, do you know it?"

"Can't say that I do," replied Jed.

Pete (Ben) kept his council but thought, *Yeah okay, little place, Shelter Island maybe but not your house, some mansion,* but, of course, officially, he knew nothing about Helen Schmidt. This round-the-table discussion could prove very interesting.

"How about you, Ben?" queried Jane with a wink, noted by Pete (Ben) but not, he hoped by anyone else.

A knowing smile fleeted across Helen's face.

"Did you not spot the accent?" he began, "I'm from the UK, little village in Oxfordshire actually. A place called Charlton, Charlton-on-Otmor, I don't suppose for one minute you've ever heard of it."

Pete (Ben) had done his homework on both his bogus alias's and prepared a vague life story together with some geographical and historical facts for both, he didn't propose to use this information, only if pressed.

"We went to Oxford a couple of years ago, didn't we Dora?" said Jed. "Love your country, so much history."

"City of Dreaming Spires, Oxford," said Pete (Ben).

"If you say so," replied Jed, his starter had arrived, and his interest was diverted in its direction.

In the meantime the waiter had placed menus in front of Helen and Pete (Ben), he returned for their orders.

"Are you having wine?" he asked.

"I have a wine package," replied Helen. "I will have a bottle of Californian White Zinfandel, is that okay?"

"No problem, ma'am, and you, sir?" he directed to Pete (Ben).

"Another coke please," he replied tendering his room charge card.

"Thank you, sir," said the waiter, noting the number and returning it.

The wine and the coke arrived in a trice followed by another waiter requesting their food order.

The four on the other side of the table had been silent as they attended the starters, they resumed conversing, mainly the two men, with occasional comment from Jane (definitely not plain Jane), Dora the dormouse never said a word.

Pete (Ben) directed a quiet question to Helen, "Forgive me if I'm being forward, you on your own, your husband not with you?" he indicated to her ring finger, the huge solitaire and a concave gold band.

"My husband died some years ago," she replied, Pete (Ben) knew this of course but…

"I'm sorry, I –"

"It's okay," she interrupted. "I can't bear to remove the rings."

"Of course, I'm sorry, I understand."

Pete (Ben) studied her closely, she had a pale complexion, unhindered by cosmetics, being fair too much sun was probably detrimental hence the lack of tan, she had blue/grey eyes, long eyelashes to which she'd applied dark tint, her mascara was a similar shade to her eyes and her eyebrows were pencilled, other than that, she wore only lipstick, a pale pink colour, her skin looked smooth and healthy.

Apart from the two rings the only other jewellery she wore was a gold choker necklace and matching gold earrings which could only be seen when her hair allowed.

Pete (Ben) told himself again, *This will be a pleasure, this is one beautiful woman, maybe a challenge too great but watch this space.*

The dinner progressed with Pete (Ben) attempting surreptitiously and unsuccessfully trying to hog the conversation with Helen Schmidt.

The three across the table, Dora being the exception, continually bombarded them with questions, stupid ones from big Jed, inquisitive, even nosey ones, from bald Geoffrey and flirtatious comments from the tarty Jane.

Pete (Ben) was pleased to see them go as they left together saying they hoped to meet again, and Pete (Ben) thinking, *"Over my dead body."*

Apart from Dora, they'd been a pain.

Both Helen and Pete (Ben) sighed with relief on their departure.

The waiter returned with the sweet menu, Helen declined, Pete (Ben) did too. "Coffee?" he asked.

"Please," she replied. "White."

Pete (Ben) advised the waiter, "Two, white please,"

"I thought all Americans took their coffee black and strong," Pete (Ben) suggested.

"Not all of us, some of us still have colonial tendencies," she laughed.

"I'm pleased to learn you know your place," he joked.

"Only regarding milk in coffee, not in important things," she rebuked with a smile.

"Your first cruise?" Pete (Ben) ventured.

"No, no, I'm what they call a cruise veteran."

"You're no veteran," he replied, an intended compliment, which was received as such.

"Thank you, kind sir," she said. "But in cruising terms above twenty is regarded as being a veteran, this is my 23rd."

"Wow, what is it, the sea air, the Caribbean, the entertainment, or what?"

"All of the above, it's easy, it's comfortable, and I get to meet nice people like you."

"Thank you kindly, ma'am," he replied, pleased to learn that his first advances had been well received.

"Can I buy you a drink?" he asked, taking advantage of the previous compliment.

"I'd like that," she replied.

48

They left the Stromboli dining room and strolled casually along the Promenade deck. "Here," said Pete (Ben) indicating the Red Lion bar, the bar he'd used as an observation point earlier.

She nodded assent, "Why not?"

The bar had filled considerably since his earlier visit, there were no vacant seats around the small tables but there were two empty stools at the bar, "Okay here?" Pete (Ben) asked.

"Sure," she replied, Pete (Ben) offered his hand as she clambered to perch cross-legged her foot swaying in the air.

He couldn't help but notice her shoe, not only was it a smart elegant design, it had a red sole, that meant only one thing, her shoes were Christian Louboutin, Pete (Ben) had read about these, the signature red soles commonly referred to as 'assistant's nail polish', the famous client list, and of course their cost, another indication of the style and wealth of this particular lady.

Helen requested a mojito, Pete (Ben) ordered a Boddingtons, a familiar English beer he was pleased to see on the drinks menu.

Pete (Ben) perched on his stool, "Cheers," he said raising his glass to hers.

"Cheers," she mimicked.

Manny's information had been pretty extensive, but it hadn't told him everything, which wasn't a bad thing, he could genuinely enquire more about her and her life without sounding false.

"Tell me about Shelter Island, it sounds interesting?" he asked.

"Well, it's at the eastern end of Long Island, you've maybe heard of Long Island."

"Yeh, heard of it, never been."

"Long Island is very highly populated, but Shelter Island is rural and green with beautiful bays and sandy beaches. It's lovely," she added.

"Have you always lived there?" He knew the answer, but it was a natural follow-up question.

"Not Shelter, Long Island yes, Brooklyn, a lot different to Shelter Island. Oh yes, I'm a native New Yorker, as the song goes."

"A bit different then," he said inviting more information.

"You could say that, Brooklyn's one of the most populated places in the Western world with well over two million people, all, or most, vertical living."

"I take it there's no high rise in Shelter Island."

"Definitely not, and I don't miss it one little bit."

"Did you live in a high rise?"

"No, an apartment yes, but not high rise, I was born in Borough Park, it's very much a Jewish community but there were a few Irish families there, we were one of those."

"Irish?"

"Oh yes, O'Flynn was my maiden name, a good old Irish Catholic family we were." Pete (Ben) got the impression Helen was enjoying this reminisce.

"My father was 2nd generation Irish-American, he was a steel erector, you know worked miles up in the air building the skyscrapers you see today, he was a good worker dad, we never went short for anything."

"And your mother?"

"American-Irish-Catholic as well, Mary, good Irish name, Flaherty, just like Dad, she was one of six children, good Catholics all," she smiled.

"Did mum work?"

"Later, when we were older, there were four of us, three girls and a boy, she was a waitress in the local deli, a little bit of pocket money it gave her," Pete (Ben) noted that if he listened carefully he detected a slight Irish lilt, or was he imagining it.

The Red Lion was busy but Helen and Pete (Ben) hardly noticed.

"Enough of me, what about yourself?" she prompted.

Pete (Ben) kicked into fantasy mode using fictitious and distorted truth to relate his history.

"Me, I'm quite boring, but if you insist."

"I do," she iterated.

"Well you asked for it, my father, George Jollif, was a teacher, a middle school teacher, and mum was the daughter of a farmer, she did jobs around the farm like tending the chickens and pigs, that sort of thing."

"So you're not a city boy then?"

"I wasn't, but I am now," he lied smoothly.

"Brothers and sisters?"

"No, only child, they took one look at me and said no more."

"Yeh, okay," she replied. "Go on."

"What, you want more?"

"Of course."

"Okay, here goes, prodigiously talented child, on to grammar school. You don't have grammar schools, do you? A secondary school for the so-called intelligentsia, although that's not true, especially if you pay."

"If you have the money, you can buy a better education in the States, not so in my case though," she added.

"Grammar school to uni, luckily got a BA, a British Degree, in Economics," he set a seed with the 'economics degree' for possible future use.

"And what do you do now?" she asked.

"I'm a famous novelist, you never heard of me?" he joshed.

"Yeah okay," she repeated, a favourite interjection.

"Yeah, you're right, how do I make my living, this and that, a bit of trading, buying and selling, I've developed a few very good contacts, sometimes get some good information," another seed set.

He turned the table back to her. "Schmidt?" he queried. "German?"

"I guess so, originally anyway, my husband's family came through Ellis Island, like my grandparents, difference was they came with some money, my family came with nothing."

"If you don't mind me saying so, you don't appear to be on the bread-line."

50

She accepted the comment in the way it had been intended, "You're right, my husband's family made plenty of money in the land of opportunity and when he died, he left me well catered for."

"Excuse me, I didn't mean to pry."

"It's okay, I'd rather look wealthy than poor."

Pete (Ben) tactfully changed the subject.

"Do you manage to see Broadway shows?"

"Sure, every two or three months, I drive downtown, three hours or more depending on traffic, then I stay overnight and return the next day."

"You must have seen some good shows, musicals?" he asked.

"Musicals, plays, sure, this last year, Jersey Boys, Cabaret, Les Misérables, that was particularly good, and your British one, Billy Elliot, that was okay but some of it went over my head."

"Yeah, I can understand that, I've seen it, it is very British, set at a very trying time politically, and of course British humour."

"Where do you stay?"

"The Bryant Park, West 40th street, there's parking, pretty good accommodation and it's walking distance to the theatres."

"Sounds good, I'll bear that one in mind, although the parking's not necessary for me."

The conversation meandered through the various shows that they'd seen, comparing the West End productions with the Broadway versions.

The Red Lion emptied around them unnoticed, only the faithful few remained.

Helen looked at her watch, a circular Longines with stainless steel strap. "My God," she said. "It's nearly 12."

"That's okay, you're not wearing glass slippers, are you?"

"I'm no Cinderella," she replied, picking up on the anomaly.

"As pretty as," he complimented.

"Thank you, kind sir," she replied, "Or should I say Prince Charming?"

"Touché, and I'm certainly no Prince Charming, Baron Hardup more like," which produced a joint laugh.

"I wasn't tired until I saw the time, I think it's time to say good night," said Helen.

"Which way do you go?" asked Pete (Ben), albeit he already knew the answer.

"Forward Level 14."

"I'm forward Level 12, we'll walk together, okay?"

"Certainly."

"Have you anything planned for tomorrow?" he asked as they walked through the Atrium open staircase area.

"Nothing organised, I thought I'd take a walk ashore and see what happened from there, and you?"

"No, nothing, I'll play it by ear, just see what the morning brings."

The lift doors opened at Level 12, "Nice meeting you, hope to see you again," said Pete (Ben) as he alighted. Don't push it, he was thinking. There's always tomorrow, *I'll see you then, you don't know it yet, but be assured, I will.*

"Good night," she was saying as the lift doors closed.

Promising start, thought Pete (Ben) as he collected the single chocolate from the bed.

"Handsome, intelligent, charming," Helen considered as she entered her empty suite, she sighed audibly as she began to undress.

Chapter 11

Pete (Ben) had just completed the first kilometre of a two-kilometre row using one of the two rowing machines in the Ship's gymnasium when he spotted Helen as she approached one of the many exercise bikes.

She wore a black sports bra top; black Capri stretch fabric training tights that finished just below the knee, and black and white patterned trainers.

In this outfit her figure was enhanced to the full, her full bust looked round and firm, made to appear larger than Pete's estimate of 36D by her narrow waist, not Dolly Parton narrow, but narrow enough, with padded hips she had what would have been called at one time an 'hourglass figure'.

Her stomach was flat with the slight hint of a 'spare tyre', her bottom was firm and her legs solid, not muscular.

She turned heads, Pete (Ben) had noticed, at least three males and two females glanced in her direction, one male ogled lasciviously.

She spotted him and waved, he acknowledged with a nod of his head as he passed the 1200-metre mark.

He was blowing hard as he completed the 2k, "Breathing through his arse," his old man would have said in his exaggerated Yorkshire accent.

He wiped himself down with the gym towel as he approached Helen Schmidt, "Morning, sleep well?"

"Head touched the pillow, gone," she replied as she removed her ear-phones still peddling at a steady pace.

"You finished now?" she asked.

"No, not yet, I'm just going to use the jogging track."

"I'll join you if you don't mind, I'll just be a few minutes."

"No problem I'll do a few weights until you're ready."

Five minutes, no more, she was stood next to him as he completed a set of arm roll exercises.

"Let's go," she said.

Pete (Ben) set his normal jogging pace, which was not exceptional, but nevertheless steady, Helen had no difficulty in keeping in step.

They didn't converse, jogging and training in general were for exercising the muscles, not the tongue, they both were serious trainers and ran in silence.

As they completed their sixth lap, the ship docked at Castries, St Lucia.

They separated, each to their own changing facility.

"Have a nice day," Helen uttered the inimitable American expression that has been adopted worldwide.

"You too," he replied. *"See you soon,"* he whispered under his breath.

Showered and changed into cargo shorts, sports shirt and leather sandals, Pete (Ben) breakfasted on scrambled eggs, buttered toast and coffee in the buffet restaurant, he watched as the crew made fast the ship and made ready for the exodus of the embarking passengers.

He was in no rush, he'd hurried through his ablutions, he had everything with him that he needed for a shore visit stowed in his rucksack of indeterminate years, he had no idea what Helen had in mind for the day, she hadn't herself, so she'd said, but Pete (Ben) was prepared for any eventuality.

He followed the first rush of the embarked sure in the knowledge, or almost sure, that he was well in advance of Helen Schmidt, he exited through the security gate and took up residence at the first bar in the village of shops that formed the Cruise Terminal reception area.

Rum, in all its guises, was the spirit of the day, as it was every day in the Caribbean, he deflected the offers of daiquiris and the like, bought a large Coca-Cola with lots of ice, and sat as inconspicuous as possible in the small interior area monitoring the surge of humanity passing by.

Two Coca-Colas later, he was still sat in the same chair at the same table, he felt sure he hadn't missed her, but doubt was beginning to fester.

Although he didn't want another drink, he felt conspicuous with an empty glass sat in front of him, he was about to order another when there she was, she looked radiant again, standing out in the crowd.

She was all in pink, button-down pink shirt knotted to reveal her flat stomach, pink knee-length shorts and pink wedge sandals with a red sole, although he doubted that, she carried a pink beach bag with a floral pattern.

He let her pass and followed at a discreet distance.

He was hypnotised by the subtle swaying movement of her hips and the rotation of her buttocks, there was no chance of losing her.

She walked passed the queues of passengers taking the Cruise ship's tours, passed the row of local taxis and mini-coaches offering more reasonable priced tours, and on into the small township of Castries.

She stopped at several shops as she strolled the busy streets, she didn't appear to be in a buying mood, merely window-shopping, the standard of shops from which she was likely to buy from, did not exist in Castries.

It doesn't take long to exhaust the sights of Castries, she found the local market arrayed with local produce, fruit, vegetables, spices, handicrafts, and a myriad of everything, the colourful scene drew her camera, an expensive-looking one, from her beach bag for a portfolio of ethnic photographs.

Pete (Ben) observed her looking about, lost, as if not knowing what to do next, a taxi was parked at the roadside, as she approached it, the driver, who had obviously seen her coming, got out to greet her, he was a huge black man, he towered above her.

Pete (Ben) approached with stealth, he could hear raised voices, this was his opportunity.

He interrupted their heated discussion. "Can I help?" he said.

Neither had seen him coming, Helen was clearly startled. "Oh, yes, oh it's you," she stammered.

"Yeah, it's me, hi, anything I can help with?"

The driver stood silent, his big eyes bulged, Pete (Ben) had knocked him off his stride, he was speechless.

Helen led Pete (Ben) gently by the arm a few yards to one side, she whispered, "This brute wants to charge me $200 for an island tour, I know I can afford it but it galls me to be cheated, I'm not paying anywhere near that sum."

"Mmmm, I agree," said Pete (Ben). "But I've found that here, like many other places, when dealing with taxi drivers it pays to be very specific what you want and expect for your money, would you like me to try?"

"I can do it myself, but here I think a man has more influence, mores the pity, so yes, if you will."

"What would you like to do, the tourist spots, and the beach, say three hours tour, two hours beach, and back to the ship?"

"That sounds good."

Together they stood in front of the taxi driver, Pete (Ben) stood eye to eye with him.

Pete (Ben) had visited St Lucia more than once and knew the main tourist spots, Rodney Bay, the Pitons, all the usual suspects, he reeled them off. "Three-hour tour, no less, two hours at Marigot Bay and back to the ship, how much, and I want a proper price, no argument when she returns."

The taxi driver pondered, "Okay, $120."

"How does that sound?" he deferred to Helen.

"Fine, that's what I had in mind, but he wouldn't listen to me."

"Pleased I could be of assistance, I'll see you later, I hope," he turned to leave.

"Ben," she called him back. "Would you like to join me?"

"That would be nice, if you don't mind?" His plan had worked.

"Yeh, I'd like that, please come."

"Then I will thank you."

The driver had watched this exchange in silence, he spoke again, "You're coming too?" he asked Pete (Ben).

"Yeah," he replied following Helen into the back seat.

"Wait a minute, for two people that will be..." he stopped, thought, and added, "$150."

"Okay, no problem," replied Pete (Ben), he had no intention of missing this opportunity.

The taxi driver turned out to be worth his fee, he had plenty of tourist type information to impart, and what he didn't know, Pete (Ben) did, for the agreed three hours together they entertained Helen with a running commentary.

Several stops were made for Helen to take photographs, twice she tried to include Pete (Ben) in the picture, but each time he cleverly avoided capture.

Two hours and 58 minutes after leaving Castries, Helen and Pete (Ben) stood at the bottom of the single road in and out of Marigot Bay waiting for the ferry punt to take them to the opposite side of the lagoon and the sandy beach with swaying palms.

The lagoon to their right was full of luxury yachts, large and small, a lone local fruit seller on a paddleboard looked diminutive as he hawked his wares weaving between them.

As if they'd been pre-ordered, two sunbeds awaited them in exactly the right places, one in the shade of a palm tree, the other adjacent in direct sunlight.

As if from nowhere, an attendant appeared for the rental fee as they parked their bags and began to strip.

How the day had changed, thought Pete (Ben). *From a poor start sat bored in a dowdy bar under a cloudy sky, to here, an idyllic sandy beach with a clear blue sky overhead in the company of a beautiful woman, I love my job.*

Helen removed her shirt and shorts to reveal colour coordinated swimwear, a pink floral bikini with a strapless top and hipster style briefs.

Pete (Ben) wore the same budgie smugglers he'd worn on the Palm Court beach.

"Last in the pond is a sissy," said Pete (Ben) already on the move toward the rippling azure blue sea.

Helen reacted quickly and was immediately behind him as he waded into the sea and down the gradual slope to the deeper water.

"What's a sissy?" she asked when she finally caught up with him stood with the water lapping around his waist.

"A sissy, oh yes, a sissy, old English I suppose, somebody that's timid, cowardly or even effeminate, it's just a word, a saying, silly I suppose."

"So I'm the sissy then?" she asked pushing him unexpectedly.

Pete (Ben) didn't see this coming and toppled over disappearing under the flat sea, he emerged coughing and spluttering, more for effect than actual discomfort.

"Thanks," he said and playfully returned the compliment in the form of splashing her using both arms rapidly.

That started a full war of splashing, both laughing and squealing through mouths full of the salty Caribbean Sea.

The bombardment came to a stop when Helen lost her footing and down she went, Pete (Ben) caught her and lifted her so that she was in his arms face to face, they stood still, looking into each other's eyes. "Should I kiss her?" he argued with himself. "Too soon," he decided.

With a fabricated embarrassed look, he coughed lightly, "Sorry," he said as he gently let her go.

"It's okay," she answered equally as embarrassed and sorry he hadn't kissed. *I thought he was going to kiss me,* flashed through her mind. *Damn, I would have liked that, but I've only known him 2 minutes, am I being silly, a silly young girl, God, I hope not.*

Bedraggled they returned to their cruise ship towels and the sanctity of beach, Helen dug out her Kindle, Pete (Ben) his book and in silence they read allowing their bodies dry in the warm offshore breeze.

Helen produced a Factor 20 sunscreen and applied it to legs, arms and stomach, she paused before returning it to the beach bag, Pete (Ben) noticed her hesitancy. "Would you like me to do your back?" he asked.

"Would you mind?" she replied turning to lie prostrate on the sunbed.

Pete (Ben) took the bottle, emptied a generous amount into his hand and applied it to her shoulders, he gently spread it downward until he reached the strap of her bikini top, he expertly undid it and continued ever south to her bottom.

Helen's head was laid to one side. "You've done that before," she said.

"Maybe," he replied non-commitally as he completed the massage and re-fastened the top.

"Thank you," she said as she turned over and sat. "Who are you, Mr Jolliff?" she asked.

Pete (Ben) wasn't expecting a question like this, but he didn't fluster, his quick mind reacted in a nanosecond. "Me, Benjamin Jolliff of Oxford, England, oh, I don't know, somebody who works hard, no that's not right, I don't work too hard, but hard enough, somebody who likes spending what he does earn on nice things, nice holidays and the like, and I like the company of beautiful ladies, and…" he stopped, he felt he'd said enough.

"Mmmm," she said, giving him a quizzical, friendly, admiring look, she liked him, of that she was sure. *This guy is getting to me,* she told herself tacitly.

The drinks and the food in the nearby beach bar were as expensive as the surrounding affluent area would suggest but the use of their facilities for changing were well appreciated, without them the options were travel back in damp swimwear or change inside a towel as when children. Bridlington beach for Pete.

Helen insisted on paying and they made their way back to the ferry punt.

Where the taxi driver had spent the last two hours Pete (Ben) neither knew nor cared, but with unimaginably good timing he drew to a stop as Pete (Ben) paid the ferryman.

The steady drive back to the Cruise terminal took less than half an hour, Helen delved into the beach bag, extracted a pink leather Gucci purse and gave the taxi driver two $100 bills, his grin stretched from ear to ear and his white teeth sparkled, why not he'd finished with exactly the ridiculous figure he'd first insisted upon.

There appeared to be more people returning to the ship than had left it earlier, Helen and Pete (Ben) joined the procession.

Pete (Ben) didn't press level 12 button of the lift, he travelled the extra floor and exited with Helen.

"Thank you for a lovely day," she said as they stood in the large lift lobby.

"Thank you," Pete (Ben) replied. "Would you dine with me tonight?" he ventured.

"Yes, I'd like that," came the immediate answer.

"Good, a drink first, say at 8, and dine at 9?"

"Fine."

"You do like Italian food, don't you?"

"I do, yes."

"Good, I'll organise a table at the Amalfi, and I'll meet you in the Red Lion bar, is that okay?"

"That will be great," she kissed him on the cheek and was gone.

Chapter 12

Pete (Ben) inspected his hair in the bathroom mirror, a little more grey dye was required, he made the necessary adjustments ensuring the same results as the original makeover.

It was the first of the formal dress nights, Pete (Ben) had invested in a new tuxedo for this cruise, he put on his black shirt, black trousers and patent leather black shoes followed by bow tie and finally his brand new, first time out, tailor-made burgundy velvet jacket with slim black lapels, the tie matched the tuxedo.

He pocketed his extra slim Canon Powershot, took a final inspection in the full-length mirror and left for the Red Lion.

Helen was punctual, Pete (Ben) had only just arrived and was sat at the bar as she entered.

"Wow!" he exclaimed, she wore a midnight blue figure-hugging long dress, low enough to reveal an exciting cleavage without being too daring and thin straps over her shoulders to a low back.

No way was this dress ready to wear, it was tailored to her shapely contours and sat perfectly on the black, definitely Louboutin shoes.

She joined him, he kissed her on the cheek and helped her on to the barstool.

His eyes fixed on her necklace, with control he avoided staring at it as he asked what she was she drinking.

"I'll have the same as you, what is it?"

"Mai Tai," he replied glancing again at the necklace and then at the matching earrings.

With the Mai Tai in her hand she raised it to say 'cheers', he did like-wise and noted the bracelet that made for a full set of matching jewellery.

"I had a lovely day," she repeated.

"I'm glad," he replied as his brain worked in two directions, their conversation, and an assessment of the jewellery.

Pete (Ben) knew a lot about jewellery and primary stones in particular.

As a university student, he'd roomed with Daniel Braun, still today his best friend even though they didn't get together much.

Daniel's family had been for several generations diamond factors in Hatton Garden in the heart of the UK jewellery business.

Together they had worked their holidays in the business.

Pete (Ben) had spent his first working day there carrying out menial tasks, fetching and carrying, but that soon changed, his intelligence, natural curiosity and willingness to learn was recognised and he was put to task doing all manner of technical tasks.

He'd learnt to recognise good stones from the less valuable, he polished stones, he valued them, the only job he was never allowed to do was the cutting of the raw stones, that was the domain of the trained skilful family members.

He knew, even from first glance, Helen's jewellery was of the very best, he determined immediately that he must have them, but how?

"You look beautiful tonight," he said fishing his camera from his pocket. "Let me capture this moment."

He snapped several photographs as she posed demurely, "Can I see them?" she asked.

"No," he replied sharply. "Not now, I'll process the best and have it framed, a present from me." Of course he didn't want her to see that he had not only taken portrait pictures of her but pictures specifically of the jewellery.

"What did you think to St Lucia?" Pete (Ben) asked intentionally diverting her attention from the photography.

"It's beautiful, and it's so green, and the beaches…"

"What of Castries?"

"It's a little bit nondescript, don't you think?"

"I guess so," he replied. "It's in a large bay you know a safe anchorage, or so we British thought, until in World War II when a German U-Boat sailed in and sank two allied ships, and not a lot of people know that," he said in his best Michael Cain voice.

The impression went over her head, but she appreciated his knowledge and his conversational skill, to her this attribute was of more consequence than good looks, and he'd got those too, so she thought.

The Amalfi restaurant was at the rear of the ship, it was much smaller than the Stromboli Dining room, the décor was similar but the lighting and ambience were more conducive for intimate couples, perfect for Pete (Ben) in his attempted conquest of the unsuspecting Helen.

Helen ordered the wine from her prepaid package, Pete (Ben) was quite happy to share the same Zinfandel that she'd been drinking on their first meeting, it being a rosé it perfectly suited all courses, antipasti, pasta and entrée alike.

They ate and conferred oblivious to all around them.

It was obvious to Pete (Ben) that the more time they spent together, the more comfortable Helen became, any early tendency to aloofness disappeared.

The plight of the jewellery was still on his mind, although he had not formulated a plan as yet, he knew that it had to be duplicated and substituted.

By simply looking at the necklace and earrings he assessed their dimensions, but the bracelet was another matter.

Resourceful as ever, he soon approximated the bracelet's circumference.

"You have small and dainty hands," he said gently lifting her left hand to compare with his own.

"See the difference," he commented as he pressed his palm to hers.

"And look at your narrow wrist, I wouldn't be surprised if I can span it with my fingers," as he spoke, he did just that.

"I told you so," and diverted the conversation elsewhere, Helen was completely oblivious to what Pete (Ben) had really been doing, now he had all the dimensions required for a copy. *Another job for Manny.*

She spoke about her husband, Henry, how they had met, and how he had made his fortune, she even let slip unintentionally that the house in Shelter Island was more than a house, but a mansion that had cost $4 million dollars to build back in 1995. *Manny's information had been spot on,* thought Pete (Ben).

With a few tears she told him about her only son, Jimmy, and how he'd died in a road accident driving his 21st birthday present, a classic Ferrari Dino.

Every so often Pete (Ben's) eyes were drawn to Helen's jewellery, each time he further appraised the quality and each time thought on how he could relieve her of them, an inkling of a plan began to form.

Several times she insisted on talking about him, but each time after a short fictitious dialogue he diverted the subject back to her and to general matters, always avoiding the conversation killers of politics and religion.

It was a fine meal, they both agreed, two and a half hours flashed by. They were the only two diners left in the Amalfi, the staff hovered patiently waiting for them to leave.

Pete (Ben) called for and signed the bill to the relief of the waiters who no doubt would be on duty again early the following morning.

They strolled unhurriedly to Helen's suite,

"Might I see you tomorrow?" asked Pete (Ben).

"Tomorrow evening, if you like, I'm taking the cruise tour of Dominica in the morning."

"You'll enjoy it, I'm sure, what about evening, what about the Theatre show?"

"That would be good, 7 o'clock, Red Lion, same seats?" she replied.

"Until then," said Pete (Ben) his arms enclosing her and drawing her close. He kissed her on the lips, she didn't resist, on the contrary, her arms went around his neck and she returned the kiss with apparent feeling.

He drew away. "Tomorrow, 7:00," he reiterated as Helen retreated watching him as she gradually closed the door.

Third day, and a kiss, I'm on schedule, he thought, business-like.

Pete (Ben) removed the SD card from his camera, slotted it into his tablet, and downloaded the pictures of Helen and the jewellery.

He then prepared a full written description of the jewellery detailing the stones, settings, chains, everything necessary to reproduce a good facsimile of the originals.

He e-mailed Manny:

'Urgent – Quality paste copies of enclosed required – Needed when I reach Barbados this coming Saturday. If this not possible MUST be in St Maarten next Tues. – Please confirm.'

He added the attachments and pressed send.

As Pete (Ben) was describing the jewellery, Helen was returning it to its velvet-lined box and placing it back in the safe.

She undressed and stood before the mirror. *"Not as good as I was,"* she said to herself as she ran her hands over her bust and down her stomach, *"But not bad for a…"* She stopped without including her age, and thought on. *Am I in love or am I in lust? Don't be stupid, woman, it's lust, and there's nothing wrong with that, enjoy whatever might happen.*

She recalled their time together on the beach, she recalled the adequate bulge in his swim shorts. Inviting, she thought. Bitch, she further thought, followed closely by*, so what, let it happen.*

She clambered into the empty bed and closed her eyes, Pete (Ben) was still in her mind, but not there with her, she imagined a time when he would be. *Let it be soon.*

Pete (Ben) re-read the jewellery description, two three-carat oval diamonds, six two-carat sapphires plus the smaller earring stones, "Must be in excess of £50k," he estimated. "£30k, maybe £40k through Daniel."

He referred to his old chum, Daniel Braun, who unlike his father and the family business, traded in a darker world.

Pete (Ben) sent another e-mail, this time to Daniel, he sent the description and the photographs. 'Are you interested? Pete.'

He stripped and was just about to turn in when the tablet bleeped, it was Manny. "Barbados doubtful, St Maarten definite. Cost – $2000 for good copies – Manny."

Pete (Ben) replied immediately. 'Make every effort for Barbados, Cost $2500 for excellent copies.'

He sat on the edge of the bed thinking of how to reach the jewellery that he knew would be nowhere else but in the safe.

There was only one way, he had to know the safe combination, for that the answer was simple, he had to see Helen enter or exit the safe, he, as yet, had not made it into her room, never mind seen the safe, but he was getting closer, his experience told him Helen was more than interested in him, but he vowed not to rush, it would happen.

Chapter 13

Pete (Ben) had the gymnasium almost to himself. *Dominica must be a popular port of call,* he thought as he powered the rowing machine, his thoughts turned to the absent Helen. *The jewellery is a bi-product, a welcome addition, but not the primary intent of separating her from her money.*

It had to be a financial scam. He hated the word *scam,* but *con* was as bad. There was no nice word for cheating someone, someone as nice as Helen, but that was soon dismissed from his mind, business was business, even if it was dirty business.

The 'scam' he had in mind was similar to one he had used before, again Manny played an integral part.

The day would be used for the sole purpose of fine-tuning the plan's various elements.

He pounded the running track, 6, 7, 8 laps – 10 was his goal. The white buildings with their green and red roofs of Roseau spread out below the deep green backdrop of the Dominican hills and mountains as he travelled the length of the landward side of the ship, he saw them only vaguely, the 'scam' plan filled his thoughts, this was his priority.

The popularity of the island of Dominica meant that there were plenty of empty sunbeds around the pools, Pete (Ben) took up residence in the sun and close to a bar, he had his book and his tablet with him.

He spent the day planning his tactics and corresponding with Manny, interspersed with the reading of the adventures of James Bond.

Manny had already weaved his magic and confirmed that the paste jewellery would be waiting for him in Bridgetown, ironically from a jeweller's shop on Palmetto Street close to the Barbados Police Headquarters.

There followed a series of e-mails between Pete and Manny preparing the way for the series of events that would convince Helen to innocently part with some of her millions.

The numbers around the pool were few, Pete's eyes surveyed the scene. No. 2 on his list of 'targets', Margaret Cellino, was lounging directly opposite, on the other side of the pool, engrossed in a book.

It was an opportunity too good to miss; he quickly determined he would introduce himself. It wouldn't hurt to have a fall-back plan, a first reserve, callous thought, but business is business.

He slipped on his shorts, stashed his effects into his rucksack and made his way to the incognizant Margaret Cellino.

"Is this bed free?" he asked.

She was oblivious to all around her; he startled her. "Err, no, help yourself," she stuttered and returned to the book.

Pete (Ben), spread his towel and unpacked his rucksack exaggerating every movement with every intention of disturbing her concentration.

She appeared unmoved, but Pete (Ben) noticed her surreptitious glances in his direction.

He returned to his book, *Moonraker*. He had reached the final episode, Bond was in the throes of despatching the villainous Drax to a watery grave and saving the earth yet again, the last few pages were a disappointment as the inevitable love interest returns to her fiancée, a fellow Special Branch Officer.

With his book closed on his lap, he studied Margaret Cellino.

The photographs provided by Manny, flattered her, the fashion magazines would have described her as having a fuller figure, Pete (Ben) thought her plump.

She wore a large, white brimmed sun hat, pretentious decorated round sunglasses and a vertically striped one-piece swimsuit, vertical stripes are supposed to be slimming, in Margaret's case they didn't work.

Unlike Helen Schmidt, she looked her age, 55; his information recorded, but age and appearance were of secondary importance to Pete (Ben).

Prostituting himself was one small part of his profession of confidence trickster and thief, he'd bedded much uglier clients to separate them from their money, his bank balance was testament to his success.

"Is it any good?" he asked pointing to her book with the interesting title *The Empire of Sin.*

She didn't seem to mind the interruption, "Yeah, it's pretty good, interesting, sex, jazz, murder, all in my home town of New Orleans," she said laying the book on her adequate stomach.

"You're from New Orleans?" he asked, as if he didn't already know.

"Sure am," she replied. "And you're a Brit," she added.

"Does it show so much?" he asked.

"Oh yes, most definitely, as soon as you spoke, you're a Brit alright."

"Is that okay, you don't mind talking to a Limey, you do still call us Limeys don't you?"

"Sure, I've met some pretty good Limeys in my time."

"I hope I can be another one," said Pete (Ben) with a smile on his face.

"Margaret Cellino," she said extending her hand.

"Ben Jolliff," he replied accepting her hand with a polite shake.

She had small hands and stubby fingers, he noted, and not exactly the smoothest skin he'd ever encountered.

Already he was thinking, *I'm pleased I chose Helen Schmidt, but if it's no go with her then Ms Cellino it will have to be.*

"Ten years now since Katrina, everything back to normal now in New Orleans?" he asked, ensuring she didn't return to her book.

"It will never be the same, a lot of people lost everything, thank God we survived," she replied.

Pete (Ben) assumed she was referring to her family with the 'we' reference. *For sure, they'd survived,* he thought, recalling Manny's report. They'd carpet bagged their way to a fortune on the misfortunes of others.

"It's getting there," she continued. "New levees, new investment, new people, we have hope."

She sounded earnest enough but Manny's report had been pretty damning. *It would have been a pleasure to relieve her of some of her millions, but not sexually,* he opined.

Keep the conversation light, his inner self instructed.

"Are you enjoying the cruise?" he asked.

"So far so good, it's early days, but it seems okay."

"Have you been into Roseau?"

"No, I've been to all the places before, I don't bother now, I just enjoy the ship and its facilities, and you?"

"I've been to Dominica before, I might get off at the next port of call."

"Can I buy you a drink?" he asked.

"You sure can, never turn the offer of a free drink down. Poppa always said never turn down a drink, but to turn down the request for anything else."

"Clever man, your poppa, what will it be?"

"A mojito, if you please Mr Ben Limey."

Pete (Ben) caught the eye of a passing waiter and ordered two mojitos.

Conversation, including make-believe, is a major element in the confidence trick stratagem and Pete (Ben) is still to this day an expert, he played Margaret Cellino like a master puppeteer.

He reached a point where he felt he'd laid the platform for further inducement if necessary, but he was hopeful that it wouldn't be. *Hurry on the return of Helen Schmidt,* he thought.

He repacked his rucksack and bade Margaret Cellino, "Adieu, hope to talk to you again," to which she replied, "I hope so."

Chapter 14

Pete (Ben) lunched alone in Buffet restaurant with his tablet open, e-mails travelled back and forth with Manny in New Jersey, everything was in place for the next phase of 'The Helen Schmidt Project'.

Helen returned, it was mid-afternoon, and the sun had started its descent but it was still hot.

Pete (Ben) had commandeered a sunbed close to the poolside, there had been plenty of vacant ones around him when he'd taken residence after lunch, but now they were occupied by the returning tourers, there was nowhere for Helen to sit except by his side sharing his roost.

"A good day?" he asked.

"Mmmm, okay," she replied.

"Not that good, eh?"

"No it was good, I suppose, but I'd rather have been with you."

"Sorry, I maybe could have –"

"No matter," she interrupted, "I'll let you off if you join me for a siesta."

Pete (Ben) was startled, he didn't expect such an invitation. He thought he would have to wait a little longer, but fine. Let's go, he thought.

Without hesitation, he replied, "Your wish is my command."

Pete (Ben's) placed his tablet on the desk, he booted it up. "Sorry, I'm expecting a call, one of my contacts asked me to stand by," he explained.

"No problem," she replied. "But if there is a call, I do hope you ignore it, at least for a while." She added with a seductive glint in her eye.

"You've got it," said Pete (Ben) as he drew Helen toward him.

For her trip to Dominica, Helen had worn Bermuda style shorts, mini-length tee-shirt exposing her midriff and the wedge-heeled sandals. Pete (Ben) had to stoop to find her lips with his.

As they kissed, his hands explored the silky skin of her back, he found the hooked fastener of her bra and expertly undid it.

She, too, had her hands-on Pete (Ben's) bare back, her long manicured nails holding him tightly holding him close.

The long passionate kiss came to an end, Pete (Ben) lifted Helen's tee-shirt over her head her bra dropped to the floor.

They embraced again but this time his hand slid down the back of her shorts, it was his turn to draw her to him, he was aroused and she could tell, it was Helen's turn now to remove his tee-shirt which she did by standing on her tiptoes, she threw it to one side.

Two pairs of shorts and one pair of panties were discarded to join the tee-shirts and bra, they stood naked locked in a passionate embrace.

The bed beckoned, together they explored each other's body, Helen finding his penis, Pete (Ben) finding an expectant maidenhead.

She was not only a willing partner, she was a good partner, the sex was good and they orgasmed simultaneous.

Helen laid with her head on his chest, their breathing and pulse rates subsided to normal.

Good choice, a good fuck, a bonus. God knows what that miserable fat bugger Margaret Cilento would be like, who cares, passed through his mind.

Helen was also thinking along similar lines, *"I'd forgotten what I was missing."*

Helen's invitation to Pete (Ben) had been for him to join her for a siesta but Pete (Ben) had read between the lines and given her exactly what she'd really meant, two highly delighted and satisfied people lay entwined on the bed.

Helen's eyes closed; she was close to sleep. Pete (Ben) gazed at the blank ceiling. *She's a handsome woman, she's trusting and she's very good in bed, the kind of woman I could...* the tacit sentence unfinished, even in thought, he avoided the 'M' word. *What am I thinking? Forget it. She's rich and she's ready for taking, don't go soft. She's a client, somebody to be shagged and deprived of money. It's business, idiot, come on man.*

Like flicking a switch his business head returned. *'Now's the time'*, without disturbing Helen he extended his arm to the adjacent desk and the open tablet, he tapped the touchpad.

Almost instantaneously a bleep indicated receipt of an e-mail.

Pete (Ben) gently freed himself from Helen's embrace, collected his tablet, sat it on his lap and propped himself up pushing the pillows behind him to rest on the bed head.

Helen moved with him, she could see the message displayed on the screen, it read: 'Shipment available immediate. R u interested? Asif.'

"Sorry about this," said Pete (Ben). "But this could be interesting."

"Go ahead," she replied, her attention roused.

He typed a reply, 'More info please. Ben.'

Seconds later Asif returned, '25 Tonnes Medium Grade Coffee now on ship bound for Rotterdam. E.T.A. 7 days. Yours for $47k. All paperwork good. Asif.'

"Is that good?" asked Helen, her eyes glued to the screen.

"It is if I can sell it on," he replied.

"What will you do?"

"I'll buy it, it's what I do. I should, with luck, make at least $10k."

"I'll send out some feelers," he added.

"But you'll buy it now?"

"Oh yes," he said, leaving the bed, recovering his shorts and pulling them on.

Pete (Ben) sat at the desk his tablet in front of him, Helen lay on her side her head cupped in her hand, she watched with interest.

His first e-mail was to Asif, alias Manny, in New Jersey. 'I'll buy. Send details of payment. Ben,' it said.

The second one read, 'Hi Pierre, I have 25 tonnes medium grade coffee. Please find buyer. Usual commission. Available in Rotterdam in seven days. Ben,' and again sent it to Manny.

Every e-mail, every word, every name, was pre-planned, there was no coffee, there would be no buyer, but Helen would never know, this was just the first phase of the scam that would come later.

During the course of the next half hour numerous bogus e-mails purporting to be to various people and banks, in each case Manny, came and went via Pete (Ben's) tablet, Helen never moved, she was transfixed.

The imaginary coffee was now Pete (Ben's), correspondence from Pierre suggested that a buyer would soon be found.

Pete (Ben) closed the tablet.

"I wait and see what happens, there's nothing more I can do," he said.

"Oh yes there is," said Helen, peeling back the sheets and beckoning him to join her.

"Why not," he said climbing out of his shorts again to reveal his readiness to oblige.

A return to his own cabin had to be made to change from the tee-shirt and shorts to acceptable evening dining wear.

He showered but before dressing he re-booted his tablet, there were no messages.

He fired off an e-mail to Manny: 'Helen Schmidt on the hook. Pete. P. S. Thanks for the jewellery package. Looks good.'

His eyes had hardly left the screen when the reply arrived, 'Your account is rising, hope you pull this one off successfully. Best of luck. Manny.'

When does he ever sleep? occurred to Pete. It didn't seem to matter what time of the day or night it was, Manny was there at his computer.

Chapter 15

Helen was well and truly hooked, the moment she joined Pete (Ben) in the Red Lion bar, she asked excitedly, "Any more on the business transaction?"

"No, not yet," he replied nonchalantly as he assisted her on to the barstool, "Maybe a few days, Pierre will sell, have no doubt."

It was the same barman on duty as the previous evening. "Your usual, ma'am," he said politely.

"Yes please," she replied even though she couldn't remember what she'd been drinking.

"Ah, a Mai Tai, thank you," she said lifting the glass of orange liquid from the bar.

"Cheers," said Helen which was echoed by Pete (Ben) as the glass clinked with Pete (Ben's) bottle of Banks' beer.

"So, what did you think of Dominica?" he asked.

"Lush, green, mountainous, beautiful, pretty good, better if you'd been there."

"Sorry, I did try, but the tour was fully booked," he lied.

"Did you get to swim at Hibiscus Falls," asked Pete (Ben).

"I did, it was great, lovely, clear and cool, I did feel a little out of place, there were a lot of couples, and I was alone."

"You mean you felt like a gooseberry?"

"A gooseberry? What's a gooseberry got to do with it?"

"Sorry, English saying, it means you're the odd one out when everybody else are in couples."

"Exactly, another reason for wanting you around."

The bar suddenly filled with an influx of fellow passengers, a group of six young people gathered at the bar immediately behind Helen.

They were loud, and one in particular was already worse for wear, he swayed like a poplar in a gale, whispering at a decibel level of at least 85.

Pete (Ben) watched him edge closer and closer to Helen, he was just about to stop him when the inevitable happened, he swayed backwards almost stumbling, his arm jolted into the back of Helen.

The glass he held in his hand stayed there but the contents soaked him from his red dickie bow down the front of his white tuxedo and pink shirt to the white belt of his black trousers.

Whatever it was that he'd been drinking was blue, probably curacao, consequently he now had a mixture of blue and purple stains on what a few moments ago had been pristine formal wear, albeit a little too effeminate for Pete (Ben's) taste.

The drunk turned angrily on Helen, "Idiot, look what you've done," he spluttered.

"Whoa!" interjected Pete (Ben). "It was your own fault, rocking like a blues singer, don't go trying to blame somebody else."

His friends stood open-mouthed, speechless.

"Mind your own business dip shit," growled the drunk, the swaying more emphasised than before.

"I think you'd better go and sleep it off before you either do or say something you might regret," said Pete (Ben) quietly.

The drunk was much the same height as Pete (Ben) maybe 30 lbs. lighter but, of course, much younger.

Helen moved to the other side of Pete (Ben) away from the drunk, he raised a finger and waved it in Pete (Ben's) face, "Please don't do that," said Pete (Ben) gently pushing the digit to one side.

Pete (Ben) could have done without this confrontation but he certainly wasn't about to back down.

"Can' you take him to his cabin?" Pete (Ben) appealed to the drunk's friends.

Two of his male friends made toward him but before they reached his side he threw a punch at Pete (Ben), it was accurate but slow, it was on the right trajectory to hit his nose, Pete (Ben's) reactions were amazingly quick, surprising even himself, with his right hand he caught the drunk's fist in mid-air and in one swift movement twisted his arm up his back, the scream of pain alerted those in the bar that hadn't been aware before.

Pete (Ben) marched the drunk to the door and handed him over to his friends. "Look after him," he said.

"Sorry about this," said one of his friends, agreed by nods from the others.

"Phew," said Helen as the buzz of the bar returned to normal.

"Were you in the military?" asked Helen.

"No, I did some martial arts when I was a kid, surprised myself a bit."

"You were great," she added.

"I think I'll have something a little stronger than a beer," said Pete (Ben), "My ticker's still pounding."

The thought occurred to Pete (Ben) that an unwanted incident like the one that had just happened had made him look good in the eyes of Helen, maybe something similar could be staged in the future.

"Where were we?" said Pete (Ben).

"I was swimming in the water of Hibiscus Falls being a gooseberry," she replied.

"A very beautiful gooseberry," complimented Pete (Ben).

"Let me see," he added, "What little known fact can I tell you about Dominica."

"Go on, Mr Know-it-all."

"Got one for you, I bet you saw the Sisserou parrot on your travels, it's endemic to Dominica."

"I don't think so, we did see some parrots, but I don't think it was them, what colour are they?"

"They're purple and green and I'm certain you would have seen at least one."

"No, don't think so."

"Did you not see any national flags?"

"Yes, lots."

"Then you will have seen the Sisserou parrot right in the middle of it."

"Now you mention it, yes, you're right."

"And another thing, the Dominican flag is the only nation's flag to have purple in it, and not a lot of people know that," he mimicked Michael Caine again, which, as he expected, bombed.

"What would you like to do for dinner?" proffered Pete (Ben).

"Take you to bed again," she replied snuggling up close.

"Don't be greedy," he teased. "Later, we have to eat."

Margaret Cellino, the first reserve on his hit list, the woman he'd met next to the pool, was sat at the adjacent table in the restaurant, she ogled him lasciviously.

Pete (Ben) acknowledged her as he took his seat at the table for two with Helen.

"She's got the hots for you," whispered Helen.

"Yeah, okay," he replied.

Tacitly he compared the two women.

Apart from their comparable wealth, there was no comparison.

In the appearance stakes, Helen won hands down, and the fact that she was good in bed, was a bonus.

Pete (Ben) was delighted with his selection and the progress made to date, already the amorous side of things was well in front of schedule and the first steps in separating her from her money were now in place, things were looking good.

Pete (Ben) had a better than average appetite for sex, which was just as well, as Helen had already proved to be his equal, the age difference meaning nothing.

The drinks and the meal proved to be only the prelude to their return to the spacious bed in L106, Helen's suite.

Chapter 16

Pete (Ben) slid from the bed careful not to disturb the sleeping Helen.

He recovered his strewn clothes and dressed in the meagre light that permeated through the closed curtains.

The corridors and staircase were empty as he made his way back to his own cabin.

Sexually satisfied and not tired enough to find sleep, he lay awake reflecting on his life.

He'd come a long way from a two bedroomed terrace house (town-house in today's vernacular) to a luxury suite on a luxury cruise liner visiting faraway Caribbean islands.

He'd never kept a diary, never had the inclination, but then with a memory akin to a computer, who needs a diary.

He could readily recall all, and there'd been many, women in his life.

Maybe not as many as Warren Beatty or the Basketball player, Will Chamberlain who were reputed to have bedded 12,000 and 20,000 women respectively, now that's impressive, nevertheless there had been a lot.

He remembered the last, Helen, of course, only a few minutes ago, and the first, many years ago, he could still visualise it now.

His virginity had disappeared when he was just 14 years old.

It would be reasonable to assume that his first full sexual experience was with a girl of much the same age, but not so.

Like a video the picture enfolded.

"Is Charlie in?" he asked when Charlie's mother answered the door.

She was a good-looking lady for an older woman, she was 35 years old, but to a 14-year-old, that was old.

"Come in," she invited.

The door closed behind him, he stood perplexed.

"Charlie's not in right now, won't be back until teatime, gone to his Nan's," she said.

He turned to leave.

Charlie's mum stood between him and the door.

"Stay a while," she purred.

Charlie's dad worked away, on the North Sea oil rigs, or something like that. He was away now, Pete was in the house alone with Charlie's mum.

Pete sniggered to himself as he likened it to Dustin Hoffman's situation in *The Graduate*. Mrs Robinson, older woman, Dustin, young man, but in Pete's case he'd still been a young boy, a long way from maturity. At the time he'd been confused, he hadn't known what was happening.

Charlie's mum wore a sheer blouse without a bra, she was large in the bust department, her nipples were dark and hard and were making every effort to burst through the taut material.

A tight mini-skirt hugged her hips and ample thighs, she was statuesque, a handsome woman, totally different to his own mum, and she was there, there in front of him.

She took his hand and led him into the living room (lounge or reception room it would be called today).

He vividly remembered the room, a stone fireplace with a gas fire surrounded by a floral-patterned wallpaper, three beige walls hung with prints and photographs and floral curtains half-covering a window opaque with net curtains.

It was, he recalled, similarly furnished to his childhood home, a plain brown three-piece suite, a china cabinet filled with glassware and a large television in the corner adjacent to the fireplace.

The floor was carpeted, and a faux Persian rug covered the central area.

Charlie's mum, Marjorie was her name, led him to the rug, she looked him in the eye.

"Don't be scared, I don't want you to be scared," she said softly.

"I'm not," he stammered. He was lying, of course, his heart was pounding. *What's happening?* he thought. *I'm not scared,* he assured himself.

Pete hadn't run this video in his mind for some while, it continued.

She took his hands and placed them one on each breast, "Is that nice?" she asked.

"Yes," he replied timidly, there was a stirring in his nether region.

He hadn't lied – they felt soft, they felt hard, they were big unlike those of the girls of his own age that he'd managed to touch before.

She was in control. Unhurriedly, she unzipped her skirt and let it drop to the floor.

Pete was too mesmerised with the sight and touch of the mounds in front of him to be distracted by the disappearance of the skirt.

Her fingers found the waist of his jeans, she expertly undid the button and drew down the zip.

Already he was hard and getting bigger and harder by the second.

She gently manoeuvred it clear of his underpants and held it in her hand.

"Wow, what a big boy," she cooed.

She moved one of his hands to her crotch, her panties were smooth, like the material of her blouse, she opened her legs, he could feel her pubic hair and the furrow of her vagina.

Before he realised, he ejaculated over her hand and on her thigh.

The sensation was unbelievable, much better than he'd masturbated, and there was more semen, of that he was sure.

"Sorry," he whimpered, "I…"

"Don't worry, it's okay," she assured him still manipulating his penis.

When he'd masturbated, his penis had gone flaccid after ejaculation, but not on this occasion, it grew bigger and harder.

She had him lie on the Persian rug; his penis stood erect.

She wriggled out of her panties and lowered herself on to his erection.

The thought evoked the beginning of an erection, the soft moistness of Marjorie surrounded his newly initiated member, it was a moment he would never forget.

"Nice, very nice," she purred as she slowly raised and lowered herself. Pete did nothing but enjoy – this was the real thing, and there'd been nothing like it before now.

If the beginning was good, then the finale was out of this world, as he orgasmed again. Marjorie did too, she screamed in pleasure. "Yes, yes, yes!"

He'd enjoyed sex many times since, and hopefully, he would enjoy it many more times, but this was his first time, and it was unforgettable.

The epilogue to the sex was something of an anti-climax, the pleasure lingered only a little while to be replaced by embarrassment, why embarrassment he'd no idea, but it was definitely that, not shame, or being sorry, he blushed for the first time ever, and as far as he could recall, the one and only time.

The atmosphere between the two was awkward as they dressed almost shyly, nothing was said, Pete couldn't leave fast enough.

That was the first of many visits to enjoy the pleasures of Marjorie.

It never occurred to him, at the time, that he was underage and Marjorie could go to prison had they been caught, he tittered to himself now at the thought.

Of course, he thought he was in love, but common sense eventually prevailed particularly after Charlie had asked him when only the two of them had been together, "Are you fucking my mum?"

"Of course not," he lied, but the fact that the question had been asked woke him to the reality of the situation, he ended the affair abruptly, he stayed away from the house, even when Charlie was there.

Marjorie had been good for him, set him on his sexual way, taught him lots as she reaped the benefit of his youthful stamina.

Never once did Marjorie ask him to wear a condom, maybe she was on the pill; when he'd raised the question she answered categorically, "No. It's like eating a sweet with wrapper on."

To this day, he'd never used a contraceptive, never had, and doubted whether he ever would.

As far as he was aware, he'd never impregnated any of his partners, so, either they had been taking precautions in some form or another, or he'd been lucky, or maybe he fired blanks. The thought of blanks amused him, he smiled to himself.

In one of the few meaningful conversations he'd had with his dad, Pete recalled his question, "Does tha use owt?," "Tha shud tha knows," "Does tha tek precautions, tha shud tha knows," he'd added before Pete could answer.

"I wouldn't know where to buy them from," he remembered saying.

"Chemists, I suppose," dad had replied. "Barbers in my day," he'd continued, "'Something for the weekend, sir?' the barber would ask before you left the chair."

He'd never bought from the chemist's, never looked on the internet, in fact never given it another thought. *"I suppose that makes me a selfish, male, chauvinist,"* he confirmed to his inner self.

In the twenty-odd years since Marjorie, he had bedded many and if need be, he could list every one, the when, the where and the quality of performance, but it would achieve nothing and at the end of the day he was not trying to break records, he was making a living, albeit a dubious illegal living.

His thoughts drifted away and sleep swept in.

Chapter 17

Tortola is the largest of the British Virgin Islands, it is mountainous and green, the forested hillsides travel down the slopes to the azure waters of the Sir Francis Drake Channel.

The cruise ship docked at Road Town in Banghers Bay, the small settlement that purported to be the capital of this island nation.

Once one of the several havens of Edward (Blackbeard) Teach and Henry Morgan, it has hardly grown since and is today still only a small town, however, on the day a cruise ship arrives its population doubles and almost trebles.

The weather was good, warm with little cloud and a blue sky, it augured well for another beautiful sunny day. Pete (Ben) pondered on his plans to further gain the confidence and intimacy of Helen Schmidt.

A relationship cannot flourish at arm's length, Pete (Ben) was fully aware of this fact and intended to make every effort to spend as much time as possible in her company.

Most of the things that he had told her were fabrications, downright lies even, but they were believable, and she had absorbed his dissertations without question.

They met again at breakfast following their individual exercise regimes.

Road Town has little to offer the discerning tourist, a few shops, a few bars and cafes, and that is it.

A taxi driver propositioned them for an island tour or a beach visit, they accepted the latter with the proviso that it was flat and sandy, and it was off the tourist trail.

There was little to see except trees, trees, and more trees as they travelled ever upward on spiralling roads that clung to the sides of the precipitous mountains.

At last they started to descend, gradually winding down to sea level to terminate at a deserted beach in a deserted bay, it was idyllic and devoid of people.

At the driver's suggestion they had stopped at a roadside store for basic provisions, water, crusty bread and local cheese which they carried in a cool bag loaned to them by the driver.

Pete (Ben) paid the driver double his asking price and promised him treble for the return journey which he set as a 3:00 p.m. prompt pick up time threatening him with a slow death if he failed to turn up, "Don't worry boss, I'll be here."

As the taxi disappeared into the distance, so did all synthetic sound, all that was left was the sound of rippling water and the occasional birdcall.

They spread the ship's towels in the shade of a group of palms, stripped of all their clothes and hand in hand entered the clear blue sea.

"I've never been skinny dipping before, ever," she said hanging her arms round his neck as her feet were no longer in contact with the floor.

"Nor me," he lied vaguely remembering a teenage episode on a Cornish getaway.

The refreshing warm water and their close proximity had similar effects on both their bodies.

Helen's nipples hardened and protruded but to a much less extent than Pete (Ben's) manhood.

Pete (Ben) nibbled each salty breast showing no favouritism to one or the other, Helen found his erection and held it gently.

With his feet planted firmly on the fine-grained sand, she surrounded his body with hers lifting herself to allow his erection to slide into her welcoming vagina.

There was little body movement, none was needed, the rippling tide did it for them.

Concurrent orgasm was inevitable, the sounds of their duet of ecstasy were heard by no one but themselves.

Disengagement was gradual, determined only by the deflation of Pete (Ben's) erection.

They exited on to the beach as they'd entered, holding hands like teenagers, except teenagers, particularly British teenagers, were hardly likely to have their first date in such exotic surroundings.

Together they lay naked under the swaying fronds drying naturally in the high sun and warm breeze.

My first fuck in the sea, thought Pete (Ben). But not my last I hope, that was a bit special.

Pete (Ben) broke the silence, with another of his Michael Caine moments.

"Did you know that Francis Drake named Tortola after the resident turtle dove?" She was, after all, a captive audience.

"How come you know so much?" she replied propping herself on one arm admiring his body.

"I don't know, I read something, see something, and I lock it away in my memory banks." He had his hands behind his head staring upward at nothing in particular.

"Lucky man, I can't remember what happened last week."

"You're kidding me."

"No, seriously, I have a terrible memory, facts, figures, faces, it really is not good," she stressed.

Pete (Ben) locked this snippet of information away, it may come in useful – her memory, or lack of it.

It was the sound of a passing speedboat that broke the relative silence of the secluded beach; until then the soporific sound of the lapping waves had been the only sound.

"Lunch," suggested Pete (Ben) as he reached for the cool bag.

"Yes please," she replied propping herself on one arm facing the busy Pete (Ben).

Pete (Ben) spread the simple fair between them and they ate looking into each other's eyes.

They were dressed and ready to go again when the taxi reappeared, the driver wore a knowing smile as he nodded a greeting to Pete (Ben).

Back on board the ship Pete (Ben) made a point of saying, "I must check to see if Pierre has been in contact," drawing Helen's attention to the imaginary deal of the previous day.

"Keep me informed," she said, something that Pete (Ben) was pleased to hear.

"I'll let you know tonight, if there is anything," he replied.

"Usual time, usual place?" she said kissing him as he exited the lift at his cabin level.

Pete (Ben) made sure he had his tablet with him when they got together for their aperitif in the Red Lion bar.

"Any news?" she asked politely as she joined at, what had become, their usual spot at the bar.

She wore a long black dress that followed the contours of her hourglass figure sweeping elegantly from her hips to the tops of her high-heeled black shoes, no doubt red-soled as were most in her wardrobe.

It had a halter neck supporting her adequate breasts revealing an interesting amount of cleavage without being ostentatious.

She wore the diamond and sapphire jewellery, it glittered reflecting the bar lighting in splashes of starlight, it complimented the dress beautifully, but then, it would complement anything, Pete (Ben) admired it again amorously. *Enjoy it while you can, he thought. It will soon be mine, if things go to plan.*

The copies better be good, crossed his mind. This is one magnificent set of jewellery, if they're not in Bridgetown Saturday, Manny gets it with both barrels.

"You look beautiful," he complimented ignoring the enquiring "Any news?"

"Thank you, kind sir," she replied adding a questioning. "Well?"

"Well what?" he was playing her subtly.

"Have you received anything from your man, is it Pierre?" she reiterated.

"Oh no, not yet, but there's time," he replied.

Pete (Ben) wore his tuxedo and dickie bow, it was the second formal night of the cruise and the majority of passengers were likewise dressed, but not one carried it better, maybe if David Beckham had been on board he might just have been outclassed, but in his absence, Pete (Ben) was a standout, and was the subject of many admiring glances.

"We would be a little overdressed in the buffet restaurant," commented Pete (Ben). "Where shall we dine, the Stromboli or one of the speciality restaurants?"

"What about the Amalfi, just the two of us, then if you need to respond to your man, you can with more privacy."

"Good idea, Amalfi it is."

Pete (Ben's) tablet sat silent on the table through starters and entrée's, at exactly 9:30 the pre-arranged communication (pre-arranged with Manny that is without Helen's knowledge) reached its destination.

Pete (Ben) read the message knowing the precise wording before he looked at the screen. "Well?" said Helen with excited inquisitiveness.

He showed her the screen, she read it.

"Great, is that the price you were hoping for?"

"A little better," he replied. "But I haven't got the money yet, agreement is one thing, getting paid is another."

"Well, it's good that you've made the sale, isn't it?"

"Yes, of course, it's good. I'm happy so far, it's now a waiting game for the money to arrive in my bank," and at that he closed the tablet.

"Sweet for my sweet?" he growled rather than lilted the title line of the old Searcher's song.

"I'd like strawberries, ripe strawberries," she sang in return.

They laughed loudly drawing strange looks from staff and diners alike, they didn't care, they laughed some more.

So far, they'd avoided hearty soup and large steaks, food not conducive to the physical gymnastics of lovemaking. They'd both by-passed these for the more delicate but flavoursome avocado with prawns and chef's Marie Rose sauce and a main course of ravioli.

Helen's strawberries were not available, instead they plumped for Tiramisu which arrived served in translucent bone china cups, a novel presentation.

An Irish coffee brought the meal to an end.

Food, food for thought, the food that Pete (Ben) ate today was considerably different to that of his childhood, back then avocado, prawns, ravioli, steak, tiramisu and the like didn't exist in his world, meat and potato pie, liver and rice pudding fitted the Holmes's household budget.

Exotic food and exotic places were never dreamed of, completely and utterly out of the question, only the rich had access to these things, and there were no rich people in Pete (Ben's) neighbourhood, Pete (Ben) had come a long way.

In the sanctity of Helen Schmidt's suite Pete (Ben) re-booted his tablet and left it open on the coffee table as they enjoyed a nightcap on the balcony watching the moonlit waves dash by.

An e-mail appeared signed by Pierre, it was Manny, of course, but Helen wasn't to know that. It read, 'Be advised, money in bank no later than Tuesday next. Enjoy your holiday. Pierre.'

Pete (Ben) didn't need to draw Helen's attention to the message, she'd already keyed into it.

"Looking good," said Pete (Ben).

"Brilliant," she replied, diverting Pete (Ben's) attention by slipping the black dress from her shoulders allowing it to drop to the floor.

Her matching transparent lacy black and red strapless bra and panties left little to the imagination. Very, very sexy they were and had the desired effect on the lucky Pete (Ben).

As Pete (Ben) discarded his own clothes, Helen further enticed him by standing legs akimbo, a hand on one hip swaying from side to side. "Come and get me, big boy," she purred.

She unclipped her bra and elegantly removed her panties, now she wore only the jewellery and a smile.

Pete (Ben), likewise naked, crushed her to him, the sight of her body and the 'come on' stance had the desired effect, the 'big boy' jibe confirmed.

The king-size bed beckoned again; their intimacy complete before the sheets were drawn.

As they lay contemplating further sex, Helen realised she was still wearing her jewellery and made to put it back in the safe.

This was the opportunity that Pete (Ben) had been waiting for, he followed closely behind her, cupping her breasts as she opened the safe.

The numbers she punched in were easy for somebody like Pete to remember with his photographic memory. Helen suspected nothing, he picked her up and carried her back to the bed.

Repeat performances followed, this time between the sheets, and then sleep.

Chapter 18

Another day, another port of call.

Helen ground out a computer-created undulating route on an exercise bike as Pete (Ben) completed a 2000-metre row, then together they pounded five laps of the ship's jogging track.

This, together with the nocturnal sexual exercise were fine ways of maintaining the health and physiques of the purported forty-odd-year-old Pete (Ben) and the fifty-odd-year-old Helen, but it is not rocket science to know which method was preferred.

St Kitts, or to give it its full title, St Christopher's Island, has moved with the times in some directions. Basseterre, its capital is home to a state of the art Cruise Terminal, but not much else.

The centre of the island is far too mountainous for human habitation, consequently everybody and everything is at sea level with a single road following the coastline.

Beautiful it might be, but the taxi tour of the island was over in next to no time.

A walking tour of Basseterre took even less time, Pete (Ben) and Helen were back on board in time for a formal lunch in the Stromboli Dining Room.

In order to maintain the pretext of the coffee sale, Pete (Ben) carried his tablet with him throughout the day hopefully giving Helen the impression that contact was imminent.

At 2:45 as Pete (Ben) and Helen lounged around the pool absorbed in their respective books, Manny, in the guise of Pierre sent the anticipated e-mail: 'Payment authorised, but hiccup at buyers end with currency transfer, more to follow ASAP. Pierre.'

The communication had the desired effect, Helen Schmidt put down her book. "What's the news?" she enquired.

He didn't read out the e-mail, he showed it to her, she quickly read it.

This communication, like all the previous ones and those still to come, was pre-planned, all of them intended to firstly fascinate the unsuspecting Helen and then draw her in to induce a financial interest. So far it was working.

The specific words, 'Currency transfer' had been included to initiate further dialogue.

'What do you mean, Currency transfer?' Pete (Ben's) return e-mail said.

'No worries, client having small difficulty exchanging currency to US dollars, time frame should still be maintained. Pierre.'

'Keep on top of it.' Pete (Ben) replied.

Throughout the exchange, Pete (Ben) held the tablet in such a position that Helen couldn't fail to see the conversation. "Just a minor snag," he said confidently. "No problem, it will soon get sorted."

The rest of the day and most of the night they never left each other's side for more than a few minutes, it was a day of little conversation, a day of just being there, the night was reserved for a more intimate activity.

Chapter 19

Friday, the last full day of the first week of the cruise, was at sea. The ship ploughed gracefully through the calm waters of the Caribbean Sea under a cloudless sky.

It was an ideal day for doing nothing, and following their daily exercise regime, nothing was what Pete (Ben) and Helen chose to do.

They passed on the cookery demonstration, the Barbados lecture and several other organised activities in favour of loafing.

As per usual on a sea day it was impossible to find a sunbed anywhere near a pool, they did, however, find two vacant beds on the port side, one in the sun for Pete (Ben) and one in the shade for Helen.

Pete (Ben's) tablet remained silent, all part of the plan, from experience he had found that a period of quiescence whetted the appetite of the client, slow and easy was the order of the day, no rush, the next phase of the operation was planned for the forthcoming Sunday, the first full day of the second week of the cruise, another sea day.

Chapter 20

Bridgetown, Barbados, was the mid-point of the cruise, and the location of the pick-up point of the paste copies of Helen Schmidt's jewellery.

Pete (Ben) had cleverly manipulated a day away from Helen.

He had invited her to join him in a tour of the Kensington Oval, the home of Barbados, and arguably, West Indian Cricket.

She had, of course, as expected, declined, leaving him free to collect the fake jewellery without her in attendance.

Somewhat peeved she'd reluctantly and under duress joined a cruise excursion tour of the island.

Pete (Ben) exited the Cruise Terminal through the so-called Duty-Free outlets, passed the inevitable steel band combo and on to the Bridgetown causeway. With the Caribbean Sea lapping the breakwater, he strolled casually in the direction of the floodlight towers towering above the sheds and warehouses.

He'd dressed for the occasion; he wore his Yorkshire Cricket Club cap and polo shirt, white Bermuda shorts and his recently acquired white trainers.

In contrast his black man-bag hung from his shoulder.

He stopped on President Kennedy Drive to admire the bronze statue of probably the best cricketer ever, Sir Garfield Sobers, the most famous Barbadian of all time whose exploits fill the annuls of cricket.

Pete (Ben) was too young to have seen Sobers play live but he had seen film of some of his record-breaking exploits, they were etched in his significant memory, his 365 not out against Pakistan in 1958 was one and six sixes off one Malcolm Nash (Poor sod) at Swansea when playing for Nottinghamshire in 1968 another, a remarkable player and distinguished man.

Pete (Ben) manoeuvred himself into the right position to take a selfie with the great man, he miraculously captured the moment first time.

The tour of the Kensington Oval that followed held him enthralled but the visit to the freshly prepared Bermuda grass wicket on the hallowed turf really had him excited.

In his mind he steamed up to the wicket in front of a full Three W's stand, he winged a 150km/hr seamer at Chris Gayle and uprooted his off stump. "Howzat," he screamed at Billy Bowden, the New Zealand umpire, the crowd hushed, no cheers. Gayle, was, after all, the West Indian hero of the day, Pete (Ben) woke from his reverie to an empty ground with only the tour group and guide to be seen.

His ploy of escaping Helen had worked perfectly. *This visit would have gone completely over her head,* he thought.

Americans do not understand or appreciate the finer arts of the great English summer sport, they have boring baseball, an adaption of the girl's game rounders, which is, believe me, much slower than cricket.

It was a hurried leisurely tour that lasted approximately one hour and a half.

The sky was cloudless, and the sun was hot; a cold Banks beer at a roadside bar gave him chance to sit and watch the world go by, people watching, the cheapest and one of the most enjoyable pastimes known to man.

Just over a week ago, he mused. There was Jude, whose surname I can't remember, and the rich Penelope Bradford Jones whose surname I'll never forget, my God, she may still be here, what if I bump into her? Oh what the hell. If I do. So be it, I only did what I normally do when not working, find 'em, feel 'em, fuck 'em and leave 'em.

Suitably refreshed he meandered into the hubbub of Barbados, central Bridgetown.

Bridgetown is not the biggest of capitals, it basically consists of one main street and a market area densely populated with colourful locals, boosted twofold by tourists when cruise ships are in port, and that is most days during the season.

Island Gems was a small jewellery shop on a side street behind the Cave Shepherd department store.

The frontage consisted of a central solid timber door and two small display windows, vertical steel bars protected the armour glass windows and an open barred gate the door, presently locked in an open position.

Pete (Ben) stepped inside, an over-doorbell rang, the shop was empty apart from an ultra-thin Barbadian with long grey hair tied in a ponytail and sporting an equally grey goatee beard, who stood behind a glass show counter.

Glass cabinets filled the sidewalls each with internal strip lights that made the inexpensive contents sparkle giving the desired effect of quality.

Apart from the display cabinets the shop was dim, lit only by an aged bare fluorescent tube, maybe that was for the best as closer inspection would reveal the shop`s desperate need off redecoration.

Pete (Ben) introduced himself.

The old man, without a word, withdrew an unopened package from a solid drawer set in a chest on the back wall.

Pete (Ben) ripped off the brown paper and bubble wrap to reveal a simple flat cardboard box.

He lifted the lid, nestling in cotton wool was a necklace, bracelet and earrings, one by one he inspected them.

They were good, very good, they fitted exactly the picture he held in his memory banks.

The grey eyes of the grey man journeyed from the jewellery to Pete (Ben's) eyeline and back, his eyebrows lifted at the sight of the necklace.

"If these were yours, and you were selling them to me, how much would they be?" Pete asked.

"Let me have a look?" these were the first words that had passed his lips.

He took the necklace, weighed it in his hand, put his loupe to his eye and turned each stone in turn.

He unhurriedly repeated the exercise with the bracelet and the earrings and returned them to the box.

"How much?" repeated Pete (Ben).

The old man scratched his goatee, he pondered, "Good paste, well made, 50, maybe 60 US but…"

Pete (Ben) interrupted, "I give you 60, you give me a receipt with a description."

"You gotta deal man," he replied recovering his receipt book from the same drawer he'd taken the package.

With the paste jewellery stashed safely in his man-bag Pete (Ben) left one happy ageing jeweller $60 US better off than he had been 10 minutes earlier.

Two more tasks and his visit to Bridgetown was over.

In no time he spotted the international green cross sign indicating a Pharmacy.

He bought a pack of Donormyl sleeping tablets, not for him, he had no problems in that direction, no, he was thinking ahead, to the time when he would leave Helen Schmidt minus her jewellery and her money.

It took a little longer to find a travel agency, but find one he did.

Using his No. 3 passport in the name of James Goodwin, he booked the first flight possible out of Barbados for the following Saturday.

He paid cash.

He returned to the ship by taxi furtively glancing around him still eager to avoid Penelope Bradford Jones should she suddenly appear.

Back on board alone in his cabin, he thoroughly inspected the copies comparing them against the photographs and the images in his computer-like memory, they were good, very good.

He texted Manny, 'Items received, well happy.'

A reply came back almost instantly, 'Good, pleased to be of service.'

Pete (Ben) sent one more text, 'Stand by for phase 2, later today hopefully.'

Again an instant reply, 'Ready when u r, await signal.'

Helen's tour finished at 3:30, she found Pete (Ben) lounging in the sun next to the main pool. He was engrossed in his new book. She sat at the foot of his bed.

"Enjoy your cricket?" she asked.

"It was great, you would have loved it," he replied.

"Yeah, I know, it sounded like a blast."

"How was your day?" he enquired.

"It was good, it would have been better with you there."

"Sorry, but I couldn't miss the chance of going to the Oval, you never know, I might not pass this way again."

She stroked his leg. "Shall we?" she said, not needing to add any more, her face and attitude said the rest.

"Sorry," replied Pete (Ben). "I really am. I have some paperwork I must do, I've been putting it off, but it must be done."

It was a white lie but even a lothario has moments when his libido falters. The excuse was feeble, but he genuinely did need a little more recovery time.

Disappointment showed on her face as she replied, "If you must, I'll see you later, won't I?"

"Of course, it's just that –"

She interrupted, "It's okay, but you will have to make up for it later," she added a cheeky wink.

"You got it," he replied, drawing her to him and kissing her fiercely.

Chapter 21

Pete (Ben's) siesta came to an abrupt end. The voice from the bridge announcing the imminent safety muster woke him from his dream, where his dream had taken him was immediately lost.

He slid off the bed, the paste jewels were still in the small box where he'd left them on the desktop.

He re-examined them, turning each individual piece in the light of the table lamp and carefully inspecting every facet.

They were excellent, really good for copies. They refracted the light sparkling like the diamonds and sapphire they imitated; they were a good facsimile of what they purported to be. Pete (Ben) was delighted with them.

Were they good enough to avoid detection? He thought so. Hopefully when Helen removed them from the safe and packed them for travel, she would only give them a cursory glance merely to confirm their presence. Well, that was the theory.

He stowed them in his safe, out of sight of the cabin steward and Helen should she visit his cabin, which was unlikely, but *better safe than sorry,* as the saying goes.

He thought about the timing of the exchange, it needed to be left as late as possible, during the last night of the cruise with Helen in a deep sleep induced by the sleeping draft.

The sun dropped into the sea and Barbados disappeared over the horizon, Pete (Ben) leant against the balcony guard rail his eyes searching the bow waves for the movement of flying fish, there were none to be seen.

He thought of Helen, unsuspecting Helen. He'd swept her off her feet, of that he was sure, he'd gained her trust and, it seemed, her love.

He was about to cheat her out of her money and steal her jewellery and vanish from her life.

In less than a week, he had ingratiated himself into her life, given her false love, made passionate love together and maybe even given her hope for the future. *Am I a shit?* he asked himself. Yes, came the answer. *But so, it's what I do, it's the way I make my living, love doesn't enter into it.*

He was distracted from his thoughts by a flight of eight, maybe ten, flying fish skimming the waves before disappearing 50 yards further away. He returned to his thoughts, *Tomorrow at sea, move to the next phase. Imaginary deal no. 2, time to take Helen Schmidt's money. Yes, I am a shit, a double-barrelled shit of the highest order, but so what?*

Chapter 22

For once the weather was inclement, the clear sunny days were replaced by a day more akin to February European climes than the Caribbean, it was overcast with a cool breeze, not a day for the sun worshipper, hence the empty upper decks.

Although the sun is a plus to most holidaymakers, it is not absolutely essential on a cruise where there are a multitude of things to do. The agenda for the day's activities was extensive including a lecture, ironically about jewels and jewellery. *Maybe prudent to steer Helen away from this,* thought Pete (Ben).

There was another cookery demonstration on offer and as Pete (Ben) fancied himself as an amateur chef and it was high on Helen's list of interests, they joined the large audience in the theatre.

In preparation for scam phase 2, Pete (Ben) carried his tablet with him but in sleep mode through the demonstration.

He re-booted the tablet as they were taking lunch, he was just about to bite into a smoked salmon canape when the premeditated communication arrived.

Helen's interest was immediately piqued.

"Is it…" she began.

"No, it's Asif," said Pete (Ben) replying to Helen.

"Mmmmm," he muted, scratching his chin.

Helen's eyes were drawn to him and to the tablet:

'Do you want to buy cotton. Asif,' it said.

Brief and to the point, precisely as agreed with Manny, Pete (Ben) had read somewhere, 'Mystery is a key factor in any illusion,' all part of the process.

"I sometimes wish that Asif would let me have more information without having to ask for it," said Pete (Ben).

He typed a reply, 'That depends, where, cost, transport, and will I be able to find a buyer. Ben,' and pressed send.

Pete (Ben) followed this with another message to his other bogus contact, Pierre.

'If I buy cotton at the right price, can you sell it? Ben.'

Almost immediately, Pierre, Manny to be precise, returned the following message, 'You buy it, I'll sell it, you know me, as you English say, I can sell fridges to Eskimos, or Innuits as they are now called, like it is taking candy from kids. Pierre.'

Manny waited a while before sending a reply in the guise of Asif.

Asif's e-mail arrived, 'Legitimate sale, 1000bales, 20 Tonnes. 1st Cut cotton. China. C & F Delivered to Home port (Southampton/Rotterdam), $0.32 US/Kilo - $64K. Cash transfer. Can U sell? Asif.'

Pete (Ben), with Helen looking over his shoulder, read it.

"$64K, that's about £40K. That's good, very good, but…" he stopped.

"But what?" queried Helen.

"I'm strapped at the moment."

"Explain strapped?" she asked.

"Strapped, oh! Sorry, very English, means short, short of money. Temporary, of course, most of my capital is tied up in the coffee, but that should come through in a day or so, I'll ask him how long I've got to raise the cash."

He did just that. 'How long have I got to say yes or no?' he asked.

The hubbub of the buffet restaurant was, as usual, a drone of hundreds of voices but to Pete (Ben) and Helen it could have been a million miles away as they pored over the tablet. Helen was captured, the hook was on the line bated and ready.

Pete (Ben) e-mailed the fictitious Pierre, "1st Cut cotton delivered to either Southampton or Rotterdam. Proposed sale price $0.48US minimum/kilo. Can you sell? Ben."

The rat-tat-tat of electronic communications came to a halt, Pete (Ben) and Helen waited. There was no further activity, just a picturesque beach under a blue sky screensaver.

"Nothing we can do now but wait," said Pete (Ben).

"But if you don't get paid for the coffee in time, will you miss the cotton deal?" asked the inquiring Helen.

Nearly there, the bated hook is in the lake, thought Pete (Ben).

"I guess so, but that's the way it goes, win some, lose some, that's business."

It was like the trout after the fly, almost there, but like playing a fish, it was not yet time to strike. Slow and easy, his brain was informing him.

Pete (Ben) knew for a fact that there would be no further communications for some time, the schedule had been agreed with Manny and to date it was working fine, the unsuspecting Helen couldn't be more intrigued.

"I'd better close down before I flatten the battery," determined Pete (Ben).

Pete (Ben) and Helen spent the afternoon at the art gallery director's lecture about Van Gogh. It wasn't the most riveting of events and at one point a nudge in the ribs stopped Pete (Ben's) snoring. Not the most successful of events, looking around he didn't appear to be alone.

The weather had improved, the sun had broken through the clouds, but the breeze was still there. There were plenty of beds to be had but only the hardy were on deck, and they were well wrapped.

Helen's balcony was as good a place as any, part shade, part sun, an ideal location for them both.

Pete (Ben) was soon absorbed in one of Wilbur Smith's gripping adventures while Helen was equally engrossed in a Kindle book.

Little was said, little needed to be said, Helen was captivated with her newfound love, satisfied just to be together alone and unhindered by anyone or anything. She was the happiest she'd been for a long, long time.

Pete (Ben) enjoyed the silence for another reason – it gave him some respite from the make-believe, the illusion and the lies. His overactive brain could close down for a while and concentrate on Wilbur Smith's fantasies; love was not an issue.

Pete (Ben) woke with a start, he hadn't even realised he'd dozed. His book had dropped to the floor, Helen had picked it up and put it on his lap, that, and the kiss on his lips had roused him.

She was not quite her usual tonsorial self, an inelegant shower cap covered her hair and she was wrapped in a towel.

She kissed him again. "You missed your chance; we could have showered together."

"What in that cupboard? I don't think so," he replied. "I've got a better idea, what about testing this sunbed?" he added, grabbing the top of the towel and whisking it off.

"Stop it!" she yelled in a subdued shriek. "Someone will see us."

"So? Let them watch."

"But –" Whatever else she was about to say was stopped by Pete (Ben's) lips on hers.

She took little or no persuading, there was no resistance as he pulled her down on to his supine body.

She was naked apart from the plastic headdress, he still wore a tee-shirt and shorts, but not for long, as Helen pulled the tee-shirt over his head, and he wriggled out of the shorts.

Now she didn't care whether anyone saw them or not, her desire for sex had taken over – she wanted him again.

The shower cap looked funny, it might have made him laugh had he not closed his eyes, the image of her face and swaying fine hair was restored, his hands found her breasts, they were alone in their sexual pleasure, and if they weren't, *'Let them enjoy the view.'*

It was Helen manipulating her body that brought them both to a climatic end.

"Wow," exclaimed Pete (Ben) as Helen climbed to her feet, picked up the crumpled towel and made to leave the balcony.

"There's more if you want it," she said, trailing the towel behind her like a lure.

Whether he wanted more or not was immaterial, she obviously did, and until the time he was in possession of her money and her jewels, he needed to keep her happy and content. He followed.

Chapter 23

Although Pete (Ben) had never said where Pierre was supposedly based, Helen had assumed he was resident in Europe, France in particular. Pete (Ben) had done nothing to discourage this belief.

The timing of the next communication from Pierre (Manny in Chicago) was set so that it appeared to be in European business hours.

As Paris time is five hours ahead of Caribbean time, Pierre's e-mail arrived at 9:00 a.m. Monday as they were docked in St John's Harbour, Antigua.

It read: 'Got a buyer willing to pay $0.50/kilo Free on Board at Cadiz. Is this OK? Pierre.'

Pete (Ben) and Helen were in the buffet restaurant; they'd been waiting all night for this communication. Pete (Ben) was acting the part of an expectant father.

Pete (Ben) had, for once, stopped in Helen's bed all night, not for sexual reasons, although sex was incidental, but to keep alive her interest in this electronic dialogue.

She read the communication at the same time as Pete (Ben).

"What will you do?" she asked.

"I don't know yet, depends what Asif has to say about buying time."

A further communication arrived from Pierre shortly after the first one of the day: 'No further news regarding credit transfer for coffee, working on it. Pierre.'

"Fuck," immediately followed by, "Sorry," burst from Pete (Ben's) lips.

"It's okay, I understand," soothed Helen, resting her hand on his.

Pete (Ben) frowned, "I'll leave it until this afternoon, then if I haven't heard…" he allowed the sentence to taper to an effective end.

"It's your show, but if I can help?"

It was the offer that he'd been working toward, the offer he wanted, the hook was through the lip.

"Thanks, I'll bear that in mind." *Not too hasty, not yet.*

They had organised nothing in the way of visiting Antigua, the so-called business communications had enthralled Helen and deterred her from leaving Pete (Ben's) side.

"Shall we go ashore?" Pete (Ben) suggested.

"Why not, as you say, we, I mean you, can't do anything as yet, might as well," she replied.

"This deep-water harbour here at St John has been a haven for ships since Christopher Columbus anchored in 1493," said tourist guide Pete (Ben) as they were stepping ashore.

"You're a walking encyclopaedia. How do you know this stuff?"

"Read it somewhere, I just remember things, and here's some other information, if you like. At that time, the indigenous people called the island, Wadadi, which means Our Own, but Columbus renamed it Antigua in honour of La Virgin de la Antigua resident of Seville Cathedral."

"Thank you for that, but in less than an hour, I will have forgotten, facts I never remember."

Another snippet of information on Helen he filed for future reference, if ever needed.

It was too late to join one of the many cruise-organised tours, but there were many local taxis offering the same itineraries at half the price, albeit the price was never an issue.

The tour details and cost were agreed before they started, Pete (Ben) had been caught before, it is imperative to be precise regarding exactly what you expect, and what price you pay for it, before you start, avoiding argument at the end, Pete (Ben) had made this a rule after his first encounter of this kind, trust nobody was his rule, which was ironic in many ways.

Mount Obama, renamed from Boggy Peak on 4th August 2009 the birthday of the US President, towers all other points of the island, it is forested to the extent that panoramic views are limited to specific created viewing points.

Following visits to Nelson's Dockyard at English Harbour, the town of Falmouth and Pigeon Point they arrived at Stingray City.

This was to be the highlight of their visit to Antigua.

The boat was small, it carried 12 passengers and 3 crew, it launched from the beach alongside two larger boats that carried passengers that they recognised as fellow cruisers.

No more than 500 yards from the beach, all the boats dropped anchor on a shallow sand bar.

Snorkels and masks were provided, and everyone dropped into the water.

Crew from each boat joined the swimmers, carrying baskets of fish bits which they spread in a small area.

The sand bar came alive with dozens of grey Concord shapes with long tails, their wings gracefully undulating as they flew, rather than swam, through the onlookers.

These were the stingrays that everyone had gathered to see and touch.

Helen's feet barely touched the bottom, Pete (Ben) supported her as she attempted to touch the passing stingrays.

"They're like velvet, not a bit scaly," she shouted with delight as one enormous fish touched her legs.

Stingrays, scientific name Dasyatidae, can be a very dangerous animal, their sting, which they use to kill their prey is actually a poison emanating from the base of their bony tail. It can severely harm, if not kill, human beings, but here they were friendly and docile, there was no history here of anyone being hurt by these gentle giants.

Throughout the leisure and the pleasure of the day, the business in hand, the con and the jewellery, almost left Pete (Ben's) mind. Almost, but not quite, it was still there hovering in the background.

She was a good person, he was a thief, that would never change, not in the foreseeable future anyway.

The inevitable memento shop beckoned as they tramped from the beach.

It was no more than a trestle table under a large canopy, it held a plethora of tourist rubbish all with a stingray motif of one sort or another.

They invested in tee-shirts. 'Stingray City' tee-shirts, black for Pete (Ben) and red for Helen. There would be memories of each other carried their different ways whatever the outcome of their tryst.

It was essential to Pete's (Ben's) cause that Helen was kept informed of every bogus move in the coffee and cotton sagas, he had his tablet with him at all times when they were in each other's company except, of course, whilst in the water.

The evening ritual of drinks in the Red Lion bar was the site of the next electronic communication.

'Sorry for delayed reply, payment for cotton required immediate, another buyer appeared. Await your instructions. Asif.'

'Bollocks, sorry,' the expletive followed by the immediate apology.

Helen saw the message at the same time as Pete (Ben).

She saw the significance straight away, "You haven't been paid for the coffee yet."

"No," he replied sullenly.

"What can you do?"

"Nothing, I'll just have to miss this one."

"It would have been a tidy profit."

"It would, but…" he stopped.

"Can I help?" the very question that all the subterfuge had been leading to, he needed to play it carefully, not too quick to accept, but not dismiss out of hand, slow and easy was the order of the day.

He replied, "It's my problem, maybe the coffee money will arrive soon."

"And what if it doesn't? You will have lost the chance of a big score. Let me help?" Helen's persistence was precisely what Pete (Ben) had been hoping for. *Act relaxed,* he told himself.

"How?" He asked innocently.

"Let me put up the money. It's no big deal, you can pay me back as soon as the coffee pays, no problem." The very words he had been working toward, if you call working wooing and enjoying sex with a beautiful woman.

"I can't let you do that, $60K is a lot of money."

"But I want to, and as I say, you'll pay me back soon, no problem."

"I don't –"

She interrupted, "I insist, what do I need to do?"

"If you're sure?" he replied with a faux sincere manner.

"I am, give me your account number, give it to me now, and I'll transfer the money right away."

Just over a week it had taken to reach this point, Pete (Ben) thought it might have taken a little longer, but he was pleased to accept sooner, rather than, later.

He found the necessary file of his tablet, brought up the sorting code and account number, slid over an unused beer mat, fished a pen from his pocket and wrote it down.

Helen disappeared for a short while, to reappear with her own tablet.

She accessed her bank file and made the transfer.

The $60K electronic money moved rapidly through two more offshore accounts before nestling in its final resting place, Peter Holmes's personal working and retirement fund.

Unlike paying out from an account which is instant, paying in, for whatever reason, takes time, sometimes a long time.

He waited an obligatory half-hour, they were still ensconced in the Red Lion bar, before firing off payment instruction for the cotton, yet again the instruction was meaningless and went to Manny, nowhere near a bank.

In order to authenticate the so-called transfer instruction, Manny returned a confirmation e-mail as if from the bank, and then half an hour later, one arrived from Asif confirming receipt from the vendors.

Pete (Ben) was now $60K richer, less, of course, Manny's percentage, and Helen Schmidt was $60K poorer, albeit $60K was a drop in the ocean to the mega-rich Helen.

Although Pete's (Ben's) main objective had been achieved, there was still some time before he could escape the relationship, and there was still the jewellery.

Maintaining the relationship would be no hardship, he decided. Although Helen was ten years his senior, she was in very good shape, her sexual appetite had been refound and matched his, the next few days would be more like a holiday than work. 'A busman's holiday' came to mind yet again.

His tablet travelled with them the rest of the evening, through dinner, through the rather poor comedians act in the Charleston Club Show Bar, and back to Helen's suite.

Pete (Ben) knew for a fact that there would no further activity, but the charade must continue right up until the end of the cruise when it would be time to make his escape.

Chapter 24

Pete (Ben) never found it a hardship making love to a beautiful woman, Helen had found an appetite that had lain dormant for some time but Pete's (Ben's) libido was more than adequate to cope.

Helen slept soundly, as was normal, he slipped from her bed to make his way back through the empty corridors back to his own cabin.

The moment his head hit his own pillow, he was asleep. Pete (Ben) had no conscience, he felt no remorse, as far as he was concerned he'd provided a pleasurable sexual service to Helen Schmidt who in turn was paying for it from her vast financial resources and with her jewellery. She was, Pete considered, still receiving good value for money, his body never did come cheap.

Helen and Pete (Ben) joined the thousands of other cruise passengers escaping from the five megaliths berthed alongside the two wharves that formed the docking area of Philipsburg Cruise Terminal, St Maarten.

St Maarten was a must call on all Caribbean itineraries, so consequently it was not new to either Helen or Pete (Ben).

The stream of disembarking passengers snaked through the bars and shops of the cruise terminal to the departure wharf where a constant supply of water taxis ferried them to the beach and boardwalk of downtown Philipsburg, Helen and Pete (Ben) joined the flow.

Philipsburg is basically formed by two main drags, Front Street, and, you got it, Back Street.

Front Street, as the name suggests, faces the beach and sea. This is the boardwalk and is the home to numerous bars and restaurants with the occasional sales outlet, the drinks are cheap and the music loud.

Drink induced reverie was well underway even though it was long before lunchtime.

Several short alleys took the growing hordes to Back Street, a shopper's dream, an American woman's heaven, a British man's nightmare.

Duty-free fragrance outlets there vie with boutiques and dozens of jewellers for the American dollar.

Both Helen and Pete (Ben) were dressed, like everyone around them, in tee-shirts and shorts. It was hot, the sun sat high in a clear blue sky, the sunbed and umbrella men were doing a roaring trade especially the ones that threw in two free cans of beer.

Helen pulled Pete (Ben) toward Back Street. He resisted little; it was inevitable that she would want to visit a boutique or two, so he gave in gracefully and vowed to make the best of it.

One boutique, became two, which became four and so on. It was in the sixth, and Pete (Ben) had voiced it to be the last, that the dress that Helen had been looking for.

Pete (Ben) had to agree, it could have been made with her in mind, it was pale grey silk with an embroidered strapless bodice and full pleated skirt to the knee, it fitted perfectly.

Matching shoes were surprisingly found, and American Express used.

"Happy now?" he asked.

"Ecstatic," she replied. "What time have you got?" she asked taking his wrist.

"I don't know, I didn't —"

"Not to worry," she interrupted.

She walked directly into the next shop which happened to be a branch of Diamond International. Pete (Ben) followed wondering why the visit here.

"Can I help?" enquired a young good looking Asian with slicked shiny black hair wearing a dark blue pin-stripe suit with blue shirt and an old school tie.

"Watches," she replied.

"For yourself, madam? We have a fine —"

"No, no. Gents please," she interrupted.

"Of course, ma'am, would you care to take a seat?" He moved two chairs to the counter and bade them sit.

"Would you care for tea, coffee, or maybe a soft drink?" he offered politely.

They both declined.

"Any particular maker, ma'am?"

"Not really, Breitling, Tissot, Omega. Let me see."

The young man whispered in the ear of a young Asian girl who disappeared through an internal door to return with two velvet-covered trays of men's watches.

Helen inspected them one by one. They were pretty eclectic, traditional, ultra-modern, colourful, plain, but no doubt with one thing in common, expensive.

"Which do you like?" she asked Pete (Ben).

"Is it for a young person, or old? That would help me advise," he replied.

"Which do you like? It's for you."

"Oh no, no, it's too much. I have a watch."

"But you're not wearing it. I want to buy you one, now don't try and stop me."

Pete (Ben) stared at the watches; they were all good.

"What about this one?" she said, touching a Breitling. "Try it on."

The Asian lifted the watch from the tray, undid the black leather strap and proceeded to fasten it on Pete's (Ben's) wrist.

Close up, it looked even better than it had sat on the velvet tray. It was a Navitimer 01.

"Let me see," requested Helen. She took his hand, "Looks good on you, do you like?"

"I certainly do, but —"

"No buts," she interrupted. "Now take it off and lose yourself for a few moments while I negotiate."

He did as bid and stood outside.

She called him back inside and handed him the watch. "For you," she said and kissed him lightly on the lips. The young Asian stood to one side, smirking as if to say, *'For services rendered.'*

With the Breitling firmly attached to his left wrist, he admired it at close quarters.

It was the epitome of a masculine watch, a stainless steel case with black face and dials, three in addition to the main chronograph face with, in the centre, the golden wings of Breitling, a very technical-looking watch. It sat well on Pete (Ben).

"I don't know what to say."

"Well, don't say anything," she replied.

"Thank you, thank you very much," he held and kissed her, causing a hiatus on the narrow walkway.

He looked again at the watch, "It's lunchtime, let me buy you the best Philipsburg lunch, step this way."

They travelled no more than 20 yards to one of the small cross alleys.

Four small round tables covered in red and white tablecloths each surrounded by four small bar stools stood unoccupied adjacent to a small timber hut with an open front forming the serving counter, this was Pete's (Ben's) selected lunch venue.

They sat at one of the tables. "Don't panic, believe me, the food is good. Are you hungry?"

"I'll eat what you feed me," she said, inspecting the hut with a dubious eye.

The shed was in excellent condition painted in a multitude of vibrant colours, all the colours of the rainbow, and then some. A potpourri of shapes and symbols, modern art on drugs, but it looked the part.

"Beer, soft drink, tea, coffee, water?" asked Pete (Ben).

"Beer," she replied, without even thinking about it.

"Yes, man," said the huge black woman smiling down from the hut.

She was as colourful as the shed; her black, heavily jowled face shone, her lipstick was a vivid red. She wore a huge yellow ribbon in her jet-black hair that matched her dress, and her fingers were covered in all manner of rings.

"Two beers and four rotis, please," he ordered.

She passed him the beers, two cans, very cold. "Two sweet potato, two chicken, that okay, man?" she asked.

"Fine," replied Pete (Ben) handing her American dollars.

She took the relevant cost, "I'll bring you the rotis, just a few minutes."

As promised, the rotis arrived shortly. Pete (Ben) couldn't help but wonder how the cafe owner fit in her hut; she was even bigger than she appeared through the counter, at the very least 20 stones and no more than 5'6" tall.

Two rotis filled each of the two plates, they arrived together with a dish of pickle. She placed them on the table with napkins, cutlery and condiments. "Enjoy," she said.

Helen and Pete (Ben) attacked the food with gusto.

Helen wiped her mouth with the napkin, "No kidding, they were great."

"Told you," he replied, "One of St Maarten's best kept secrets."

"Well it won't stay secret for long if I have my way," she said.

Pete drained his can, "Ready to go?"

"Sure, where to now?" she asked.

"Wait and see, come on," he rose and stepped to the kerb of Back Street.

A stream of traffic constantly crawled one way down Back Street, it was only a matter of seconds before a taxi arrived.

The two bundled in. "Maho beach," Pete (Ben) advised the driver.

Twenty-five minutes later, they were sat at the Driftwood Boat bar off Beacon Hill Road overlooking Maho Beach and the Caribbean Sea.

"It's nice here, but we could have gone to the beach in Philipsburg."

"Yes, we could, but there's more to see here."

"Like what?" she asked.

"Like this," he replied pointing out to sea.

A dot appeared in the sky; it grew bigger by the second.

"A plane," she said.

"Look behind you," Pete (Ben) suggested.

"Airport!" she exclaimed.

"Right," he confirmed.

The approaching plane was, at first, no more than a dot, then it had shape, and then it had colour. Soon the carrier could be determined, the livery clear, bigger and bigger it grew, lower and lower it came.

The bar was a mere 40 metres away from the end of the runway which began immediately behind the beach.

The Jet Blue Boeing 737 appeared to miss the perimeter fence by a couple of feet as it raced toward the tarmac, Helen and Pete (Ben) waved manically to the faces filling the windows.

"Wow!" exclaimed Helen, barely heard above the screech of the jet engines.

"We'll get nearer for the next one," suggested Pete (Ben) as the engine noise subsided into the distance.

"Yes please," she confirmed.

They had drink refills until the next arrival, it wasn't long, they left the bar to join the crowd that had already gathered immediately below the aircraft's beach crossing point to the runway.

From a dot to the red white and blue of American Airlines to the wheels and the undercarriage, it thundered closer and closer. It was an awesome sight; it was directly above them, the sound was deafening. Some people stretched their arms skyward as if to touch it, others cowered low as if to avoid any contact.

The sound waves and engine jets buffeted them almost knocking them off their feet, their hands flew to their eyes to give protection from the flying sand.

"That was brilliant," she said as they made their way back to the boat bar and a taxi back to the cruise terminal.

"I haven't given you a useless fact about St Maarten, have I?" Pete (Ben) asked as Helen snuggled up to him in the rear seat of the taxi.

"No, you haven't," she said resigned to fact that one was on its way.

"Let me see now," he considered rubbing his chin like a professor of archaic knowledge.

"The airport, the one we've just left, that is Princess Juliana Airport, and Princess Juliana became Queen Juliana of the Netherlands in 1948 ruling until 1980. Now here's today's fact, there's a minor planet orbiting the sun named after her – 816 Juliana it's called, but don't ask me what the 816 means."

"I won't," she promised.

There were no messages on Pete's (Ben's) tablet when he booted it up in the confines of Helen's suite.

He didn't expect any, but Helen did need reassurance from time to time that her money was safe, a loan, although Pete (Ben) knew otherwise.

"Nothing from Pierre yet," he said.

"Okay," she replied, showing little interest. She had that twinkle in her eye again. She had other thoughts; she snuggled close lifting her head in anticipation of a kiss. Pete (Ben) obliged, he obliged with more than a kiss.

Helen wore the new dress and shoes, the diamond and sapphire jewellery stayed in the safe. She wore a simple gold choker and matching bracelet.

Her jewellery may have been simple, but it was beautiful in its simplicity, interwoven flat braid gold that sat flat on her pale neck and hung only slightly loose on her narrow wrist.

Pete (Ben) admired his new watch. *Very generous of Helen, he thought. Another $2,000 profit,* he further thought cynically, never for a second did he feel any remorse.

It was another gala evening, another one which they would spend together but this time in the company of others first in the Stromboli Dining Room and then on the cabaret dance floor.

The night, as had become habit-forming, was spent entwined in one and other's arms until the early hours when Pete (Ben) made his way back to his own cabin.

Chapter 25

"It's okay," was Helen's response to Pete's (Ben's) advice that 'Pierre had not come through with payment yet'.

"There's still a hiccup with the coffee money, why God knows, and he's still in negotiations for the cotton," Pete added.

"No worries, I'm in no hurry, we've lots of time," she said, as she squeezed alongside him on to his sunbed as they lounged in the shade shipside away from the prevailing wind.

"I have to go back to the UK, but I'll come to you after that, if that's alright with you," he lied.

"Make it as quick as you can."

"I will," he compacted the lie, a kiss gave her assurance.

"I'll miss you."

"And I'll miss you, a couple of days, maybe three," he assured her.

As per usual they had exercised and breakfasted together and proposed to spend the rest of the day together.

It was another day at sea, another day of organised activities, should they wish to take part.

Pete (Ben) considered the itinerary, Helen read it over his shoulder.

"General knowledge quiz," she read. "You could win that easy," she said.

"I'm glad you think so," he replied. "Not my bag, I'd rather bug you with snippets of useless information."

"Okay, what about fruit carving?"

"Do I look like a fruit carver? I don't think so."

"Line dancing?"

"With my two left feet, not a chance."

"Me?" she suggested with the customary twinkle.

"Very tempting," he replied.

"Only tempting," she nudged him sharply in the ribs.

"Later," he added, kissing her forehead.

"How about we go to 'Your Cruise Ship', talk by the 1st officer and staff?"

"If you want, it's not exactly hot laid here."

The sky was blue with white clouds scampering by on the breeze which together with the forward effect of the ship lowered the temperature to an uncomfortable level, one for the hardy, far too cool for Helen and Pete (Ben).

They gathered their belongings together and made for the theatre.

Hundreds agreed with them regarding the weather conditions, the theatre was well attended.

Facts and figures amazed the audience but only Pete (Ben) would probably remember them, it was interesting, it must have been, no one appeared to drop asleep.

Following a very light lunch and an ice carving display by the Filipinos Pete (Ben) introduced Helen to English afternoon tea.

It was presented in true British fashion, crustless sandwich triangles with egg mayonnaise, salmon and cucumber and ham filling, followed by cakes and scones presented on tiered cake stands.

The bone china tea service completed the Englishness of the occasion.

Helen was one of only three Americans in attendance. "They don't know what they're missing," commented Helen which amused the many Brits sipping their tea with their pinkies raised high, a successful hour's dalliance.

Helen was not amused when Pete (Ben) declined to join her for a siesta. "I must do some work," he insisted.

"If you must," she replied, intentionally sporting a frown.

"Afraid so," he confirmed.

They parted with a passionate kiss as Pete (Ben) exited the lift.

For once Pete (Ben) had not lied, he was working, working to complete the Helen Schmidt con, with the aid of his tablet he had a meaningful conversation with Manny. 'Asif' had done his work but there was still 'Pierre'. Helen's 'loan' had to be protected with empty, but plausible promises, two more days and he'd be out of her life.

Chapter 26

The following two days passed in different ways for Pete (Ben) and Helen Schmidt.

For Pete (Ben) they dragged. The end was in sight, Saturday he would be gone, $60K and whatever he could get for the jewellery better off, but until then he had to keep Helen amused both mentally and physically, albeit that was no particular hardship.

Helen Schmidt was also aware that come Saturday she would lose Pete (Ben), although as far as she was aware, it would be temporary, he would be back in her arms in a matter of days.

Her days passed in a flash, his not so.

Thursday, they disembarked for a tour of the Island of St Vincent, the largest of the St Vincent and Grenadines in the Windward Islands archipelago.

The day was perfect for sail boating, an azure blue sky with a huge golden sun and a light breeze, they joined a small party of a dozen on a catamaran round the island tour.

The tour turned out to be a perfect choice, it had something for everyone. The near silence of being under sail, the only sound being the wind and the canvass, swimming and snorkelling in crystal clear waters, the tranquillity of almost empty fine white sand beaches, and a seafood and beer lunch.

The island of Spice, Granada on Friday, was a different entity, an island tour in an air-conditioned mini bus along with six others they toured the north of the island starting and finishing at St George.

Another successful day of sights, sounds and smells of Granada's delights.

Inevitably, each day Pete (Ben) astounded Helen with an unusual, or if you like, useless fact.

"St Vincent," he advised. "Was dominated by an active volcano." He even remembered its name, 'La Soufriere'. "And it last erupted on April 13, 1979, Friday the 13th, Good Friday."

The Granada snippet was somewhat different. "You remember we drove past the National Stadium, mainly for cricket, I said," began Pete (Ben), when she'd deigned to nod a yes, he'd continued, "$40 million it cost, paid for by the Peoples Republic of China who also provided 300 labourers to build and repair it."

Both evenings were spent in the Red Lion bar, where the barman never failed to judge their drink of the day, in the specialist dining rooms, and at either a show or in the casino.

Friday evening, late, Helen's mood had gradually changed from light to sombre, their time together was nearing the end. Pete (Ben) read the signs.

"It will only be a few days," he said.

"I know," she said, tears forming.

"I'll phone you, you can phone me. You have the number, don't you?"

"Yes, I think so."

"Check," he suggested.

She took her mobile from her handbag, pressed a few buttons and read out the number.

"That's it," he lied. He'd long since given her the number of an old defunct phone of yesteryear. He was confident she wouldn't use it until after they had separated.

"There you go, I will only be on the other end of the line," he said, compounding the lie.

"Don't be surprised when I'm not here in the morning, I have an early start, I know you don't."

"That will be awful, I'm not looking forward to that," she replied.

"I know but I must go, the money, the $60K. I haven't got it yet, I'll –"

"You'll either send it or we'll sort it when I next see you," she interrupted.

"I was just going to say, it's safe, you'll get it soon," he lied professionally.

"I know, it's you I'll miss, not the money."

Pete (Ben) drew her to him. "Let me take you to bed," he whispered.

They left the Red Lion bar with Pete (Ben) carrying a bottle of Shiraz and two glasses. "A nightcap," he explained.

Pete (Ben) had been waiting all night for Helen to leave him alone for a few moments.

At last that time arrived with Helen visiting the bathroom.

Quickly, he poured two glasses of the Shiraz, took the small package of ready crumbled sleeping tablet from his pocket and stirred it in to the one intended for Helen.

He held it up to the light, the powder had dissolved, it could not be seen.

As Helen rejoined him, he offered her the glass. "To the future," he proposed and drained his glass.

Helen followed suit, placed the glass on the dressing table and draped her arms around his neck. "Make love to me," she purred.

Chapter 27

Pete (Ben) gently moved Helen's head on to her own pillow. She snored lightly but didn't wake, the sleeping tablet was working perfectly.

He unhurriedly dressed as Helen slept on.

Using his mobile phone as a torch, he removed the fake jewellery set from his jacket pocket and crept on tiptoes to the safe. It would have made little difference had he made lots of noise, Helen was not about to wake now or for some considerable time to come.

He opened the safe. The real jewellery was on the bottom shelf peeping out from below a flat document case.

Pete (Ben) peered round the dividing wall, Helen slept soundly.

Silently, he exchanged the real set with the fake careful to ensure they sat in exactly the same places.

The pale blue light of the phone glinted off the faceted stones, false and pure alike. In this light, there didn't appear to be any difference. "Hopefully, the same would apply in natural or better artificial light," he thought.

His best guess was that Helen would quickly check the box before packing merely to confirm the jewellery's presence, he didn't expect her to inspect it thoroughly. Why should she? That was his theory, he hoped he was right.

With the real jewellery secreted in his pockets, he kissed Helen on her forehead and whispered sarcastically, "Cheerio and thanks."

He left with Helen in the deepest of sleeps.

Dawn was breaking as he opened his own balcony door to see land on the horizon. "Come on, skipper, put your foot down," he said. "Let me be away from this ship before Helen wakes." The following two hours to the Bridgetown Cruise Terminal appeared to take four, Pete (Ben) willed it to pass quicker, but no, an age it seemed.

Slowly the huge ship docked, ropes were secured to capstans and the first gangway was put in place.

Pete (Ben) watched and waited impatiently his luggage packed and ready to go the moment the call came over the tannoy.

At last, it came.

His cabin steward had been good, and as far as he was aware, he had no inkling that Pete's (Ben's) bed had only been half used, he left him a generous gratuity and left.

He was the first passenger to disembark, the steel band were still setting up their instruments and the shops were just opening.

He grabbed the first taxi in the line and rode into Bridgetown alighting on the main thoroughfare, Broad Street as it was just coming alive.

Out of the taxi and into Cave Shepherd Department Store, he scampered entering through one door and immediately exiting through another.

On the previous Saturday, he'd spotted a small backpacker style hotel in a back street, he went there and paid for one night's accommodation.

The room he was allocated was dingy but clean, a minuscule box of a room, a single bed, an ancient dressing table and a flat pack wardrobe filled the room exposing hardly any of the floorboards ingrained with years of Barbados grime.

Under normal circumstances, Pete (Ben) would never enter the front door of such an establishment, never mind the bedroom, but on this occasion, it was perfect for his requirements.

He dumped his case on the bed, it was rock solid. The springs twanged and the case bounced.

The view from the bedroom window was, as expected, that of a drab alley home to bins and loose rubbish, perfect, all that was required now was a devious exit.

A reconnoitre down the stairs and along an unlit corridor confirmed his hopes.

The door was locked from the inside using an internal Yale, he opened it to be greeted with the dubious odours of a variety of rotting vegetation and animal remains, the long tail of a scabby cat disappeared below a plethora of garbage.

He propped the door open and intrepidly strode over the mountains of mire to the rear alley.

Mission accomplished. He backtracked along the corridor and out the front door and out into Bridgetown.

He glanced around furtively as he made his way to the market area he knew to be littered with numerous street vendors.

He bought a small limited wardrobe of clothes, underwear, socks, a couple of shirts etc. enough to be accommodated in the nondescript carry-on bag that he also acquired.

Back to the hotel he sped, unseen, he hoped, by anyone that might have recognised him, the generous Penelope, for instance.

He sifted through his cruise luggage and located everything he needed for his onward journey, passports, money, documentation, and particularly the necklace, bracelet and earrings.

These were transferred to either his pockets, the new carry-on or his faithful old duffel bag.

He'd had better bathrooms, but this had to suffice. He filled the cracked washbasin with the tepid brown water that trickled from the Verdigris covered tap, and with aid of hair dye neutraliser, he removed the silver grey from his dark hair.

That done, out came his well-travelled professional make-up case. He selected a none too droopy moustache, and fixed it firmly in position. He checked his handiwork and compared his appearance with his passport photograph; he was pleased with the result. Enough of a change from Ben Jolliff, but not too much as to not be recognised from any of his passport photographs.

With the duffel bag over his shoulder, the carry-on bag in one hand and the large case of cruise clothes in the other, he crept down the stairs again and out into the rubbish dump area.

The duffel bag and carry-on he set to rest by the alley gate while he emptied the case and scattered the contents willy-nilly in and under the stinking debris.

That done, he dumped the empty case into a bin, collected the two waiting bags and departed the dump, the alley, and central Bridgetown.

And so began his devious journey to the airport, his pre-determined disappearing act, Ben Joliff was about to vanish.

Over the Chamberlain Bridge, he strode and on to Bay Street to pick up the south coast bus route.

Minutes later, his ears were being assaulted by the constant excessively loud reggae that thundered from the speakers of the dolmus-style mini bus as he passed the Palm Beach Court Hotel on his way through Hastings.

Jude the nympho; I wonder where she is now, he thought as the green painted hotel building flashed by.

His thoughts briefly turned to Helen, Helen Schmidt, *She should be awake now, she'll be okay, as long as she doesn't spot the exchange, nothing I can do now, forget it, if only.*

The strains of Bob Marley gradually diminished as the dilapidated people carrier disappeared into the distance, leaving Pete (no longer Ben) stood at the junction of Worthing Main Road and Lawrence Gap. The time was 10:05.

Chapter 28

Back on the cruise ship, Helen Schmidt was woken by a female member of the crew.

She'd slept through three telephone calls instigating a visit from senior staff.

She'd woken with a start, a feminine hand shaking her exposed shoulder.

She hadn't expected to find Pete (Ben) next to her, but she certainly did not expect to be roused by anyone else.

She pulled the sheet up to her chin covering her naked body.

"Who, what –" she began.

"We couldn't locate you. It's way past your departure time, we tried to find you using the PA System, tried your phone, and now…"

"I, I don't understand. I never sleep this late," Helen stammered.

"Well, you seem okay. We'll let you get ready, quick as you can, if you don't mind, ma'am,". The small entourage left.

Her travel clothes and carry-on bag were on the settee, she dressed quickly, the rest of her luggage was sat in the cruise terminal awaiting collection, it had gone the previous evening.

She collected her documents and valuables from the safe, offering a cursory glance into her jewellery box at the necklace set. All appeared okay, she packed them into the carry-on and left.

She was still drowsy as she left the ship and passed through Security and Customs, she wondered why she'd slept so long.

She was angry that she'd missed saying adieu to Pete (Ben) even though he'd said he was away early.

"Damn," she uttered. "A few days, just a few days, that's what he'd said."

Little did she know that she would never see him again, neither would she see the return of the $60,000 so-called loan or her diamond and sapphire necklace set.

The time was 11:08.

Chapter 29

Two occupied taxis raced past before Pete acquired a free one.

The taxi journey to Grantley Adams International Airport was short and uneventful.

Helen will be on the move soon, he mused. I should be away before she arrives at the airport, assuming my plane is on time.

Pete arrived at the airport with time to spare, but not a lot, he held aloft his James Goodwin passport and his boarding pass as he passed through Passport Control and Security on his way to the departure gate for the 12:20 flight to Grenada.

At the gate, with boarding imminent, he took a seat at the rear of the waiting lounge, pulled the neb of his baseball cap down and attempted to look as inconspicuous as possible.

When the boarding call was announced, he waited until the queue had disappeared and then made his move, he was the last to board.

His seat was 3rd row, aisle. He quickly stowed his carry-on, sat, and fastened the seat belt.

Four minutes later, Flight LI727 was in the air.

Peter Holmes had arrived in Barbados, Ben Joliff had taken his place, now both no longer existed.

He gladly accepted the coffee offered. Until now, he hadn't stopped. Breakfast had gone by the board, as had lunch, priority one had been to escape Barbados unadulterated.

He relaxed a little; first phase of his disappearing act had been successfully carried out, phase two beckoned.

The flight was short, 55 minutes; the ride was a little bumpy. "Turbulence unavoidable," advised the captain but the landing was professionally smooth.

Granada was relatively new to Pete, now travelling in the guise of James Goodwin, he exited the terminal building.

Only the previous day, along with Helen, he had toured the island visiting the obligatory hot spots, but being there now alone was a completely different entity.

He thought of Helen, where she might be, *had she suspected any wrongdoing?* He considered it hardly likely but there was still some uncertainty. Only when he was back in the UK as himself, Peter Holmes, would he feel completely safe and secure.

He was intent on keeping a low profile just in case Helen did eventually blow the whistle and either the police or private investigators tried to find him.

With his new temporary identity, he felt he could relax a little, no one knew him here, but still caution was the order of the day.

There was no doubt Helen could afford the financial loss. The $60K now in Pete's offshore account would hardly make a difference, but could she afford the embarrassment of being conned by a toyboy?

Still, caution was better than a devil-may-care attitude at this time.

Three taxis and four private cars stood at the kerb immediately outside the terminal exit doors. Pete (James) passed them by and walked casually to the dust covered yellow and blue bus parked on the other side of the road.

The handful of passengers that collectively had ridden the 7-mile journey to St George all alighted together.

Pete (James) felt the first pangs of hunger. He hadn't as yet eaten, the quick escape from Barbados had enforced an unwanted fast.

The centre of St George had certain similarities to Bridgetown, the colours, the smells vibrant and acrid, a mishmash of small shops and at first glance no eateries.

He found a small cafe filled with locals. A good sign, the limited menu consisted of chicken. Chicken or chicken cooked in a variety of ways. He chose curried chicken West Indies style.

To say it was hot would be an understatement; the accompanying Coca-Cola did nothing to soothe his damaged tongue, his palate was gone forever.

The best tourist hotels were, to be found outside of the city, aligning the beaches. The town hotels, as far as Pete (James) could see, were the type that catered for itinerant locals or island hopping reps.

He walked around the block and returned to a hotel not three doors from the cafe where he'd lunched.

Still using the name James Goodwin, he checked in for one night.

The room was a clone of the Bridgetown hotel room except this one looked over the main street, not the garbage dump.

He surveyed the scene, the room was claustrophobic, but he thought it prudent not to venture far.

A siesta without sex was a first for a while. Sleep came easy, tension, he hadn't realised was there, disappeared.

It was dark when he woke, weak yellow light from the street permeated the thin curtains. He showered under a trickle of tepid water and changed into a nondescript outfit of jeans and faded blue shirt.

He ventured out; he needed Wi-Fi, that was not available in the hotel.

Pete wandered the deserted streets of St George to no avail, nowhere was there Wi-Fi, not an internet cafe, not a library, not a hotel, businesses that may have had internet and Wi-Fi were all closed.

He found a single taxi with a sleeping driver parked outside a tiny bar from which pounded the inevitable strains of reggae. He woke him and asked him to find him an internet connection.

"You want a beach hotel, boss," he said, rubbing his eyes.

"Take me to the nearest and wait for me, okay?"

"No problem, boss."

The 15-minute moonlit ride took them along the coast to the tourist area of Grand Anse. The taxi came to a stop outside the four-star Beach Resort.

The complex was low rise colonial style set in elegant tropical gardens. Pete ventured in; the internal décor was in keeping with its external facade.

Pete wandered through the bright modern reception area and found the bar.

He ordered a Pina Colada and requested the Wi-Fi password, the barman in his smart white coat provided both together with a huge smile.

Apart from two young couples, he had the place to himself. He took occupation of a settee set behind a low table, he set down his drink and opened his tablet.

From where he sat, he could see that the dining room was well attended, only then did he realise he was hungry, he promised himself a good meal once he'd finished on his tablet.

Surfing the internet for flights was not new to Pete, he had his pet sites and in no time at all he had organised his travel back to the UK.

The journey would take him via Miami, passing through the USA, it was, therefore, a must he travel on his Peter Holmes passport as he only held an ESTA in his true name. No problem, he had anticipated this and Granada was as good a place as any for James Goodwin to disappear.

The aroma of fine food permeated from the dining room. He paid for his drink, went outside and advised the taxi driver he was dining. "No problem, boss, I'll wait."

The lunchtime curry had been good and nourishing but the fine seafood meal served in the four-star hotel was much better. He accompanied his meal with white Zinfandel for which he'd acquired a taste. He toasted Helen Schmidt, more for her money and her body than any feeling of lost love.

As Pete expected, the taxi driver was snoring his head off when he returned for his ride back to the dingy town hotel.

Pete retired with a happy stomach and the driver with a happy pocket.

Chapter 30

Helen Schmidt had just about recovered from her rude awakening, but she was still feeling a little drowsy when she was reunited with her luggage.

She was one of the last passengers to leave the ship and exit the cruise terminal.

She taxied to the airport arriving thirty minutes after the Liat flight had left for Granada totally unaware that Pete (Ben) was on board.

She was disappointed and distressed that Pete (Ben) had left without any goodbyes, there much she had wanted to say to him.

Sat in the departure lounge of Grantley Adams airport, she speed-dialled the mobile number Pete (Ben) had given her.

The unobtainable sound buzzed in her ear.

She tried again, same thing.

She tried without speed dial, carefully tapping in the number. Nothing.

Little did she know that the phone she was trying to call had been dumped by Pete (Ben) some time ago and had probably by now been recycled into a car, or a TV, or even another phone.

Before she boarded the US Airways Boeing 737 for Miami, she tried again without success. She was confused. Why was she unable to contact Pete (Ben)? It never occurred that he'd given her a redundant number, tears trailed her cheeks taking mascara with them as she made her way to the gate.

During the 97-minute layover in Miami, she tried Pete (Ben's) number several times, all to no avail.

Realisation dawned that she'd lost contact with him, for what reason she knew not, she wept into a tissue avoiding the glances of fellow travellers.

"Why, why, why?" she asked herself. "Is it accidental, is it intentional? It couldn't be intentional, could it?"

The thought that she'd been swindled out of $60K never entered her head, neither did she think about her jewellery. She had no cause to, as far as she was concerned, she'd put that in her carry-on bag and there it was, still.

While Helen transited in the South Terminal, Pete (Ben) was in the International flight North Terminal.

Neither were aware of this fact. Had they been, Helen would have been overjoyed whereas Pete (Ben) would have been mortified. As it was, one was sad, very sad, and the other alert and wary.

It took a while but eventually Helen became resigned to the knowledge that Pete (Ben), for whatever reason, was no longer contactable. She still lived in hope that he would phone her.

Helen Schmidt arrived home to her near-empty mansion overlooking the angry Atlantic Ocean. The weather was as sombre as she, dense grey cloud covered the sky and intermittent rain fell.

The house would have been totally empty had it not been for the presence of her long-time housekeeper, Molly Boyle.

Molly Boyle had been Helen's housekeeper from the moment she and her husband, Henry, had moved into the house, at the time when their finances were on a steep incline.

She reflected: They had been good times, Henry and her deeply in love, their young son, Jimmy, with money in their pockets, happy and content.

Henry's death had left a huge void in her life, they had met and married when young, barely were they out of college, a time when they could hardly afford their apartment rent, never mind live the high life.

She had wanted to die herself when Jimmy had been killed, he and his father had been close. His father's death had induced a wildness, a head-strong streak in him. He had driven too fast, but, she had fought through the depression like the stoic person she was.

Now there was another void, another loss. She'd met, got to know, and learnt to love, Ben Jolliff in less than two weeks, and now he was lost to her. Why, she didn't know.

The presence of Molly Boyle made no difference. She'd greeted her like the old friend she was, she'd made her a drink, run her a bath. She was there, but still the place seemed empty. She was lost, she cried, out of sight of Molly, she cried, and she cried, and she cried some more.

Chapter 31

As Pete had paid cash the previous night for the 'not so delightful' room, there was no reason for him to check out.

There was no one about anyway as he crept quietly down the stairs and through the entrance lobby.

It was still dark, 5:30, at least an hour to sunrise.

He played a hunch, and he was right. The taxi and driver of the previous evening were parked in exactly the same spot. Pete woke him again. "This is becoming a habit, boss," the driver slurred.

One baggage desk was in operation at the airport but there was nobody in attendance except a surly black woman of undetermined years yawning with boredom.

Passports and security were formalities through which Pete passed unhindered.

The sun gradually lifted its head to a fine day with a fair breeze, Pete could see the runway windsock in a horizontal position.

The American Airlines Boeing 737 in its distinctive silver and red livery with Pete and no more than 20 others on board left for Miami on time, 8:25.

Pete hated passing through American Airports and Miami, he found, was no different to the rest.

Since 2001, the attack of September 11, security in American International Airports has been raised to an extremely high level.

No doubt the precautions are necessary but the time it takes for travellers to move from one gate to another is, to say the least, eventful and annoying.

It doesn't help that in every uniform there is a brusque, sometimes rude, individual that had forgotten how to smile and be courteous before reaching puberty.

Pete wasn't a great fan of American beer, but the Sam Adams he was drinking from the bottle was much better than a Budweiser, the other beer on offer.

He had nearly five hours between flights, but the time it had taken through officialdom meant that this had been reduced to just over three. He sat at the bar watching the surfeit of basketball that appeared on every screen.

If the beer had been to UK standards, he would have fallen off the barstool long before his flight was called, but that wasn't the case, he was more bloated than drunk.

The next port of call, reached in just over two hours, was Charlotte/ Douglas. Again flight on time, American efficiency, or so he found sometimes.

It seemed to Pete, to be a devious route, but it had appeared to be the quickest and most efficient one on offer, soon he would be back on home ground.

It was the same tiresome route through bureaucracy as it had been in Miami except this time instead of the voices being mainly Latino here it was a Southern drawl that accompanied each threatening expression.

North Carolina may be a beautiful place, but through the large plate glass window of a modern airport looking over a floodlit concrete runway in the dark of night there's no way of knowing, one could be anywhere.

A Starbuck's latte and chocolate muffin filled Pete's time and sated his appetite as the enforced additional layover slowly passed.

He bought a magazine and sat in the half-empty departure lounge watching the clock whose hands seemed to be frozen.

At last, it was time to board.

Pete made his way down the left-hand aisle of the American Airlines Airbus A330 pushing his carry-on bag in front careful not to bump anyone already seated.

He was one of the early boarders and the seats were sparsely occupied as he shuffled toward the very back window seat, his seat of preference whenever he flew.

He couldn't help but notice the occupant of seat 25B, an aisle seat.

She was petite; very pretty. Blonde hair with pink highlights.

She wore a tight white tee-shirt through which her breasts and nipples showed clearly.

She was maybe 35, no more than 40.

His eyes were drawn first to the shapely mounds before moving up-ward to her face and into her bright blue eyes.

How did I not see her in the lounge? he wondered.

She looked directly back at him and smiled showing a perfect set of white teeth.

As Pete brushed by, she turned to watch his progress down the plane.

Pete stowed his bag in the overhead locker and watched the ground staff go about their business and the crew settle the remaining passengers in their seats.

Into the night sky soared flight no. AA732, Charlotte to Heathrow.

No sooner had the seat belt sign been extinguished, the animated crew sprang into life serving the obligatory drinks and so-called celebrity chef-designed meals.

As quickly as the meal had appeared the remnants were removed faster.

The cabin crew disappeared; and the lights were dimmed into sleeping mode.

Passengers wanting to read or use electronic equipment became reliant on the overhead directional downlights.

One by one, seats were reclined, and blankets were utilised.

Pete followed suit and began to doze.

He was in the twilight zone when he detected movement. The woman from seat 25B came up the aisle, passed him and ducked through the curtain to the toilets and staff area immediately behind him, she glanced in his direction as she went by.

Pete eyed her from top to toe, in addition to the tight white tee-shirt she wore a white skirt, tight at the hip flaring to just above her knee revealing a fine pair of shapely legs. She was barefoot moving noiselessly through the cabin. *"Nice pair of pins,"* he could hear his dad say.

"Excuse me," she said. "Do you mind if I sit here?" Seat 25B had reappeared through the curtain and hovered over him with the white tee-shirt covered protruding nipples pointing in his direction.

"No, not at all," he replied, thinking, as most men would: Nice, very nice.

She sat, buckled the seat belt, reclined the seat and covered herself in her blanket which she'd carried with her unnoticed by Pete.

Whether he slept, he was not sure. He felt movement on his knee, it was his neighbour's hand with probing fingers, he did nothing.

The hand moved upwards and stroked his thigh, his penis became alert.

If you can play, so can I, he thought. He explored beneath the blanket. His left hand found her left thigh; she moved only slightly, definitely not away.

Pete was temporarily disappointed when she removed her hand, he need not have been, it was only for her to raise the dividing armrest, which she did, moved closer and returned her hand.

She reached his fly and deftly undid the zip.

As her hand explored his boxer shorts, his hand was finding that she wore no panties.

She held his erect manhood as he found her bush.

She slowly and pleasantly manipulated his penis as his fingers found and massaged her clitoris.

Together they pleasured each other until she shook and whimpered restrainedly, Pete held himself in a practised way.

Her hand left his penis, she pushed off the blankets, climbed over him, lifted her skirt and lowered herself on to him. There was no movement elsewhere, no sound, only that of the droning engines.

He half lay, half sat as she raised and lowered herself pushing up and down using the arm rests, his hands found her firm breasts and stiff nipples under her shirt.

It was his turn to orgasm. It didn't take long; she let go the armrests and accepted his full length. She joined him throwing back her head, muting her ecstasy.

She did not move for, what seemed to Pete, minutes, but was probably only a few seconds.

She sat back in her seat, adjusted the blankets to their original positions and produced, as if from nowhere, cleansing tissues, she had literally come prepared.

No one else stirred.

He adjusted his zip as she straightened her skirt and shirt. She kissed him lightly on the lips and returned to seat 25B.

Not a word had been spoken and no one had seen.

Pete had always been lucky, but never in his wildest dreams, and there'd been a few of those, had he ever believed that he would qualify for the mile-high club.

Hardly surprising, he slept until woken by the noise of breakfast being served.

Chapter 32

The day was cold and dank, grey clouds rubbed shoulders with more grey clouds. It felt like it could snow, a typical February day in London.

Peter Holmes was himself, in his own adopted city, yes a far cry from his childhood surroundings, but now he was a time served Londoner, albeit still a Yorkshireman at heart.

He'd seen little of the city to Paddington from Heathrow, the periphery had flashed by the windows of the Heathrow Express and the rest of the journey had been underground.

His apartment was a small one-bedroom affair, bijou, the advert had said, and bijou it was.

He'd decorated and furnished it himself. It was functional rather than decadent, the furniture was angular, modern, in pastel shades, which together with the white walls made for bland surroundings.

The apartment matched Pete's inner self, apart from his womanising, his life as a hustler, he was, in truth, a solitary, erudite person who enjoyed his own company, the numerous books on many subjects strewn around were testament to this fact.

When he was in residence, which was not often, the apartment was given the once over each week by the janitor's wife who was under strict instructions not to touch the reading matter wherever it lay, and it was everywhere, even in the bathroom.

The cheap clothes and carry-on bag he'd bought in Bridgetown had served their purpose. He dumped them in the basement garbage area before climbing the stairs to the apartment.

He was totally relaxed, the journey home had been interesting, to say the least.

Home, where was home? England was home, but not the apartment. That was somewhere to live. Back in Yorkshire, when he'd been young with Mum and Dad, that had been home. When he'd made enough money and retired from hustling, then he'd find a home, a proper home, with a proper partner. Well, that was his dream, maybe someday.

The apartment was somewhere to read and learn and to rest his head. It was rented; it suited his purpose. The majority of the money he accrued was deposited in his offshore account, now it was boosted by Helen Schmidt's $60K and soon it would be increased further with the proceeds of her jewellery.

He'd realised some time ago that once past fifty, his appeal to the ladies would diminish and his working life as a conman would grind to a halt.

His aim was to accumulate more than enough funds to retire and enjoy the fruits of his not-so-hard labours before then.

He discarded the clothes he'd travelled in, showered and dressed in tee-shirt and shorts. For the moment he was going nowhere.

It felt good to be back in quality clothing, the dowdy cheap Barbadian clothing had served their purpose but being able to choose from his extensive wardrobe of Saville Row and Designer label clothes was much better.

It was time to curl up with one of his many books. Which one, was an easier decision to make than the many he'd made over the last couple of weeks, now for some rest.

The stolen jewellery of Helen Schmidt had travelled all the way from the cruise ship berthed at Bridgetown Cruise Terminal, via Grenada, Miami, Charlotte and Heathrow undetected, next step was to take it to Daniel.

If, by any chance, the jewellery had been found, by customs or security, he had the receipt for the fake set to support his claim that it was a surprise present for an imaginary fiancé, surely a lowly security officer manning an x-ray machine would not be able to tell the difference between real and fake gems.

Lounging in his favourite white plastic half-egg shaped bucket seat, he phoned Daniel.

Daniel was his roommate during his days at university whose father he'd worked for part-time in Hatton Garden but now had his own independent gem business.

Daniel's business was 95% legitimate, but Pete was interested in the other 5%, the 5% that was more under the counter than above.

Pete gave him the gist of his latest scam and a description of the acquisition that he had for sale.

Chapter 33

Peter Holmes and Daniel Baum met in the Crown and Two Chairmen, an ancient pub situated on Dean Street in the heart of Soho. It was early evening and the stalwart few were in residence.

They greeted each other like the old friends they were, briefly attracting the attention of the silent drinkers.

Each armed with a pint of Truman's Runner, recommended as best in the house by the landlord, they sat in a quiet corner.

Pete sipped the already flat beer. "Bloody rubbish," he commented, grimacing. Beer was one of the things he missed from his native Yorkshire, a good pint with a good creamy top that lasted until the last drops were drained.

"Look at it, it's as flat as a fart."

"Some things never change," replied Daniel. "Your good looks, you jammy bugger, and your complaints about our Southern beer," he added.

They exchanged pleasantries regarding friends and family and the dire weather before Pete broached the main purpose of their meeting.

They occupied a table in the corner furthest away from the bar and the majority of customers but Pete was alert to inquisitive eyes, he surreptitiously slid the box containing Helen's jewellery from his jacket pocket. He opened it on the upholstered bench seat between them, below the level of the table.

"Fuck me!" whispered Daniel, "You've scored here, brother, they're fucking beautiful."

"Not bad eh?" replied Pete.

"Are you fucking kidding? It's been a while since I've seen anything as good."

"How much?" asked Pete, the famous Yorkshire adage appearing unerringly.

"How much do you think?" threw back the shrewd Daniel.

"Well, I reckon they'll be more valuable left intact than broken up, but –"

"You're right," interrupted Daniel. "But they may be recognised. I take it they weren't a gift, shall we say you acquired them?"

"Yeah, that sounds right, I acquired them."

"I suppose it's fair to say you acquired them without the owner's knowledge?"

"Correct, but what I don't know, is if she'll spot that what she has now are copies, albeit good copies, and what she'll do if she does. Will she go to the police and the insurance company? I don't know."

"In that case, best play safe, break them up. Shame but prudent," said Daniel in a decisive tone.

"Right," continued Daniel. "Good stones, good colour, clarity fine, even without a loupe I can see that. You going to leave them with me, I'll do the necessary and give you my best price."

"So be it, let's drink to that."

Pete raised his glass of barely touched insipid liquid (to Pete it looked insipid, the locals no doubt were more satisfied), clinked Daniel's and sipped the abhorrent brew with another grimace.

Daniel pocketed the cardboard box careful to avoid prying eyes.

A light-hearted conversation ensued about nothing in particular accompanied more drinks, but not beer, gin and tonics was more suited Pete's palate than the 'dishwater' he'd been attempting to drink earlier.

By the time Pete got back to his apartment, the alcohol was beginning to take its effect, he felt lightheaded. "Tipsy," his Mum would have called it.

The adrenaline rush of the jewellery theft, the devious journey, the broken sleep on the flight from Miami interrupted by a nymphomaniac stranger and latterly several high-octane drinks – no wonder he was light headed, his body was knackered, no other word for it.

He slept like the proverbial baby.

Chapter 34

Peter Holmes soon reacclimatised to the inclement British weather and resumed his search for knowledge visiting the numerous museums and galleries London has to offer.

Two days after their meeting in the Crown and Two Chairmen, Daniel called. It was a no-frills call, straight to business.

"You've hit the jackpot, you lucky bastard," Daniel opened.

"Good, give me the good news then."

"Two excellent diamonds, four sapphires of equal size and quality, two small diamonds, two small sapphires and some gold chain, all separated and valued."

"Okay, cut to the chase, how much?"

"To you, £40K," replied Daniel.

"That's good, so, their value to you is at least £58K?" goaded Pete.

"Peter, Peter, would I –"

"Yes you would, try again."

"Because we've been friends a long time, £45K," he returned.

"And because I love you like a brother, £53K?"

"What you trying to do, kill me?" a well-used phrase used by traders of the Jewish faith.

"£50K. And they're yours. I know you, you'll still make a bundle."

"Some friend, some brother, okay. £50K, it is."

"And I don't want any of your dirty cash. I'll take nice clean numbers from your off-shore to mine, you still got the details?"

"Yeah, yeah, check it out tomorrow. Your pension fund will have grown."

"I owe you a drink," said Pete.

"I'll take it out of the gold chain," Daniel snapped back.

"You crafty Jewish bastard," said Pete and closed the call.

Pete renewed his dalliance with Marianne, his need for sustenance in the sexual department needed to be sated. There was always Marianne.

Pete and Marianne went back years. They'd met when they were both working their way through university at the same escort agency.

She, of course, looked after the men, well not always, while he looked after the ladies, never the men.

Her background was working class, as was his, but from different parts of the country, him from Yorkshire, she from Somerset.

They had much in common including the acquisition of neutral accents.

Marianne had originally been simply Anne but she'd changed to the more middle/upper-class Christian name shortly after leaving home for university.

Her surname had changed three times, having married two of her elderly rich clients.

Originally she'd been Anne Gardner but had become first Marianne Gardner and then Marianne Green.

Two years later, the aged, exceedingly rich Mr Green departed this world following a heart attack, leaving Marianne very comfortable. What brought on the heart attack was the subject of much debate but which came to nought.

She had very much enjoyed the 'escort' work, getting paid for something she would have given away for free, and very soon she met and married Mr Right, literally Mr Wright, but with a W.

Mr W was somewhat inadequate in the bedroom department, which was hardly surprising, at 81 most people are well past their sexual best, at 35 Marianne was in need, Mr W's loss was Mr Holmes's gain.

Escorting was by now a thing of the past, but she still required maintenance, and that was where Pete came in.

The arrangement was satisfactory to both parties, filling a sexual void for each of them.

Pete and Marianne were not cheating on Mr W. They had been, but then he suffered the same fate as Mr Green, so that their relationship was no longer adulterous, just pleasurable without strings attached.

They never intruded on each other's space, fornicating in either one's apartment was a no-no. Pete's dad had always told him, "Never shit on your own doorstep," wise advice that he remembered and never took any woman into his home or temporary home, like a ship's cabin.

Twice or three times a week, they met for drinks and extras which they performed in a salubrious, but clean and comfortable hotel that catered for expensive one-night stands.

It was only on these nights that Pete spent a full night in the same bed as his partner.

Breakfast in the hotel dining room was always an interesting affair, making comparisons between the relative age and merits of the various couples became a regular pastime.

It was rumoured that some of the couples were real-life partners and were adding spice to their otherwise mundane lives by living a night charade. If it rocks your boat, why not.

Enjoying a leisure period was all well and good but Pete's bank balance was diminishing exponential to his growing boredom, his feet, or his groin, were itching for new pastures.

Winter had turned into spring although there was little change in the London weather.

March into April was the wrong time of year for the sun-worshipping American and European rich leaving the likes of St Tropez, Monte Carlo and the Amalfi coast bereft of potential clients.

Cruise options were limited to the Canaries, Scandinavia and the Baltic Sea, hardly good hunting grounds for prospective pseudo affairs with wealthy ladies.

He looked to the Middle and Far East and even the Antipodes, the possibilities there.

Although the Caribbean had extensive itineraries from various starting ports, Pete thought it foolhardy to contemplate a return there for some time, maybe it would be safe, but maybe not.

Pete spent a full day anchored in front of his laptop, Google worked overtime as he visited numerous cruise company and airline sites to determine his next venue.

After much deliberation, he made his decision. The Far East, in his opinion, offered the best odds for finding single, or, if necessary, unaccompanied married ladies of wealth, from whom he could extort additional funds for his coffers.

He had been installed back in his habitually tidy and organized flat surrounded by his books for four weeks and in that time he'd thought of the hapless Helen Schmidt only once, and that was the thought of her body next to him as he laid in his own e empty bed.

She, on the other hand, had thought of him almost constantly a week or so for her to realise that he was gone never to return.

She had found love again, she'd been happy in Ben's arms but now he was no longer there and never would be again.

The realization that he and her $60K were gone eventually dawned. The $60K meant little, yes, she'd been duped and cheated, but it was Ben she missed, not the money, that meant nothing.

"Would she go to the police?"

"No."

"Admit that she, a mature woman, could fall for the wiles of a handsome conman and be separated from her money?"

"No, the embarrassment would be too much, try and forget it."

Helen was oblivious to the fact that the sapphire necklace set that sat in the house safe was a copy, maybe she always would be, the thought that it was not the original might never have enter her head.

Helen's melancholy had not gone unnoticed by Molly, her retainer and confidante, but she was powerless in mending what she didn't know was broken.

Singapore, the departing port for many of the Far East cruises, was readily accessible from London, from Australia, and America, the homes of many of the world's wealthy widows seeking late-life adventure in pastures new.

A visit to Saville Row and Oxford Street replenished his departed holiday wardrobe, that, if found, would be languishing on the back of a local layabout. A smile came to Pete's face as he imagined the sight of a grubby dishevelled hobo wearing a maroon tuxedo asleep in some Bridgetown back alley, not a pretty sight, but amusing, at least to Pete.

The lost tuxedo was replaced with a perfectly cut white one which he would wear with the tailored black trousers complete with pencil sharp horizontal creases both made by the same celebrity tailor.

Chapter 35

The flight from Heathrow to Singapore was for Pete 13 hours of boredom.

Unfortunately, there was no mile-high surprise sex on this flight, quite the opposite.

He found himself in a window seat hemmed in by an elderly couple who would insist on asking personal questions, where was he going, what was he doing when he got there, who was he doing it with, and so on.

He tried to shock them with imaginary and erotic answers but that only whetted their appetite, the questions kept coming.

He feigned sleep, that worked for a while, but the moment his eyes opened, they began the inquisition again.

Singapore has to be the cleanest city in the world, dropping litter, apparently, is punished with a heavy fine, hence the place is immaculate and modern, yet green and airy.

The taxi from the airport was spotless with the driver smart in chauffeur's livery complete with peaked cap. Unlike many cities, the drive to the hotel was quick and interesting, pristine roads and streets interspersed with greenery.

The famous Raffles Hotel was a little above his budget for the over-night stay before embarking on the cruise, but the Shangri-La was more than adequate, salubrious without the same expense.

Singapore was well known to him and following an afternoon siesta, he ventured out into the Orchard Road area to join the throng of late afternoon and early evening shoppers.

A table outside Starbuck's was a perfect location for people watching, a veritable league of nations passed him by, including a host dressed in national and international dress.

A visit to Singapore is not complete without a visit to the Long Bar in Raffles Hotel to sample an original recipe Gin Sling in the place where it was invented.

Peter Holmes leant at the bar sampling the famous drink where Ernest Hemingway and Somerset Maugham had stood in the days of yore. The drink was much overrated; in his opinion, he would have much rather had a beer, but when in Rome etc.

It was, he was assured by the impeccably dressed barman, made to the original recipe, two parts gin, and one part each of cherry brandy, orange juice, pineapple juice and lime juice, all ingredients fine on their own, but not together, not to Pete's taste.

He did, however, manage to drain the glass, after all he was a Yorkshireman, and at something like £11, he certainly wasn't going to leave any, not one drop.

His second drink was a more conservatively priced Tiger beer presented in a tall glass, no drinking out of the bottle in Raffles.

The purpose of his visit was twofold, one to visit the famous colonial style hotel, and two, to see if he could acquaint himself with an unsuspecting rich female.

He casually surveyed the room, the bar was exactly as the name suggested, long, very long, something in the order of 30 yards long., Running almost the full length of the room the bar was a carpenter's dream, the whole room was for that matter, timber fixtures, timber ceiling with exposed timber beams, everywhere wood, polished, perfect wood and woodworking.

The floor, in contrast, was covered in patterned ceramic tiles.

The stools at the bar, of which there were at least a dozen, were yet again wood, dark wood, maybe mahogany, but Pete was no expert. They were occupied by several casually dressed tourists.

The sitting, drinking area in front of the bar was filled with wicker chairs and wicker tables with glass tops, these were interrupted halfway along the room by a wooden circular staircase going upward to who knows where.

The wicker chairs were the further domain of tourist types, they were occupied by groups and couples nursing the obligatory gin slings and local beers, there didn't appear to be any need for him to stay, no prospective ladies of wealth to be seen. I start again in earnest tomorrow, he told himself as he left.

Chapter 36

The earlier siesta and refreshing shower had revitalised him, it was still early evening, he'd eaten, he'd sampled the disappointing Gin Sling, now he was ready for a little nightlife.

The taxi driver was most obliging. "Take me to a good music bar," Pete requested.

"No problem, sir, one music bar coming up."

He wasn't a chatty inquisitive taxi driver like the London cabbies, he just drove, weaving in and out of the Singapore night traffic expertly, along main thoroughfares and down dimly lit back streets.

"This good place," he said in his pidgin English as he pulled to the kerb outside a canopied door, the illuminated sign read simply 'Music Bar'.

Pete paid the asking price plus a generous tip.

"I wait few minutes," the driver said. "You no like, I take you somewhere else, I wait."

"Thanks," Pete replied, turned and approached the door guarded by two burly doormen wearing tuxedos two sizes too small for their broad shoulders.

He nodded to them as he pushed the door and sighed with relief when there was no opposition to his entry.

It was like many of the night clubs of London, New York and probably the world, diffused lighting gave the place a dim eerie feeling. Not romantic, but secretive and seductive. It took a few moments for his eyes to adjust.

"A table, sir," asked another tuxedo, not of the same size as the two outside, but big enough, the equal of Pete, and then some.

"Not at the moment," replied Pete. "I'll take a seat at the bar, maybe later."

"Fine, sir, please follow me."

It wasn't a huge place, maybe twice the size of the Long Room that he'd just left, the tuxedo led him on a winding path through tables and chairs to the bar in the far corner of the room.

From the bar, Pete could see the full extent of the Music Bar.

It was tastefully decorated in Art Deco style, tables and chairs filled the centre of the room, there were three side booths with padded Ottoman style seating surrounding semi-circular tables.

A stage surrounded by suspended lighting booms filled the far corner.

The stage was set for a live combo, a piano, a set of drums and a double bass occupied the space but without the musicians.

The recorded voice of Michael Bublé filled the air.

The chairs were sparsely occupied, it was after all early, maybe they would fill later, at least Pete hoped so, he didn't want a raucous night but neither did he want to be in a dentist's waiting room.

He ordered a beer, a bottle of Tiger was set beside him, no glass.

As he sipped, he further surveyed his surroundings.

Through the gloom he could see that one of the booths was filled completely with young women.

Even from a distance, he could see they were all quite beautiful. Asian girls with jet-black hair, small facial features, it was their narrow dark eyes that gave away their ethnic origins.

They all appeared to be looking his way, appraising him as he was them. It felt strange, he averted his eyes.

The few people in residence appeared to be all couples, it seemed he was the only single in the club.

The musicians appeared from a concealed door adjacent to the stage, the background music faded to nothing as the combo opened with the iconic 'Take Five' jazz number made famous by the Dave Brubeck Quartet in the pre-rock and roll era.

This they followed with 'Fly me to the moon', the frequently recorded jazz standard made popular by Frank Sinatra.

Four of the Asian girls took to the small dance floor.

They were all quite tall and slim, narrow at the hip and even narrower at the waist.

They all wore full-length evening gowns, a sight rare in the present day Western world, the tight-fitting dresses accentuated their slender bodies.

The dresses followed a similar style but were of different colours, patterned, plain and sequinned, all were accompanied by a sash worn shoulder to hip, similar to that worn by Miss World.

As they swayed to the music, Pete's eyes roved from one to another.

It was the sashes that fascinated Pete, each one had a different number, they varied from 500 to 2,500. Pete pondered on their significance.

Pete was a man of the world, not naïve in any way. He had a good idea what the numbers indicated, but only one way to find out.

The barman confirmed his thoughts. "The cost of being your escort for the night," he said. "Extras are negotiable and expected," he added, "Interested?"

"Maybe," replied Pete mulling over the thought. *Could be interesting.*

The four dancers left the floor to be replaced by another two similarly dressed, now they swayed to a more upbeat number.

One of the girls was slightly taller than the rest, her dark hair was coiled into a top knot exaggerating her long slender neck, she had high cheekbones and a sharp chin.

Her pink eye shadow and peach lipstick enhanced her lightly blushed face, long drop earrings added to the effect of making her appear taller.

She moved slower and more seductively than the others.

128

Her dress was red with a floral pattern down one side, her sash was silver with black digits. 2,500, the top number, Pete could see why.

Pete pointed her out to the barman, "Would you ask her to join me?" he requested. "I'll take a booth seat," he added.

"Fine choice," commented the barman with a wink.

"Hello," said Pete as the vision in red joined him on the Ottoman.

"Hello," she returned offering her slender hand.

Pete rose slightly from his seat and kissed the back of her hand in a gentlemanly fashion.

"Pete," he said.

"Puteri," she replied.

"Nice name," Pete complimented.

"Thank you, it means princess in Malay," her English was near perfect, hardly any trace of an accent.

"Very apt," said Pete as another bottle of beer and a glass of champagne were delivered by the barman.

"House rules," the barman said before Pete could ask. "The drink of choice for the ladies."

Puteri looked embarrassed as she sipped the drink.

"Sorry about this, I don't even like it," she grimaced.

Pete found her good company, she was well educated, from a good family. She had plans, she was careful with her earnings, and she didn't intend to be an 'escort' for long.

Pete empathised with her but didn't share his escorting experience.

When she asked of his occupation, he replied simply, "Businessman."

Pete looked at his Breitling watch, for an instant, he thought of Helen Schmidt. It had ticked around to 11 o'clock. "Shall we leave?" he asked.

"If you wish," she replied. "I'll say bye to my friends."

Pete beckoned the barman as Puteri joined her fellow escorts, there were giggles and glances in his direction.

Pete paid the exorbitant bar bill after the mandatory 'How much?' comment.

Puteri guided Pete through a door concealed behind a curtain adjacent to the bar. "Enjoy," said the barman in a jealous tone.

The door led on to a similar dimly lit corridor to the one through which he'd entered the club.

A rickety four-person lift, circa 1970, took them to the fifth floor. Puteri looped her arm through Pete's.

An identical corridor to the one at ground level greeted their exit from the lift, there was complete silence other than the rattle of the lift gate.

Puteri unlocked the third door on the left, pushed it open and turned on the light, Pete followed her in.

This was not a dingy, decrepit hotel room of the Bridgetown and St George standard, quite the opposite. The room was tastefully furnished and decorated in a western style.

The room was large comprising two distinct areas, a living area with a small table with two upright chairs, a comfortable upholstered chair and a TV, the other was the bedroom area filled with a wardrobe, dressing table and double bed.

Two doors led off the living area, Pete assumed these to be a kitchenette and a bathroom.

"Coffee?" Puteri offered.

"No thanks," Pete replied.

Pete took in the surroundings, he hadn't known what to expect, but he certainly hadn't expected this.

Never before had he paid for sex. He'd been paid himself for the service, but this was new, he was at a loss how to begin, he sat on the corner of the bed.

Puteri took the initiative.

She stood in front of Pete and dropped the sash and red dress to the floor.

Pete's eyes travelled upwards from her sling-back high-heeled shoes, rose to her slim, almost thin, long legs to the thong, upward to her flat stomach, and her small brassiere-clad breasts, and on to her pretty oval face.

She kicked off the shoes and removed the bra, her breasts were small and pert, the nipples proud and erect.

Puteri assisted in the removal of Pete's jacket and shirt.

The thong disappeared to reveal a hairless mound of Venus. *Different,* thought Pete.

Puteri turned off the light and slid between the sheets.

Pete dispensed with the rest of his clothes and joined her.

Was it expected for him to take the lead, or her?

The question was answered for him, she gently found his penis already hard.

He cupped one tiny breast, it was firm and soft to the touch.

Her manipulation of his penis was tender, that of an experienced hand. He delighted in her pleasuring him.

Her hairless vagina was an unusual find, very different to the usual short and curlies. There was no stubble effect, just a very smooth and soft approach to a moist and receptive slit.

He was paying, she was working. She mounted him.

She leant back, rotated her hips, undid her coiled hair, let it fall, she rode his penis energetically bringing him to ejaculation, which she appeared to enjoy herself. Whether this was real or professional, he'd never know, but he didn't care, it was good, very good.

She lay next to him as he recovered. "More," she said.

"Soon maybe," he replied.

Puteri made black coffees before he paid her handsomely and left.

The experience had been worth every penny. *What's the opposite of a busman's holiday?* he thought as he rode the taxi back to the Shangri-La.

Chapter 37

It was a different ship of a different line that Peter Holmes boarded at the Singapore Cruise Terminal. But, as he found from his hour-long tour through the public areas, all cruise ships are pretty much the same, some bigger, some smaller, but all have similar facilities in similar areas.

Different themes, different décor, but generally speaking the same luxurious amenities and environment.

His genuine Peter Holmes passport was not in use for this cruise, he was on this occasion James Goodwin resident of Bury St Edmonds.

Pete (alias James) sat on his level 10 balcony overlooking the Singapore Cruise terminal watching the ant-sized passengers make their way to the boarding ramp, *could one of them be his next client.*

His trusty tablet sat open on the balcony table up and running ready for sending and receiving communications to and from Manny Strauss.

Manny Strauss was an indispensable cog in the wheels of Peter Holmes's operations. He didn't come cheap, in fact he was expensive, but as dear old dad used to say, "If you pay peanuts, you get monkeys," Emmanuel Strauss was no monkey.

When Pete's old friend Daniel Baum had broken away from the family jewellery business to set up his own legal, and not-so-legal, company. He had dealings both sides of the counter with similar businesses in Maiden Lane, Lower Manhattan, the US equivalent to Hatton Gardens, London.

It was here that Daniel became acquainted with Emmanuel Strauss.

Daniel was well aware of Peter Holmes's line of business and his need for good information.

Daniel arranged for the two to meet.

Pete travelled to New Jersey, to Emmanuel Strauss's operational centre.

Manny's offices comprised three workrooms and facilities at one end of a derelict warehouse building.

Manny's office was the bigger of the three, it was simply furnished.

It was dominated by his large mahogany traditional desk upon which sat two laptop computers, a silver-plated pen stand and desk tidy and a telephone, nothing else.

A well-worn dark brown fully upholstered leather swivel chair sat behind the desk with two comfortable guests' chairs in front.

The only other furnishings in the simply decorated office were a book case full of hardback books and a modern workstation laden with two PCs and associated monitors.

Although from alien backgrounds and of a different generation there was an immediate rapport.

The two sat in the two guests' chairs and talked.

At first, Pete thought he'd seen Manny before, his face and appearance were familiar. His hair was long and completely white and wild, he had cotton wool balls for eyebrows and below his aquiline nose his moustache was thick and bushy. He was a clone of Albert Einstein.

He wore a white collarless long-sleeved shirt under a black waistcoat, his trousers were grey and his shoes black and shiny.

A gold Double Albert chain stretched from one waistcoat pocket to the other terminating at a gold fob watch of which only the stem wind could be seen.

They exchanged histories between numerous cups of strong black coffee that was served at regular intervals by Manny's personal assistant, his niece, Rebecca.

It didn't go unnoticed by Pete that Rebecca was giving him the eye which he had trouble in ignoring, she was a looker of much the same age as himself. *Shit and doorstep* came to mind.

Manny's biography was literally a rags to riches story.

His father Ishmael Strauss escaped Nazi Germany in 1937, was processed, like millions of other immigrants, through the now defunct Ellis Island, and took up residence in Borough Park, Brooklyn alongside fellow Jews.

He was a tailor by trade and soon established a small business in a tenement basement.

Ishmael met and married Esther and begat two boys, Emmanuel and his brother Arron.

Money was always in short supply, but Ishmael and Esther managed to send the two boys to a local Yashira for a traditional Hebrew education.

Both boys were academically inclined, their build was slight, not suited to the athletic nature of American sports. Books were of more interest than balls.

Sandy Koufax was a neighbour of Manny's, Manny knew him well, he, unlike Manny, was inclined to sport, all of Brooklyn and New York were proud when he made the Baseball Hall of Fame,

Manny remained unknown, as he liked it.

In the 1950s and 60s New York, street gangs ruled, the real life Sharks and Jets, the Brooklyn Bishops, and many more, it was inevitable that these touched the lives of everyone especially in the poorer districts.

Manny was no fighter, he had nothing to offer or nothing to protect himself in this direction, but he did have a brain, a very active brain and a strength of character that carried him through the tough gang times.

He became an 'accountant', a money man, an organiser. More useful to the gang, which he never named, than just another pair of fists or a baseball bat.

He not only survived but grew in stature, not physically, but financially and in standing.

Manny had outgrown the gang and managed to 'retire' unscathed.

The contacts and information he'd accrued formed the basis of his new business.

He moved across the Hudson River to his present location and never looked back.

Manny had embraced the advent of computers, they increased his knowledge, his contacts and prospective clients, he formulated his own personal Facebook.

Manny explained that his only permanent staff were Rebecca, himself and Solomon, his nephew, Rebecca's cousin, who resided in the adjacent office.

Manny employed externally a small part-time army of young computer whiz kids, kids that he unearthed from top universities and software companies. These formed the backbone of his information-gathering business – he was a rich man, and getting richer, but it didn't show.

Manny had called Solomon to join them. He was a younger version of Manny, same features but with dark hair already with streaks of grey. He was about the same age as Pete.

Solomon was being groomed for the mahogany desk and would be Pete's contact in the not too distant future. Pete liked him too.

From that day on, Manny's information had become pure gold to Pete, essential in his amorous adventures, aiding and abetting in the growth of his offshore bank account, his retirement fund.

Chapter 38

It was Manny's e-mail that disturbed Pete, now James's, reverie, it read simply: 'Where are you? Manny.'

'On board, waiting for the manifest,' he replied.

'Ready when you are,' came the instant reply.

Pete (James) barely heard the knock on the door, he investigated.

Two porters positioning luggage outside cabin doors were the only ones to be seen on the narrow corridor.

But as expected, an envelope protruded from his post box, he collected it and returned to the balcony.

He peered over the parapet, there was no movement on the dock below, the ship's access had been removed, he could see the bridge crew making ready for sailing.

He tore open the envelope.

As on the Caribbean cruise, it contained a list of the occupants of the suites together with their details.

Quickly, he scanned the contents and then returned to the top to analyse each one a little slower.

It was an eclectic list; twenty nations were represented but the majority were Australian and American.

It was the 40+ age group that interested him most, but the details of a pair of sisters, ages 35 and 37 caught his eye.

They were from Perth, Australia and occupied one of the most expensive suites. He marked an asterisk next to both.

A 55-year-old from Brisbane was a possibility but her photograph was not very flattering. So what? he thought. *You don't look at the mantelpiece when you're poking the fire,* he thought remembering another old adage, another asterisk.

A further asterisk was marked adjacent to a 49-year-old from Sacramento, California and one more, to a 58-year-old from Nice, the Cote d'Azur, France, a tester for his fluent French.

There was one more possibility, a 47-year-old from County Cork, Ireland. She too acquired an asterisk.

Several English ladies fitted the bill, but no, too close to home for comfort. They were discounted.

He typed the basic details of each one to an e-mail and sent it to Manny.

He heard the muted tannoy call for passengers to present themselves at their allocated muster stations. With his life vest under his arm he made his way to the Theatre, the designated station for him and most of the forward ship suites.

Sat toward the rear of the theatre, he surveyed all below him his, photographic memory was a boon when it came to locating and identifying his unsuspecting asterisked passengers.

He spotted the Brisbane lady. Her photograph had actually flattered her. She was not exactly a handsome woman and she was well built, no, she was large, obese large. Pete (James) immediately scrubbed her from his list.

The 47-year-old from Cork tripped daintily down the stairs to take a seat next to a woman of a similar age wearing a straw bonnet, they were immediately in conversation.

Pete (James) marked her as a possibility. She was petite, dainty even, a small pretty face surrounded by long, dark hair which appeared to have a natural curl.

The French lady flowed past him, she was tall and slim, elegant in a floral-patterned chiffon dress that swayed seductively with every movement. She looked fresh from a catwalk, every inch a model.

Pete (James) eyes travelled downward, her dress finished at her knee revealing shapely legs enhanced by extra-high heels.

He switched to her face, a photographic model face, long and narrow with minimal makeup. Her hair was blonde, a young style, spiky on top and shaped over her ears to the nape of her long neck, she was a definite maybe, particularly in the looks department.

He couldn't see the two sisters, maybe they were on the lower level but he did eventually locate the American from Sacramento.

Pete (James) could only see her in profile, a little more when she turned to speak with her neighbour. She wore a San Francisco 49ers cap concealing her, what must be, short hair. Large, red-framed glasses sat on her pert nose. She was neither handsome, pretty or not-so good looking, ordinary would best describe her.

She wore a red 49ers short-sleeved tee-shirt with the no. 17 and the name Meg printed on the back. She had a tattoo on each arm, big enough to be seen but not of sufficient size for Pete (James) to make out their nature.

She was a big girl, broad-shouldered and big-busted, Pete (James) thought she looked butch, but Manny's reports would tell all.

At last, the necessary instructions on what to do in the unlikely event of an alarm situation was over, Pete (James) returned to his cabin.

His tablet indicated a communication.

Manny had again come up trumps, yet again, two hours to produce a lengthy report on each of the 'asterisks' was there for Pete (James) to assess which one would be his target.

Ms Sacramento was the first to be discarded, as he suspected. She was a lesbian, rich, but according to the report, 'definitely not interested in men'. He read no further, a challenge he could definitely do without.

The photographs attached to the report on Samantha (Sam) Potter, the 55-year-old from Brisbane were not at all flattering.

As a young woman, she'd been slim, no beauty but not unappealing to the eye, but in middle age her girth had expanded to obesity.

She had been married and divorced, she had three children, all married with families.

Her ex-husband owned a chain of hardware stores who had admitted adultery. Sam's lawyers had extracted a very healthy divorce settlement from him which together with her inheritance from her deceased parents had left her more than comfortable.

She lived alone in a state of the art penthouse suite in the newly built Brisbane Skytower located on the bend of the Brisbane River next door to the Botanical Gardens overlooking the city and the suburbs.

Her bank balance was in excess of $5 million Aus. distributed world-wide.

How Manny found out about individuals finances was one secret he never revealed but his information was always accurate.

Samantha Potter was a strong contender despite her appearance, that he could live with.

The two other Australians, the sisters, also presented individual possibilities.

Manny had produced a report on each.

The eldest, the 37-year-old was a divorcee who had reverted to her maiden name Sophie Kouris.

Her father Nicholas was a first-generation Australian of Greek extract who had emigrated north from the Melbourne Greek enclave to find work in the bauxite minefields.

He had started at the bottom and finished at the top, a millionaire director.

His wife, Sophie and Sister Stella's mother, had died when they were teenagers. When Nicholas died suddenly in his 60th year the sisters became millionaires.

Sophie's divorce settlement amounted to little as it was she who was the correspondent but that was of no matter, she was wealthy in her own right.

Pete (James) was impressed with the pictures of her, particularly the one where she was wearing a bikini.

She was a handsome woman, not pretty, handsome, long jet-black hair, olive-skinned with piercing blue eyes and full smiling mouth revealing perfectly white teeth.

She was well-endowed in the bust department, narrow-waisted and broad at the hip.

She had long shapely legs exaggerated by the high cut of the bikini which also exposed a large amount of rounded bottom.

All in all, impressive, very.

The last of the attached photographs was of her house, a single and two-storey terracotta-roofed waterside property with its own jetty, a tethered white and blue speedboat was central in the picture.

The address was Waterside, Mandurah, described as an enclave of Australian millionaires approximately 45 miles south of Perth.

Pete (James) pegged her as a definite, but what about the sister?

Stella Kouris, Sophie's 35-year-old sister, also owned her own similar property on another of the canals of Mandurah.

From her photographs they could have been twins, the two were almost identical.

She had, the report said, never married but was never short of an escort, trysts with several celebrities had not gone unnoticed by the Australian press.

Pete (James) considered Stella another definite.

The report on the tall French woman confirmed Pete (James's) first thoughts. She had indeed been a model, a model of many years, sharing the catwalk with the likes of Naomi Campbell and Elle Macpherson, her name was Collette Bernard.

Her photographs served to confirm Pete's (James's) own eyesight. 58-year-old she may be, but her beauty was unquestionable, what was her bank balance like? Pete (James) read on.

Her bank balance was fine, she'd made a small fortune from her modelling career and a couple of failed marriages had expanded her fortune further.

She'd invested wisely and was worth millions.

She had homes in Paris, New York and Nice, where she lived most of the time.

Photographs, external and internal of each of these confirmed that she was far from the bread line, a very rich woman.

Pete (James) didn't have to think twice, she was a most definite.

Already, before considering the County Cork resident, he had earmarked four candidates, would she be another?

He'd been engrossed in the reports to the extent that he hadn't noticed the ship was on the move, a change of direction and a blast of wind alerted him to the fact, he had to grab the reports to stop them flying, what a disaster that would have been.

With the read reports safely stowed inside, he began reading of Ms County Cork.

Her name was Meara Connolly, an unmarried self-made woman that lived in a converted stone barn overlooking the Celtic Sea in the village of Allihies near the tip of the Beara Peninsular.

From the photographs of her house and surrounding area, Pete (James) thought it looked an idyllic place to live, the kind of place he had in mind for his retirement.

She hailed originally from a poor area of Cork City but from a lowly position as a local reporter with the Cork Echo she had risen through the ranks to editor.

She had turned to writing books, novels of the romantic kind which she published herself.

She published works of other young unknown authors and became so successful she was made an offer she couldn't refuse from one of the world's largest publishing houses.

She gladly accepted to become a full-time writer with a healthy bank balance, enough to be of interest to Pete (James).

In the photographs that Manny had copied, Pete (James) could see that she was small and pretty but not very modern in her dress sense, old fashioned and mundane best described it, he imagined her in more progressive clothing, the picture he got was much better than those before him.

She passed the Pete Holmes test; she was another candidate for his attentions.

Pete (James's) cabin was, like on the Caribbean cruise ship, on the port side, the hotels, amenities and giant Ferris wheel of Sentosa Island were, like the high rise of Singapore, retreating, getting smaller and smaller.

He lay back in the balcony chair, put his bare feet on the table and studied his possibilities, which of the candidates topped his list and what would be his modus operandi.

The cruise had a ten-day itinerary, hardly enough time to run the set-up and con as on the Caribbean cruise. Knowing this, Pete (James) had resurrected a sales scam for which his forger friend and Manny had provided some fake documentation, who would be the mark.

Pete (James) was finding it difficult to make up his mind as to which of the five women would have his pleasure. "First come, first served," he decided, meaning, which one he met first, would be the one.

Pete (James) scanned the original list provided by the anonymous crew member, all of the women had requested freedom dining, that ruled out a specific time and dining room encounter, he decided to troll the bars starting with the equivalent to the Red Lion bar, he consulted his pocket-sized ship's plan, the Explorer's Lounge.

Chapter 39

There was a knock on the door. It was the cabin steward, Benjie, another Filipino. Pete (James) wondered if all stewards on all cruise ships were Filipinos. In his experience they were.

His luggage had arrived, Pete (James) meticulously stowed his clothes, hanging suits, trousers and dress shirts, and putting the rest into drawers.

His passports and documentation went into the safe.

He showered and applied the grey hair dye, the distinguished look seemed to appeal to the fairer sex.

He changed into smart casual as directed by the Cruise daily itinerary, nothing too ostentatious, a Ralph Lauren short-sleeved dark blue polo shirt, pale blue slacks and beige loafers.

He made for the Explorer's Lounge.

The Explorer's Lounge was L-shaped with a long bar on the inside wall and a small stage in the outside corner, an entertainer who introduced himself as Eddie Something-or-other played guitar and sang with the additional help of backing tracks.

Pete (James) sat on a high stool at the end of the bar so that he could see all areas of the lounge.

Eddie the entertainer gave his rendition of John Denver's 'Annie's Song' as Pete (James) surveyed the lounge, not bad, but he'd heard better.

Samantha Potter, the large Brisbane lady sat investigating the contents of her huge handbag.

Shit, thought Pete (James). *Not the one I was hoping for but…*

He searched the rest of the room; a party of seven/eight were leaving. Probably for dinner, maybe because of Eddie, in Indian file they maneuvered their way to the exit door.

Through the line Pete (James) spotted Sophie Kouris, the eldest of the two Perth sisters. She was browsing a copy of the cruise daily itinerary a blue-coloured cocktail sat on the table in front of her.

He looked from one to the other, no contest, Sophie Kouris it was to be.

Casually, he carried his half-empty bottle of Singa Thai beer across the room. "Do you mind if I sit here?" he asked.

She looked up from the itinerary. "Help yourself," she replied in a cultivated Australian accent, her voice reminded him of Cate Blanchett's.

He took residence in the low comfortable chair, resting back and crossing his legs, one foot planted, the other reaching for the ceiling.

Sophie Kouris set the itinerary on the table next to her cocktail, glanced at Pete (James's) foot and then in his eyes.

"How much is £75 in Aus.?" she asked.

"£75, about $140, why?"

"Is that your price, or the price of the shoes?" she smiled and winked exaggeratedly.

"Oh, the shoes, I'm much cheaper than that," he replied returning the smile and the wink.

A superficial glance confirmed that Sophie Kouris was a beautiful woman. *I'll look forward to seeing more of you, Miss Kouris,* he thought lasciviously.

It was not a gala night, but she wore a long elegant figure-hugging dress of charcoal grey satin material. It was low revealing an ample cleavage, and had thin shoulder straps.

Her shoes were extremely high heeled, sandals with a metallic finish, no red soles but they had an expensive look about them.

At her neck she wore a gold choker in the Egyptian style, her fingers were adorned with several rings and numerous bangles and bracelets covered both wrists.

Her jet-black hair sat on her shoulders and she wore minimal make-up, just lipstick and a hint of mascara.

To say she was easy on the eye would be an understatement of mammoth magnitude, she was stunning.

"James Goodwin," he said, offering his hand.

She took it and shook it gently. "Sophie, Sophie Kouris," she replied.

The ice was broken, easier than Pete (James) thought it might have been, he continued tentatively.

"You, err, you on your own?" he enquired although he knew the answer.

"No, I'm with my sister, she's gone off on her own somewhere," she replied.

"Leaving you all on your own?"

"I'm not on my own now, am I?"

"True," a slight pause. "I'm James Goodwin, James if you like."

"James is fine, pleased to meet you, James Goodwin," she said, offering her hand again.

"I don't need telling you're Antipodean, but where from exactly?" he asked.

"Australia, Perth, to be exact Mandurah, do you know it?"

"No, sorry, been to Sydney and Brisbane but not Western Australia."

"You need to try it sometime, it's beautiful."

"I'd love to, I've been to the SCG and the Gabba, I'd like to add the WACA to my list."

"You like your cricket then?"

"Do I, Yorkshire and England," he hadn't forgotten that his James Goodwin passport read Bury St Edmonds, but that was in Suffolk, a county without Senior cricket, Yorkshire was the real county of his birth, that she'd never know.

"Whitewashed you last time, your Pommies were bloody useless."

"Hands up in the air, you've got me there, next time our place, we'll see."

140

"No bloody chance."

"Okay, I give up, can we change the subject?"

"You got it, Mr Goodwin, tell me, how do you make a crust?"

He could hardly tell her the truth – *'out of unsuspecting women',* instead he used the cover story for this cruise: "I'm a gentleman geologist."

"A gentleman geologist, what does that mean?" she asked.

Eddie's version of Rhinestone Cowboy assaulted their ears, Pete (James) ignored it and leant closer, "I'm lucky enough to have independent means, that's English for I'm not badly off," he whispered. He continued, "So I go to different places, far and wide, looking at rock structure, it's a hobby but I might find something interesting, you never know." It was the first tentative step to gaining her interest.

She bit, "What do you call interesting?"

"Gold," he quickly added. "But no, I haven't found any but who knows, oil would be good, but there are other things, cobalt, bauxite, all sorts of things that are out there waiting to be found, and I go looking for them."

"Bauxite? Daddy mined bauxite in the Darling Range," she said proudly. "He started driving a machine and was MD when he died."

"Sorry," Pete (James) interjected.

"Don't be, he's been dead a few years, he wasn't the best dad in the world, but he left me and my sister comfortable."

"Oh!" exclaimed Pete (James) as if he didn't know. "Do you work?" he asked.

"Hell no, we still have some shares and a few dollars in the piggy bank."

"So you're a lady of leisure as we Pomms would say."

"Too right," she replied her sophisticated accent slipping a notch.

"So you're not short of a dollar or two?" she ventured.

"I'm okay, like yourself I inherited a few bob, made one or two good investments, lets me do my own thing."

"Good on ya," she responded in true Aussie fashion.

Her cocktail had gradually disappeared. "Another?" he asked.

"Why not, Blue Booty, please."

Pete (James) returned with a tall glass of the blue liquid with a slice of pineapple perch on the rim, and another beer for himself.

"I watched him make that," said Pete (James). "Three kinds of rum, blue Curacao and juices, hope you've got a good constitution."

"No worries, ace," she replied ignoring the articulated straw to imbibe a good quarter of the Booty.

"So far so good," thought Pete (James). "Probably the easiest intro I've ever had."

He pressed on.

"If your sister's otherwise engaged, are you free for dinner?"

"Are you asking?"

"Yeah, I guess so, if you'd like it official, may I request the pleasure of your company for dinner?" he said in his best BBC English.

"You're so kind, sir, I'd love to," she mimicked.

Eddie had finished his set and been replaced by a duo, a large grey-haired man in a tuxedo played the piano accompanying a younger woman dressed in a glittering evening dress, with music and voice, they were per-forming their first number as Pete (James) and Sophie rose to leave.

Their way was obstructed by Samantha Potter's large frame. *You don't know how pleased I am you were here,* he thought, referring to the beautiful Ms Kouris.

In the carpeted area immediately outside the Explorers Lounge they faltered, "Where would you like to dine?" Pete (James) enquired.

"I'm fine with the Botticelli, as long as we have a table for two, I want you to myself," she replied looping her arm into his.

A short walk and a short wait later the waiter attended them.

"Evening, madam, evening, sir. I'm Marco, I'll be looking after you tonight," he said, presenting the menu. "Would you like the wine list?"

"No wine for me," said Sophie. "Could I have a Blue Booty?"

"No wine for me either, a Singha please," added Pete (James).

They studied the extensive menu in silence.

The drinks arrived. "Are you ready to order?" requested Marco.

"No worries," said Sophie and recited her selections, not missing a course.

Pete (James) did likewise, Marco scurried away.

"You have many rings," commented Pete (James). "Is one of them a wedding ring?"

"Yes," she replied. "But it doesn't count. I've been divorced a long time, I suppose I should take it off but I just haven't, what about you?"

"No, never had time," he replied honestly.

"You're not gay, are you?" she said with another wink.

"No, definitely not, nowt wrong with me," he replied in the deepest voice he could muster.

She laughed and Pete (James) joined in.

The intermittent conversation between courses was about each other, Sophie giving honest accounts about friends and family, Pete (James) fabricating his stories.

Apart from the overweight Samantha Potter, the other possible targets, including Sophie's sister Stella, were conspicuous by their absence, that pleased Pete (James).

Back in the Explorer's Lounge sat in almost the same places they'd been before. Sophie Kouris was well down another Blue Booty, Pete (James) sipped his Singha beer, "You've told me about family and friends, but not much about where you live, you said, what was it, Mandurah, near Perth."

"You've a good memory."

"Afraid so," he replied.

The duo was ruining the Carpenter's 'Yesterday once more', but who wouldn't, there could only ever be one Karen Carpenter.

"We used to live in Perth, but now both Stella and I live in Mandurah, different houses. My God I love her, but we couldn't live under the same roof, not now. It was bad enough when we were kids, if I had it, she wanted it."

Pete (James) ignored the sister jibe. "Mandurah, never heard of it," he lied. "Nice name, sounds good."

"It is good, second Western Australia city after Perth, black fellas called it Mandjar, meeting place, but the settlers mispronounced it to Mandurah."

"Second city, so it's a big place?"

"No, not really, 80 odd thousand, that's not very big, and it's on the coast, and we get great weather, and it's terrific."

"I guess you like living there."

"Bloody oath."

"Sorry."

"Aussie, sorry, can't help it, I mean that's certainly true."

"Got yer now, Aussie slang, I love it. I love accents. I don't think I've got one mores the pity, used to have a Yorkshire uncle, every time he was in the company of Southerners he'd exaggerate his accent, they didn't have a clue what he was talking about."

In truth it was his father he was referring to, not some fictitious uncle.

"You haven't said where you're from, London I guess?"

She was right but the false passport he was using said Bury St Edmonds so he kept to the script he'd written in his head, hoping she'd never heard of it.

"Americans think all us Brits come from London. No, I live in a little village called Horringer just outside Bury St Edmonds, it's in Suffolk and it's about 80 miles from London as the crow flies."

"Never heard of it." He was pleased to hear.

"G'day," a female voice boomed in Pete (James) ear.

Before he could turn around, the full skirt of a dress brushed past him and a younger version of Sophie appeared.

"Hi sis, who's this?" she said turning to face Pete (James).

Even if she hadn't said 'sis', Pete (James) would have had no problem in recognizing Stella. She was a replica, maybe an inch or so shorter, but identical in features and figure.

The dress that had touched his shoulder was olive and brown patterned flora and fauna with horizontal black stripes around the bottom of the skirt which finished about three inches above the knee.

She wore chunky, laced black boots with high heels and one-inch-thick soles, her legs were very shapely and from where Pete (James) was sat there was a lot of them to see.

"Stella, James. James, Stella."

"Hi, James," she said, leant over and kissed him on the cheek, a view of her ample bosom was offered which didn't go unnoticed.

There was a little cough, a clearing of the throat from behind Pete (James).

"Oh, sorry, this cobber is Joey, he's Aussie, met him earlier," said Stella.

Pete (James) knew Stella to be 35, Joey was no more than 23/24 unless he looked younger than his years, Pete's dad would have said she was 'baby snatching'.

Joey was a big lad, 6'4"/6'5" built like the *'Proverbial brick shit house',* again to quote dad, a handsome bloke with a mane of blonde hair and a permanent tan, he could have been a poster boy for Bondi Beach.

"He's an athlete, shot putter, that's right, isn't it?" she directed at Joey.

"Yeah, shot putter," he replied. *Not a conversationalist,* thought Pete (James). *Maybe he's got other attributes.*

"We're not staying," said Stella. "Disco, nightclub."

Stella grabbed hold of Joey's hand. "See you later," she winked at Pete (James). "Don't wait up, I've got my key card," she directed at Sophie.

They were gone.

"I don't think she'll ever grow up," commented Sophie. "One for the road," she added tendering her empty glass.

Pete (James) escorted Sophie home, it was just as well, she might not have made it on her own.

With her arm looped in his, she swayed and staggered to the lift, leant in the corner until they reached the right level, lurched out, grabbed Pete (James) around the neck and hung on until he'd dragged her to her door.

"I think I hit the turps tonight," she slurred, Pete (James) read that to mean *'she was pissed'.*

She searched unsuccessfully in her handbag for the key card.

"Do you mind if I look?" he said gently removing the bag from her hands.

He located the key card, entered it into the reader and pushed open the door.

"Are you coming in?" she asked bumping the door jamb.

"Not tonight," he said politely, his experiences of sex with drunken women had been frequent, but only once enjoyable, he felt confident that there would be a better opportunity to come. "Good night, see you tomorrow. Explorers Lounge, same time, if I don't see you during the day."

He gently encouraged her into her cabin and let the door shut.

He heard a muted, "G'day," as he about-turned for his own cabin.

Chapter 40

Joey, the shot putter was pumping iron, slow arm curls using huge dumbbells, one in each hand alternatively lifting them to his bulging biceps.

The Collingwood vest he wore was soaked with perspiration, he nodded to Pete (James) as he passed to take the seat of one of the rowing machines.

It was early morning, the first of the two sea days before reaching Benoa, Bali, apart from the staff, Pete (James) and Joey were the only two in the gymnasium.

Pete (James) was a creature of habit, when working (his kind if working) on cruise ships he liked, if at all possible, to train each morning, the same exercises, the rowing machine and a fast jog around the ship, this morning was no different.

Pete (James) was about to enter a shower cubicle when the door of the adjacent one burst open, it was Joey towel in hand, smoothing back his long hair with his fingers.

Naked he looked bigger than dressed, he had a narrow waist, an exaggerated six-pack, sculptured pecs and extremely broad shoulders, he would be a contender in any bodybuilding contest.

Pete (James) could not help but notice he was large in another department, especially when he grasped it with one full hand. "That Stella's a bonzer biddy, old but fair dinkum," he boasted.

"I get the gist, but too much information," replied Pete (James).

The muscles and penis were hidden by an extra-large tee-shirt with a Sydney Harbour motif and white athletic shorts respectively when next they met in the communal changing room.

They had, what turned out to be, a one-sided conversation.

"You enjoy the disco?" asked Pete (James).

"Okay," replied Joey.

"The band good?"

"Okay."

"You like Stella Kouris then?"

"Okay, she's fair dinkum in the sack." Joey boasted ignoring the 'too much information' jibe.

"No Joey, I repeat gentlemen do not discuss their exploits, especially with strangers," spat Pete (James) who sometimes, surprisingly, could be something of a prude, especially when his line of work was considered.

The smile disappeared from Joey's handsome face to be replaced with a scowl, he clenched his fist and moved toward Pete (James).

Pete (James) ignored the attitude change, entered the shower cubicle and closed the door.

Through the frosted glass of the cubicle door Pete (James) saw Joey about to turn the handle, at the last second he changed his mind and stomped away. "Thank fuck," Pete (James) said out loud, he didn't fancy his chances with Mr Australia.

Breakfast was not difficult to find, Horizon Court, the Lido deck buffet restaurant served everything a man could want, and then some.

He plumped for an English style breakfast, the eggs were fine, the bacon was okay but the sausage (supposedly English) left an awful lot to be desired, he ate it anyway, washed down with a couple of cups of insipid coffee.

It was still early and it wasn't a hot day, but still the majority of the sunbeds around the pool areas were taken, not necessarily occupied but adorned with towels.

Pete (James) scanned the pool area and other possible sunbathing areas, there was no sign of Sophie Kouris or her sister.

He did, however, see Samantha Potter and Meara Connelly, the Cork ex-publisher.

Samantha Potter had managed to accommodate a large proportion of her body into what appeared to be a too-small swimsuit, but not all, not a pretty sight, a good decision to eliminate her from his list of candidates.

Meara Connelly, on the other hand, looked demure in Bermuda shorts and blouse. She was reading Harper Lee's classic, *To Kill a Mockingbird. She would be a challenge*, he thought. *But I'll stick with Sophie Kouris now the ice has been broken.* He made no effort to engage in conversation.

Pete (James) took up residence on a sunbed along the port side of lido deck, the cloud persisted not allowing the sun to break through but it was hot, made to feel hotter by the high humidity, rain and possibly thunder had been forecast, but to date it had not appeared.

He began reading the first of the two books he'd bought from WHSmith, Heathrow. A Clive Cussler, The Spy, an Isaac Bell adventure set in pre-first World War 1 America.

It was late morning when the two sisters, Sophie and Stella Kouris, walked by. He saw them, but whether or not they saw him was debatable.

Either they didn't see him or they did and ignored him, Pete (James) watched them pass following them with his eyes attempting to determine their destination.

They both wore shorts and tee-shirts and carried beach bags, Pete (James) surmised they were intent on sunbathing but whether they'd find two sunbeds together was unlikely.

He waited ten minutes or more and made to find them.

How they'd managed to find two sunbeds together close to one of the pools was nothing short of a miracle, but they had.

They had both stripped off the shorts and the tee-shirts and lay bikini-clad under the still cloudy sky.

The bikinis covered what was necessary, but only just, one was white, that of Sophie, and the other a pale lemon both accentuating their naturally tanned olive skin.

Many a male eye wandered in their direction.

There was nowhere for Pete (James) to sit, so he hovered above them.

"Morning, ladies," he ventured.

Two pairs of reflective designer sunglasses turned in his direction.

"G'day," they replied in unison.

"How are you this morning?" he directed at Sophie.

"Cactus, sorry fragile, I hit the turps a bit too strong last night," Sophie replied.

"A little bit," he concurred.

"Did we, you know, did we, sorry I don't remember if we did?"

"No, I left you at your door."

"Good, I would have hated to miss it," she said cheekily.

Stella remained impassive her head pointing in Pete (James) direction, her eyes concealed behind the reflective lenses, she could have been as-sessing him but it was difficult to say.

"You could have joined us but –"

"Yeh, never mind, how about we meet tonight, Explorer's Lounge, 7:00?"

"Why not, but easy on the booze, I don't want to miss anything," re-plied Sophie.

"Don't worry about me," interjected Stella, "I'll be okay."

"Thought you'd be with man-mountain Joey," said Sophie.

"No chance, wham-bam and not even a thank you ma'am, bloody use-less, but no worries I've seen another guy that could be interesting," retort-ed Stella.

"Until 7:00," said Pete (James) and left to the tacit *'lucky bastard'* from a host of the males who ogled from close proximity.

Around the corner Pete (James) almost bumped into the massive frame of Pal Joey, he was entertaining the immediate sunbathers with a physical exercise routine, women ogled, and jealous men muttered, *"Show-off bastard."* Pete (James) instantly became wary, trouble in public was the last thing he wanted.

Joey wore only a pair of Bondi swim shorts his attribute forming an adequate bulge which most certainly attracted the eyes of the teenage girl in the sunbed across the way.

"She dumped me, gave me the boot," said Joey.

Pete (James) had no answer.

"She told me to fuck off, said I was fucking useless, the bitch."

Pete (James) still had nothing to say.

"Bugger her," said Joey extending his arms making small circles with his hands, his muscles rippled.

"See you around," said Pete (James) walking away attracting some of the female eyes away from Mr Muscles.

He continued his stroll around the ship, first outdoors and then inside. *Strange,* he thought as he passed through the shopping mall. *I know it's a big ship but I would have thought that in a couple of days I might have seen Collette Bernard.*

No worries, concentrate on Sophie Kouris, or even her sister, both promising, very promising, he told himself.

Chapter 41

The Explorer's Lounge was nigh on full of diners sipping their aperitif of choice as Stella Kouris made her entrance.

Heads turned as she strode flirtatiously to meet Pete (James) waiting at the corner of the bar.

She looked elegant yet again, on this occasion she wore a figure-hugging dress, high at the neck and knee-length, it accentuated her hourglass figure.

She'd coiled her long black hair into a top bun which had the effect of narrowing her oval face and making her appear taller.

She wore sheer black patterned tights or stocking which complimented the midnight blue dress and 5" high shoes.

She greeted him with the inevitable 'g'day'.

He leant to kiss her cheek, she let him. "G'day," he echoed.

"Drink?" he asked.

"A fruit cocktail, no alcohol, please."

"You meant it this morning, no booze."

"Bloody oath," she replied in her best Aussie tongue. "No turps, more control," she added.

"Shall we sit?" Pete (James) asked indicating the free comfortable seats at a low table.

"Why not," she replied.

Pete (James) carried the drinks as Entertainer Eddie murdered, no that's not fair, assaulted another country and western classic.

They continued the conversation from the previous night, small talk with a hint of the personal.

"You didn't say whether you were married or not," Sophie ventured.

"Neither did you," was the riposte.

"You first," she countered.

"Nope, never. Never found Miss Right I suppose, how about you?" the answer he knew already but the game had to be played.

"Not now, have been twice, first time he played away, second time, I did," she said openly, almost boastful.

"This your first cruise?" asked Pete (James).

"No, I'm a regular, we've been on a few, first time in this neck of the woods, how about you?"

"First one," he lied. "Just been to Africa looking at minerals and rocks, thought it would be nice to have some R and R, flew to Singapore and here I am."

"Did you find anything interesting?" she asked more in a conversational way than any real interest.

"Mmmm, maybe," he replied playing a patient game.

"I don't suppose you find your minerals and rocks in the city," she enquired as if she had a reason.

"Too true, we were out in the bush, five weeks," he added reading from the mental script.

"You'll be ready for some physical exercise then," she said casting her eyes from his face to his trousers and back seductively.

"Maybe so," he replied returning the flirtatious glance.

For thirty minutes or so that they sat and conversed oblivious to the efforts of Eddie the average entertainer. "You can buy me dinner in the Crown Grill if we can get a table," suggested Sophie.

"We'll get a table, be assured," replied Pete (James) positively.

Pete (James) was prepared to backhand the Head Waiter a substantial tip to ensure a table, but it wasn't necessary.

The décor in the Crown Grill was a combination of dark wood and rich colours with subdued antique lighting, a cultured ambiance promising a fine meal.

The dinner was, indeed, good, excellent even, the steaks were enormous and looked delicious, but both of them chose a lighter menu, both anticipating a future event.

Sophie's selection was Marinated Goats cheese and tomato salad starter, lobster tails for entrée.

Pete (James) chose the more macho Black and Blue Onion Soup and Rack of Lamb.

A bottle of Gewurztraminer Alsace white wine was recommended by the Sommelier, a fine choice drunk mainly by Pete (James), Sophie sipping at only single glass.

Neither could resist the Molten Dutch Chocolate Fudge Obsession.

They returned to the Explorers Bar as the same duo as the previous night began a harmonised version of Moon River. It sounded okay but Sophie and Pete (James) were rapt in their own company.

True to her word, Sophie steered clear of alcohol, Pete (James) had a good idea why, and was looking forward to it, if he was right.

"Are we likely to see Stella tonight?" asked Pete (James).

"Who knows," Sophie replied nonchalantly. "Last time I saw her, she was stalking a fresh-faced college kid hardly old enough to shave."

She paused. "I prefer a mature man," she added running her long-manicured fingers along his thigh while looking into his eyes suggestively.

The duo disappeared further and further into the background as Sophie drew closer and closer to Pete (James) the small talk thwart with suggestive innuendo.

It was not late, far from it. "Shall we go?" said Sophie not saying where to.

"When you're ready," replied Pete (James).

"Oh, I'm ready," said Sophie taking his hand and leading him from the now busy bar.

The lift door had hardly closed when Sophie's arms went around Pete (James) neck and she kissed him passionately, he responded by squeezing her to him his hand on her rounded firm bottom.

From the lift she hurried toward her suite dragging Pete (James) in her wake.

There was no kiss and goodnight, she opened the door and pulled him inside.

She omitted to turn on the lights, the dim blue light of a low moon in a cloudless sky reflecting off the flat sea and white of the balcony was the only illumination.

It was sufficient for her to guide him past the twin beds to the lounge area in front of the dressing table/desk and settee, again she hung around his neck, their lips met, Pete (James) hands explored her back, he found the zip of her dress and made to draw it down.

Sophie released her hold and gently pushed him backwards until his calves met the bed, she bade him sit.

Silhouetted against the moonlight she unzipped the dress herself, let it drop to the floor and kicked it one side.

Her hands she put on each hip and posed seductively. "Like what you see?" she solicited.

"Oh yes, yes please," he replied.

Her ample breasts were contained by a lace bra which left nothing to the imagination, they sat round and full, her nipples already protruding invitingly in his direction.

The patterned hose turned out to be stockings suspended by a matching suspender belt sat on her shapely hips.

Her dark pubic hair were visible through the sheer lace of her minuscule panties.

He reached out toward her. "No," she whispered pushing her hands away. "Not yet."

She kicked off her shoes, placed her right foot on the edge of the bed between Pete's (James) legs, her toes under his groin.

Pete (James) penis had woken to the potential situation on entering the suite, now it grew and hardened with every passing second only his boxers and trousers restricted its movement.

"Take them off," she whispered, referring to the stockings.

One by one Pete (James) undid the four supporting straps and rolled down the stockings.

Each one disappeared over her head as she flicked it from her toes to join the shoes.

Sophie peeled Pete (James) shirt over his head and hurled it backwards.

In turn, she lifted each of his feet removed his loafers and socks and despatched them likewise.

The suspender belt and bra joined the other discarded garb, only her panties remained, but not for much longer.

These she removed, twirled them on her finger and consigned them to somewhere behind her.

Without invitation, Pete (James) stood, undid his belt, hooked his fingers into the waistband of his trousers and removed them and his boxers together. At last his released erection rose to the occasion noted with a smile by the aroused Sophie.

The vertical embrace and amorous kiss were short-lived, the bed beckoned.

Pete (James) used all his experience and expertise in satisfying the lustful Sophie. With foreplay alone Sophie orgasmed loudly, she pleaded for full sex, he made her wait.

She forced him on his back, she could wait no longer, she mounted his erection with a 'Yes'.

It was her turn to dominate, she did it slowly, gyrating her hips to manipulate Pete (James) penis, she undid her hair and shook it wildly.

He unsuccessfully controlled his orgasm, but not before Sophie had, more than once, with screams of ecstasy which surely must have been heard in the corridor, she didn't care.

They lay and recovered, their heartbeat rates returning to normal.

The cool of the air conditioning encouraged them to take refuge under the duvet.

Sophie's sex drive was matched equally by Pete (James) libido, more urge and more action were inevitable.

Eventually they slept.

Pete (James) was woken by the door opening and corridor light flooding into the room.

It was Sophie's sister, Stella.

Pete (James) watched her tiptoe passed the beds to the scattered clothes, she stood in almost the same position as had her sister earlier.

She wore another flared mini dress, but not for long.

Sophie was asleep, Pete (James) watched with interest, his dormant penis beginning to stir.

Her bra and pants followed the dress, she was not exactly the double of Sophie but her attributes were similar as was her face and her hair.

Whether or not she knew Pete (James) was watching was debatable but she smiled salaciously at the two close-knit bulges.

"Move over," she said climbing in beside Pete (James).

The movement woke Sophie. "What –" she began.

"It's only me," replied Stella. "Remember sis, shares."

"I suppose," said Sophie.

Stella's hand found Pete's (James) erection, other hands found his chest, he was the meat in the sandwich of two randy female Aussies.

Experienced as he was, he had never before encountered a *ménage à trois,* a first that he enjoyed with gusto.

Fortunately Pete (James) was in excellent physical condition, fit enough to satisfy the demands of the two sisters.

Stella was asleep in her own bed, Sophie likewise next to him. Pete (James) woke in the small hours, the moon had long since moved, the room was dim.

With difficulty he located all his clothes with the exception of one sock.

He left the two sisters to their reverie, his rule of not spending all night in a partner's bed intact.

Chapter 42

Again the gymnasium was sparsely occupied.

Pete (James) by way of a change was cycling an undulating electronic course when the muscle-bound Joey passed him to take residence in the weights section.

He sneered in Pete (James), direction but did not speak.

Pete (James) followed the cycle with his usual jog, searching for the two sisters, Sophie in particular, as he ran.

It was the second day at sea and the sunbeds were filling, or at least they were again being reserved by the presence of personal clothes or towels.

Still there was no sign of them, it would appear that they were not early risers like himself.

It was nigh on lunchtime when he came across them, two beds together in a prime position, it begged the question was somebody, a staff member, saving them for the two handsome women.

"G'day," said Pete (James) in his best Aussie accent.

The two sisters totally ignored him looking straight through him.

"G'day," he repeated undeterred.

"Fuck off," whispered Sophie.

"What?" said the startled Pete (James), "Did you say –"

"Yeah, I said fuck off," she repeated.

"But –"

"You're not needed, you're superfluous to requirements. You've served your purpose, now fuck off."

"Okay, got it, thank you and goodbye," said Pete (James) as he turned and walked away.

What was that about? he asked himself as he sauntered dejectedly toward the bar.

It was still a little early for an alcoholic drink, but he had one nevertheless, a double scotch.

A double first, he thought. *Two in a bed, and the big E, that's fucked the job.*

He downed the whisky, it didn't help. He was angry. *Where did I go wrong, what did I do?* He tried to analyse the situation.

He found no answers, he shrugged. What the hell, forget it, move on.

Almost two days of the ten-day cruise gone and Pete (James) was back where he started.

He had backed the wrong horse, although the seductive Sophie Kouris could hardly be called a horse.

She had been an attractive prospect, but she had dumped him unceremoniously. He was in shock, he wasn't used to being spurned, and he didn't like it.

It was imperative that he find a new payday, and quick.

It had to be the bookish Miss Cork, Madame France or even the obese Samantha Potter, but he was hopeful it didn't come to her.

Three thousand or more passengers in a large floating hotel, it should have been relatively easy to locate any one of the three, but not so.

Pete (James) scoured the ship from top to bottom without a sighting, he retraced his steps for a second time.

Inevitably it was Samantha Potter he found first; she was at the pool bar overhanging a high stool sipping from a bottle of Singha beer.

He shook his head and determined to look further for either Meara Connelly or Collette Bernard.

He lunched in the buffet restaurant picking at his food still in shock at being given the 'Heave-ho', not since his school days had that happened, and that was because he'd tried it on too soon.

Unlike his normal self, he left half his food, something he would normally complain about when he saw others doing the selfsame thing, but he wasn't in the mood for food.

Had the two remaining prospective clients got invisible shrouds, he was beginning to think so, apart from the suites and cabins he'd looked everywhere, neither hide nor hair of them was to be seen.

He looked in the Explorer's Lounge for the third time, a few ardent drinkers inhabited the bar stools but not the two ladies, he walked on.

The door to the library-cum-reading room was unusually open, he peered in expecting to be, yet again, disappointed.

To his amazement, both Meara Connelly and Collette Bernard were there in the same room.

Petite Meara Connelly sat at a table poring over an encyclopaedic tome, a reference book of some kind. She was totally engrossed oblivious to all around her, she could have been researching information for a new project or just advancing her knowledge.

She looked older than her 47 years wearing clothes more fitting of a much older woman, her white blouse was full at the neck with a large bow and long sleeves that flared at the wrist.

Her lower half was concealed by the table, but her visible waist suggested that the blouse was worn with a black skirt.

She wore rimless glasses that sat on her pert nose.

Pete (James) recalled Manny's report, her academic and successful past would make her a challenge. Was he up to it, that was the question.

The library was all but full, men and women all preoccupied with their book, tablet or laptop, it was, as one would expect of a library, quiet.

One red leather chesterfield chair remained vacant.

Pete (James) moved it a fraction to make it more accessible, the legs squeaked on the herringbone timber floor. Only one person looked up, it was Madame Collette Barnard.

She acknowledged his presence with a minimal smile and returned to her book.

Unlike Meara Connelly, Collette Bernard belied her years in the opposite direction.

She also wore glasses, without a doubt they were a designer brand, Gucci, D&G, Ray-Ban or the like, large pink framed with gold-tone arms, they complemented her complexion and short blonde hair.

Collette Bernard might well have been a retired model, but she still wore the style of clothes that could be seen on a present-day walkway.

She wore a white shirt, also long-sleeved, but there the similarity ended. Collette's shirt had a traditional open-necked collar and was buttoned down the front, a stylised Chinese pattern of natural shapes in tones of black and grey ran vertically down the front and back.

The middle front of the shirt was tucked into black sheen trousers with each side hanging loose, she looked equally as elegant here in the library as she had on the historical photographs in Manny's file.

Pete (James) had travelled light as he'd reconnoitred the ship, he carried with him only his current read. How fortuitous was that, he made himself comfortable in the soft chair and opened it at his bookmark halfway through.

In his book Isaac Bell, the top Van Dorn detective was busy attempting to find the identity of the spy intent on destroying the new dreadnought battleship being built in the pre-World War I New York shipyard, it was a riveting yarn that Pete (James) was enjoying immensely, he had no problem looking comfortable in the Library surroundings.

Patient as ever, he bided his time until a suitable moment arrived for him to make his move, he had made up his mind which of the two it would be.

In his book the hero, Isaac Bell had just turned down the oblique offer of sex, Pete (James) paused. It set him thinking about the ditching he'd just received.

His thoughts travelled back to when he was sixteen, the back row of the cinema, the film *Independence Day,* the girl Marie Cooper.

He remembered it vividly, as he did all his sexual encounters, she'd said no several times as his hand had found her small breasts and then worked its way up her skirt to her thigh, her pleas had been ignored.

But that was as far as she had reluctantly allowed, as his fingers had found her knickers and tried to get in, she had pushed him away with a loud 'no' and fled from the cinema. He recalled attempting to sink into the seat as heads turned.

The day after, Marie's best friend Steph Briggs brought him a three-word note, 'We are finished'. No worries, he fucked Steph instead.

He chuckled to himself then thought of the two sisters. He thought he'd satisfied them, he thought there'd be more, only to find himself ditched. It had hurt his pride, his professional pride.

Forget it, he told himself. *Concentrate on Collette Bernard, wait for the right opportunity.*

The opportunity arose when she raised her head and removed her glasses.

Pete (James) was sat close enough to touch her, he leant forward and whispered, "Good book?"

"Mais oui," she replied quickly adding. "Sorry, my natural tongue, yes it's very good."

Her accent was hardly noticeable, a little nasal, a typical French trait.

"You're French," he replied, stating the obvious appearing surprised, which of course he was not.

"Very French, but I have travelled everywhere. Is my English okay?"

"Very okay," he replied. "I studied French a little at university, worked for a while as an interpreter, but that was a long time ago. Would you mind if we converse in French?"

"No, no problem," she agreed, reverting to her first language.

Pete (James) followed suit.

He could see that her book was a paperback, a white cover with an English title, he pressed on with his opening gambit, "You seemed absorbed, it must be good."

She tapped the cover with her long slim fingers, her nail varnish glittered. "Jackie Collins, Goddess of Vengeance. Good title, good story. I can relate to Ms Collins, I like all her books," she replied still in the whisper that they'd both adopted.

"Have you finished reading for now?" he ventured.

"I think so," she replied, sliding her glasses into their case and putting them into a black handbag together with the Jackie Collins.

She made to leave, Pete (James) rose from his chair. "May I buy you a coffee?" he asked hopefully.

"Mais oui," she replied. "I'd love one."

Pete (James) knew from Manny's report that Collette was tall, but he had not until now realised how tall.

The trousers she wore were of silk, hence the sheen, and narrow cut, which together with black high-heeled shoes accentuated her height, she stood almost eye-to-eye with him.

"Beautiful ship," Pete (James) commented as they descended in the scenic lift overlooking the ornate atrium to level 5 on their way to the International Cafe.

"Very beautiful," she agreed.

Collette took the lead as they approached the cafe, her carriage confirmed his information that she had been a model, she moved across the floor with impeccable deportment and grace, she took a seat with equal elegance crossing her long legs.

"Coffee, tea, what will it be?" he asked.

"Café au lait, if you please," she replied.

"A cake, gateau perhaps?"

"Non, no thank you, I try not to…" She tapped her flat stomach.

"You don't need to worry, I'm sure," he said hoping the compliment would be noted.

She smiled, it had been the opening gambit of his charm offensive, and it appeared to have worked.

Pete (James) returned with two coffees and sat across the table opposite Collette.

"Merci," she said. "I think perhaps we should introduce ourselves, I am Collette, Collette Bernard, and you are Sir Galahad, I have the name right, yes?"

"Yes, you have the name right but I'm no knight in shining armour. James, James Goodwin, that's me, at your service, ma'am," he replied inclining his head in a mock bow.

She smiled with her eyes as well as her mouth.

She had a long oblong face that complimented her stature, her eyes were sapphire blue, she had high cheekbones, an aquiline nose and full lips.

Her make up appeared as if professionally applied, Pete's (James's) pal, the make-up artist, would have been impressed. She wore a lilac mascara, her cheeks were lightly rouged and she wore a pink lipstick, the overall effect was subtle complimenting her features, no way did she look nearly 60 years old.

Pete (James) could see why she had been successful on the catwalk and in front of a camera, she was photogenic now, she must have been stunning as a young woman.

She was, he recalled, 59 years old, much older than his normal clients, would she be amenable to sexual advances or would a different approach be required? It would be what it had to be, he decided, his initial introduction would be the same as usual anyway.

"Are you travelling alone?" asked Pete (James) as if he didn't know.

"Quite alone," she reverted to English.

"Please indulge me, speak in French, it's been so long," he requested.

Si tu veux. "If you like," she replied.

That's a start, at least she's agreed to a conversation, he thought.

"And you?" she returned the question.

"Oh yes, just me, a week or so's rest and relaxation, I'm looking forward to it."

"Do you work?" she enquired.

"Sort of," he replied. "I'm a gentleman geologist, I work in Africa mainly." He liked the 'gentleman' bit, it had worked with Sophie Kouris, maybe it would work again, it did.

"What does sort of and gentleman geologist mean?" a quizzical look appearing on her face.

"I'm an amateur really, a very good amateur, if I say so myself. My father left me well provided for, I don't have to work, but I studied at Oxford, a degree in French and a PhD in Geology. I love rocks and the like, so I spend a lot of time in the field, but here I am some R and R."

"It sounds interesting."

"It is," he replied and changed the subject. *Move slowly,* he told himself.

"Do you live in Singapore?" he asked, fully aware that she did not.

"No, no," she replied. "I live mainly in France, Nice or Paris, but sometimes in New York."

"Very nice," commented Pete (James) trying with every fibre to not sound envious or sarcastic.

"I am very lucky," she replied. "I have a beautiful house in Provence, near Nice, I spend most of my time there, but sometimes I have business in Paris and New York, so I have small apartments there too."

Pete (James) recalled the photographs of all the properties, he would hardly call the apartments small, and the Provence house was a grand villa with manicured gardens and a swimming pool overlooking the Mediterranean. *Yes, she was lucky.*

"Your husband is not with you?" he asked.

"No, no, I have no husband, just me, you are not married?" she returned.

"Me married, no, never had time, I'm not gay though," he added quickly.

She smiled again; her teeth were as perfect as her face. "Never doubted it for a minute," she said.

The cups were almost empty. "Another?" suggested Pete (James).

"Why not," she agreed sipping the last drops.

The conversation resumed following Pete's (James's) return with two more coffees.

"Where were we?" asked Pete (James).

"You were just assuring me that you were not gay," Collette replied.

"Oh, yes," he coughed.

"I wouldn't have minded if you were," she assured him. "In my business you meet all kinds of people with different persuasions."

"And what or is, your business?"

"I was a model, fashion and photographic, I still work a little," she replied matter-of-factly without any hint of boast.

Pete (James) appeared interested, it wasn't difficult, although he was adlibbing he was still working around a basic pre-determined script. "Sounds fantastic, tell me more, who, where, what, tell me, it must be an interesting life."

"It is not all glamour, not all you see on TV and in the press, but it has given me a good life I must admit," she replied, gracefully sipping her coffee.

Pete (James) drained his cup. "I'm sure you have many stories to tell, will you have dinner with me and tell me some of them?" he asked.

"Are you, as you British say, chatting me up?" came the response.

"Yes, I suppose I am."

"But I am much older than you."

"No you're not, and anyway what does that matter."

"I don't want to be called a sweety mother," she replied.

"I think you mean a sugar mummy, and you're not, you're attractive and intelligent and I like your company, please say you will."

She thought about it before answering. "I'd love to," she said.

"I'm honoured," he replied. "Where and when shall we meet?"

"How about there, 8 o'clock," she said pointing to the wine bar across the atrium.

"Until 8," she said, rose and sauntered toward the lift lobby.

Pete (James) watched her go. *That went well, he thought. I think it deserves a drink.*

The Explorer's Lounge was half-full of lunchtime drinkers including the sisters Sophie and Stella Kouris, they were surrounded by a group of young men aged between 16 and 25.

They saw him at the same time as he saw them, their eyes followed him to the bar but neither of them acknowledged his presence in any way.

Fuck you, sprang to mind. *But then I have, both of you, F.F.F.L.,* he thought. *Find 'em, feel 'em, fuck 'em and leave 'em,* his own criteria, he smiled, but this time it had been reversed in his direction.

He ordered and dismissed a scotch before leaving.

He then spent a quiet leisurely afternoon on his own balcony.

He took the opportunity to communicate with Manny Strauss giving an update on his progress, or lack of it.

They discussed a tentative timetable of e-mails intended to convince his new client, the hapless Collette that Pete (James) was a gentleman geologist as he claimed and that his soon to be so-called findings were bonafide.

The Kouris sisters interlude amused Manny, drawing a 'you're losing it' comment and an electronic guffaw.

The rest of the time was taken up with wave watching for dolphins – they were conspicuous by their absence – reading *The Spy* following Isaac Bell's progress, and inevitably dozing.

It was evening when he woke from his reverie, the moon shone bright in a clouded sky, the breeze created by the moving ship was still warm with a hint of humidity and spray, it was time to shower and dress for his evening with Collette Bernard.

Chapter 43

Leaning at the rail overlooking the Atrium, Pete (James) surveyed the scene as he waited outside the Wine Bar for Collette Barnard.

A string quartet played their version of Bohemian Rhapsody as fellow passengers paraded in their gala night finery; it was one of the best places for 'people watching' he'd ever been.

Pete (James) felt good in the first public airing of his Saville Row white dinner jacket and black trousers.

A black dress shirt, black bow and shiny black shoes completed his outfit, he felt good and hoped that Collette would be suitably impressed, he adjusted the bow as he waited.

Once a model, always a model, Collette glided effortlessly through the throng that as always on gala nights accumulated in and around the Atrium.

"Have you been waiting long?" she asked in her almost accent-less English.

"No," he replied truthfully. "You look beautiful," he added.

"Thank you," she replied demurely.

She wore a full-length evening gown of dark blue velvet with a high halter neck, open shoulders and open back, it followed her slim bodyline and was adorned only by a gold loop belt.

Pete (James) knew little, or nothing, about fashion, but he would have gambled that Collette's dress had come from the workshop of Chanel, Yves Saint Laurent or the like.

Pete (James) led Collette to the one empty table; she sat as he hovered. "What would you like to drink?" he asked.

"Just a tonic, I'll save myself for a wine with dinner," she replied.

On his return, they resumed the conversation from earlier but this time in English.

"You were telling me about modelling," he began.

"So I was, you have a good memory. It was hard work sometimes, it may not look it, but believe me it was, but it was fun, we were paid a lot of money, more than I'd ever seen as a child, and we travelled, all over the world we travelled."

"Do you travel much now?"

"Not so much working but holidays, yes, I cruise whenever possible, so relaxing, flying is so irksome and boring."

"I know nothing about fashion," admitted Pete (James). "But I've seen the occasional Paris or Milan shows on the TV News, you all look so elegant and so much in control even though some of the clothes look a bit outlandish, at least to my Neanderthal mind."

"We don't always like the clothes we wear, even we think that some of them are crazy, and as for control, not always. I have fallen on the catwalk a few times, but it was not publicised like dear old Naomi's trip in Paris, 1993, Vivienne Westwood's show, now that made the news and the papers big style, poor dear."

"I don't remember that."

"You wouldn't. You'd still be at school, enough of me, tell me about you?"

"If I must," he said with feigned reluctance. "I'll tell you at dinner," he paused. "Are you ready for dinner?"

"Why not," she replied.

The same waiter that had served Pete (James) and Sophie Kouris the previous night brought the menus for their perusal, he eyed Pete (James) suspiciously but gave a courteous, "Sir, Madame," made a couple of suggestions and left them to collect their selections.

"Wine, any preference?" asked Pete (James).

Without reference to the menu, she replied immediately, "A Chianti Classico, please."

"I thought perhaps you would choose a French wine."

"No, no, a friend introduced me to the Classico when we were in Rome a long time ago, it's been my favourite ever since."

"So a Chianti Classico it shall be."

The confused waiter returned and took their order.

"You were about to tell me about yourself," Collette prompted.

"Okay," he said. "Stop me if I'm boring you."

He referred to the mental file he had prepared for James Goodwin, he began.

"I was born in Bury St Edmunds, that's a market town about 130 kilo-metres north of London, do you know it?" he thought not but was pleased to hear that she did not.

"My father died when I was young, he was big in the city, he left mother and I,. I've no brothers or sisters, financially well provided for."

All codswallop, the only bit that was true was that he was an only child, he continued.

"Mother died when I was at university, I'd be just 20, I still miss her."

She leant across the table and touched his hand. "Sorry," she said sympathetically.

"Oxford's a lovely city, ever been?"

"No, never," again it was pleasing to his ear, if he had to invent names and places she wouldn't know.

"Oxford, City of Dreaming Spires, great city for students and I was a student there for a long time."

The waiter brought the wine and offered a sample to Pete (James). "No, the lady," Pete (James) re-directed him.

Expertly Collette held the glass to the light and examined the colour and clarity, she swirled the glass and used her nose before finally taking a small tasting sip. "Fine," she declared.

The waiter completed the wine serving and left.

"Go on," Collette prompted.

"Maybe I'm lucky," Pete (James) resumed. "I'm a bit of an information soak, I've got a very good memory."

"I'd better watch what I say," she said jokingly.

"Yes you'd better," he agreed with a smile. "So learning I find relatively easy, I did two-degree courses in tandem, quite diverse subjects, Geology and French."

"That is why your French is so good, and did you know you have a Paris accent?"

"I didn't know, but maybe the six months I spent at the Sorbonne accounts for that."

As soon as he'd said this, he regretted it. She knew Paris and knew it well, if she asked him where he lived and spent his time it might be a problem, he had been to the Sorbonne and knew the area a little, hopefully more than she did, but with luck she wouldn't go there.

"Maybe so, but then the Geology became my number one, a Masters and a PhD, another three years or so, I was like a professional student."

"So now you are a gentleman geologist," she mimicked.

The conversation came to a temporary halt as the waiter returned with their first course, a salad of greens and peppers with a balsamic dressing for Collette and a lamb carpaccio with gooseberry chutney for Pete (James).

"I didn't really know what to do when I'd finished at uni," Pete (James) continued when the food was in front of them. "I did this and that, an interpreter for a while, some laboratory work, something here, something there, a bit of a rolling stone."

"And then?" she asked eating sparingly.

He finished the mouthful of food. "I suppose I started doing what I really wanted to do, travel and actually do some kind of work, real work."

"Fieldwork, as I recall, that's what you called it fieldwork," she'd remembered, that was good.

"Yeh, fieldwork, here, there and everywhere that I might find important minerals."

"Like gold, silver, oil?" she asked placing her knife and fork across the half-eaten salad.

"I should be so lucky, no most of those are pretty much accounted for but I have had some success," he took the opportunity to begin his offensive.

She took the bait, so to speak, "Interesting, can you tell me?"

"Yeh, no problem, as long as I'm not boring you?"

"I wouldn't ask if I wasn't interested," she scolded.

"No you wouldn't," he agreed. "8 or 9 years ago I found manganese in DRC that was good, good for DRC anyway."

"DRC, what is that?"

"Sorry, Democratic Republic of Congo, the government commandeered the land and extracted the manganese."

The main course arrived, curtailing conversation.

Having eaten in the Crown Grill the previous night, Pete (James) was fully aware of the size of the portions, he had ordered accordingly.

An 8-ounce Filet Mignon (still large) with sautéed mushrooms and fries was his choice.

Collette was served a lobster tail with grilled asparagus.

Apart from the odd remark about the food, Pete's (James's) artificial narrative was suspended whilst they ate.

Two almost empty plates said everything about the food. *As good as it gets,* thought Pete (James).

Collette, who must have eaten in some of the world's best restaurants also appreciated it and sent 'compliments to the chef' via the waiter.

Sweets were offered and declined but *café au lait* was requested.

They drank the last of the wine which Pete (James) had to agree was a fine choice.

She prompted him again to resume his biography.

"Where was I, oh yes, DCR, I keep going back there and Africa in general, keep looking, it's good, I love it, but I do need to recharge the batteries."

"And that is why you are here, but no more manganese, no?"

"No, no manganese but maybe something promising," he set the wheels in motion, she noticed.

"Is it a secret?" she asked.

"At the moment, I'm waiting for some reports."

"I hope it goes well for you," she said with genuine tone.

Pete (James) requested and signed for the meal adding a generous tip for the perplexed waiter.

It was not late, Pete (James) suggested a drink in one of the many bars, she declined.

"I have had a wonderful evening, thank you James, but I think I'm ready for my bed, I have a relatively early start in the morning."

They walked toward the lift. "You have something planned for tomorrow?" asked Pete (James).

"Yes, I love art, I paint a little myself, I understand Ubud is the place to go in Bali for local and international art."

"Would you mind if I tag along? I'm no art expert, perhaps you could teach me," he had his fingers crossed behind his back, this was a deciding moment.

He need not have worried, "I'd like that, sometimes a woman alone in a different country can feel vulnerable, yes I'd like that."

They reached Collette's cabin door, "Until tomorrow," said Pete (James).

"Yes, breakfast at 8, the dining room, will you wait for me?" she offered her hand.

"Of course," he replied taking her hand and lightly kissing it. "Good-night."

"Goodnight," and she was gone.

It was too early for Pete (James) to retire, the Explorer's Bar beckoned.

It had to be coincidental, the man and wife duo, he assumed they were man and wife, began harmonizing 'Chanson d'Amour', the Manhattan Transfer hit of

1976, on the face of it rather apt under the circumstances, French, yes, Collette was French, but amour, no, that was not an option; affection and physical love, if that became available, a means to an end.

He stood at the bar, a Sam Adams in hand, he cast his eyes around.

The Explorer's Bar was full, every table and every chair occupied.

The glamorous Kouris sisters were there again, their retinue of fresh-faced college kids replaced by a pair of bald bookends, brothers at least, twins possibly.

The new beaus were as opposite to the sisters as they could be, they looked like punk wrestlers or boxers complete with rings in their cauliflower ears and tattoos on their thick arms, maybe they could sate the sister's sexual appetites, but Pete (James) somehow doubted it.

The sisters acknowledged Pete (James) presence with sardonic smiles.

Samantha Potter, the Brisbane heavyweight was spread in a low leather armchair, she wore an evening dress of no doubt quality but somewhat inappropriate for her ample dimensions, far too much flabby flesh was on view.

At the other end of the bar, perched on a stool, was the American lesbian, in total disregard to the evening's dress code, she wore the same 49ers tee-shirt she'd worn on the first day of the cruise.

She was in deep conversation with another equally butch-looking woman wearing a pinstriped suit, collar and tie, and black trilby hat.

Meara Connelly, the passé Irish ex-journalist sat with her nose in a book toward the rear of the room oblivious to the duo and all around.

Pete (James) thought it strange, amusing even, that all the candidates on his list of possible targets, with the exception of the sleeping Collette, were gathered together in one room.

He chuckled to himself as he summed them up as *'a pair of nymphomaniacs, a fat lady, a dyke and a bookworm'.* Cruel, but true in his eyes. *Thank God, Collette was the chosen one for him, maybe not for her.*

His eyes were drawn to the sisters and the two ugly Kojaks, *Only last night, three in a bed, arms, legs and other body parts entangled in a sexual frenzy, he recalled vividly* and amused himself by further thinking, *I didn't know which way to turn.*

Was there such a thing as Manage et Quatre? Is that what they've got in mind, good luck to them, the baldies will be yesterday men tomorrow. At least I don't have the problem of attempting to satisfy the unsatisfiable.

A couple of beers later, tired of the duo and bored of watching the Kouris sisters enticing the two uglies, he sauntered back to his cabin.

It was 11 o'clock local time on the Java Sea approaching Bali, which meant it was 11 o'clock in the morning in New Jersey. Manny Strauss acknowledged Pete (James) e-mail by return.

Several communications later the two had determined a strategy and a rough timetable of forthcoming events, all aimed at relieving the oblivious Collette Bernard of a large number of her Euros.

165

Chapter 44

The gymnasium was fast becoming the venue for a gathering of the Kouris sisters discarded lovers.

In addition to the weight pumping Collingwood Joey and Pete (James), the two hairless Neanderthals were also in attendance.

It was an assumption that the two ugs were now ex-lovers as more than eight hours had passed since Pete (James) had seen them with the sisters, and that appeared to be more than enough time for them to have been used and dismissed.

His finishing line was in sight, only 200 metres ahead, he increased his stroke rate to 40 SPM pumping his legs and pulling the handle as hard as he could.

It must have been the close proximity of the trio of Kouris sisters' ex-lovers that initiated his mind wander.

He had never before compared his sex partners, but for some reason, he found himself doing that now.

His old friend, and occasional partner, Marianne, was always gentle and loving, as had been Helen Schmidt.

Puteri, the Singapore Music Club prostitute had also, at least, given the same impression, albeit she was a professional and faking it was part of the service.

Sophie Kouris had, when they were alone, been gentle and sensual, but that had changed dramatically with the arrival of sister Stella when she had changed, and like her sibling, become frenetic, raunchy and carnal.

Joey, the two skinheads and even Pete (James) had, he suspected, received lessons in libidinous sex and in all likelihood, all failed to sate the lustful desires of the two sisters, and what about the bevy of college kids?

He decided, he was best out of their lives, yes, a possible client lost, but now he had gained another better prospect.

His 2000 metres complete Pete (James) showered, changed into tee-shirt and shorts and went to meet Collette Bernard.

Collette was already in the Dining room foyer when Pete (James) arrived. "Sorry, I'm late," he said and took the liberty of kissing both her cheeks.

"No problem, I've only just arrived," she replied. "I've already organised a table for two."

The headwaiter led the way, Collette followed with Pete (James) behind.

The sky was clear blue, and the temperature was climbing, Collette was dressed accordingly, she wore pink, cropped jeans together with a pink-collared sleeveless pocketed cotton shirt buttoned and tied at the waist showing a hint of her flat stomach.

On her feet were leather-strapped, cork-wedged sandals and she carried a large floral-patterned beach bag which appeared to be carrying very little.

Established at the table, they ordered, and resumed the conversation of the previous night.

"Ubud, that's where we're going, have I got that right?" asked Pete (James).

"Exactly right," she replied, "I understand that there are many museums of art and galleries there."

"So I believe, maybe we will see Balinese dancers, maybe even see them do the Tek Tok dance," he said to impress.

It did.

"Tek Tok dance, what is that, and what is more, how do you know about it?"

"I must have read it somewhere, a guidebook maybe, I'm blessed with a photographic memory, I read I remember, the Tek Tok is the sound made with the mouth with the music and the movements."

"You're a mine of information, that's what you say, right," she said.

"That's what we say, I am apt to quote trivia from time, please tell me if it is boring you."

"No, I like information, but I soon forget."

"Sometimes I wish I did," he replied not knowing whether he believed himself or not.

Like the previous evening, Collette was by far the more frugal eater of the two, fruit juice and muesli started her day whereas an English breakfast replaced the calories that Pete (James) had left behind in the gymnasium.

"I hope you don't mind," began Pete (James), "I have my tablet with me, if we get to somewhere with Wi-Fi I would like to check my e-mails, I'm expecting an important report."

Time was passing and he needed to move with the con.

"No problem, not oil, not gold, but something else maybe?"

Exactly the reaction he was hoping for.

"Maybe," he responded non-committally.

Organised tour groups gathered outside the small Benoa Cruise terminal and more added to them by the second as more and more arrived from the ship, 40ish to each tender.

Collette and Pete (James) bypassed the milling crowd and made their way to the row of waiting local taxis.

Pete (James) led the necessary negotiations leaving the driver in no doubt what was expected of him at the agreed price, there would be no further negotiations on their return to Benoa.

The landscape of Bali is spectacular, numerous shades of green created by the forests and the terraced rice fields interspersed with vivid colours of flowers and blossom.

Around every corner was a temple or a village with locals ferrying their offerings of fruit and flowers on their heads, beautiful slim women in colourful dresses, their menfolk working the fields.

Through the sprawl of Denpasar City they drove vying with the thousands of mopeds and motorbikes, four on one motorcycle was not uncommon, Dad driving, Mum at the back with two kids in between, and there was hardly a crash helmet to be seen.

An hour and a half of city and country and they were in the shanty outskirts of Ubud, already works of local art were on display and for sale.

The taxi dropped them in the centre of Ubud unpaid, it was the only sure way of guaranteeing his return, they agreed a pickup time of 3 o'clock giving them plenty of time for the journey back.

"Before we start our tour of the galleries, do you mind if we take a coffee, I'd like to check my e-mails?" reiterated Pete (James).

"No problem, a coffee would be good," she agreed.

Pete (James) had already spotted an internet cafe on the other side of the road, but getting across to it was another matter.

Motorbikes outnumbered cars at least 8 to 1, they passed 3 and 4 abreast and nose to tail, and no pedestrian crossings, it was a case of 'going for it'.

Pete (James) took Collette's arm and skilfully guided her across zigzag-ging between bikes and cars alike, a relieved Collette sighed audibly as they reached the other side, "That was worse than the Champs Elysees at rush hour," she exaggerated.

The internet cafe was well-occupied, mostly Western tourists, all, or most, poring over laptops and tablets.

With two white coffees and the Wi-Fi password Pete (James) joined Collette at a window seat where she sat mesmerized by the procession of two-wheeled vehicles.

"Excuse me," said Pete (James) booting up his tablet.

He cleverly angled the tablet out of the direct sunlight but more importantly to where it was readily seen by Collette.

He went directly to his e-mails.

There was plenty of junk mail but nothing from Manny purporting to be the minerals laboratory, not that he expected there to be, not as yet, this particular exercise was to maintain Collette's interest, the report would be next.

"Mmmm," Pete (James) uttered, appearing disconsolate.

She swallowed the bait, obviously remembering their discussion of the previous night. "Your reports, they have not yet arrived," she said in a conciliatory manner.

"Not yet, I'm just anxious to find if my theory is right," he replied.

"I'm sure it will be fine," she reassured.

As Collette was attracted to the melee outside, Pete (James) swiftly sent a pre-drafted e-mail to Manny. It simply said, 'Now.'

He packed away the tablet and joined Collette in peering through the window.

It was a colourful scene, tourists and locals alike vying for position on the narrow pavements.

From their vantage point they could see two Museums of Art and two galleries in addition to numerous shops selling tourist tack.

"Are you ready?" asked Pete (James).

"Most certainly," she replied. "I'm really looking forward to this."

Before taking their lives into their hands again they explored the side of the road they were on, another two galleries were side by side not 20 metres away.

Pete (James) was not particularly interested in art but neither was he an ignoramus, but on this occasion, it was in his interest to at least appear attentive and even inquisitive.

Collette was, as Pete (James) dad would say, "Like a kid in a sweet shop."

"Look at this," she said in awe, "And this, and this."

Paintings and pottery, sculptures and tapestries, all took Collette's eye.

She was knowledgeable and gave Pete (James) a running commentary as she stopped to admire a particular painting or artefact.

The second gallery was equal to the first, paintings festooned the walls and, in every nook, and cranny there were other delights, colour, colour and more colour.

Collette led, Pete (James) followed, not always agreeing with her preferences, after all as is said, "Beauty is in the eye of the beholder."

A fine woodcarving of a naked Balinese woman in kneeling position took her eye.

It was about 12" tall and in art deco style, it was dated 1930 and possibly attributed to I Rodja, a name that Collette recognised but meant nothing to Pete (James).

Pete (James) agreed that 'even to his untrained eye, it was beautiful'.

Collette asked the price. "Fucking hell," said Pete (James) under his breath.

Collette had determined to have the piece, she negotiated and bought it at a marginally reduced price.

Wrapped, and double wrapped it went inside the floral pattern beach bag.

Time had slipped by unnoticed, it was lunchtime, time again for the tablet which Pete (James) knew harboured the erroneous mineral report from Manny in New Jersey.

Collette agreed, they returned to the internet cafe which in addition to coffees and internet access had a small adequate menu.

They made their selection at the counter before returning to the same table at the window that they had occupied earlier.

Junk mail filled his e-mail box but among them was the one Pete (James) had been waiting for, in truth, expecting.

It was headed UK Minerals Laboratory. The Lakes Commercial Park, Tewksbury, together with a host of untrue references and registration numbers.

It was titled 'Report for James Goodwin'.

Enclosed were six separate lists of chemical elements with figures and percentages the like of which would be found on genuine mineral deposit analyses.

The figures on each list were not the same, but very similar.

Collette scanned the pages with Pete (James), they meant nothing to her, little did she know they meant little to Pete (James) either, but they would mean a lot to genuine geologists.

Pete (James) made as if absorbing all the details, a smile crossed his face.

"Good news?" queried Collette with genuine interest.

"As I suspected, yes, sorry, yes, great," he stammered, "Bloody hell, eh, sorry."

The waitress interrupted with Collette's bowl of fresh fruit, Pete (James) salad sandwich and two coffees.

Pete (James) feigned pleasant shock. "Bloody hell," he repeated.

"You are surprised, maybe?" asked Collette.

"Not really, I was pretty sure, but I needed the proof, and here it is," he replied feigning mixed emotions of pleasure and relief.

Pete (James) was a good actor, he had to be, it was a necessity in the world of confidence tricks, without it he wouldn't have lasted two minutes.

He had at one time considered an acting career, a degree in drama and RADA, or the like, but he chose French instead. Joseph in the Junior School Nativity and even King Lear at Rodillean Secondary were a long time ago.

Acting came naturally to him, like his memory, it was a given gift, a natural fortunate attribute.

"Now I have to do some real thinking," said Pete (James). "These pieces of paper could be worth millions, I have some options I need to think about," he added but did not expound further.

"I am no engineer or financial expert, but if you need someone to talk to, a sounding board, do you say, then here I am."

Again the very words he was hoping to hear, she was going to hear more anyway, it was her money that was needed to finance his future but in the first instance the forthcoming so-called land deal.

Pete (James) closed the tablet. "That can wait a little while, until we get back to the ship anyway, no way am I going to spoil your pursuit of art," said he.

"You're not to lose a deal, we can go back now if you like, we can phone the taxi I have his card."

"No way, galleries, museums, art it is, at least until 3 o'clock," he replied, rising to move Collette's chair in a gentlemanly fashion.

Several more galleries were scattered along the main high street and down narrow side streets; before they'd run out of time they had visited four of them.

The carving in Collette's beach bag was joined by two rolled canvasses, one a very traditional Balinese painting of two white starlings in a Jalak Bell fruit tree, the other a contemporary Paddy fields scene by an American who had taken up residence in Ubud, it was, Collette advised him, in the Cubist style, Pete (James) preferred the Balinese to the modern, but Collette was delighted with both.

In addition, she bought a large sculpture, a carved limestone shape with holes, it was called Bella for some reason, maybe Bella was a woman, but it didn't look like a woman to Pete (James), Collette thought it did, she loved it and it was her money that was paying for it.

Including the delivery to Nice, it was a large four-figure dollar sum, which like all her other purchases she paid for with a diamond credit card, a card not available to the ordinary Joe, Pete (James) recalled Manny's report, Collette, was indeed worth a lot of money and he was eager to get his hands on some of it.

Although they had spent many hours in the various galleries Collette had ensured that they had sufficient time to visit an Artists supplies shop of which there were several in Ubud.

Being in and around the countless numbers of art forms, her own yen to paint had been kindled big style, she had not brought her own equipment intentionally, rest had been her priority, but now she felt the need and she had a subject she wanted to paint.

The large pink beach bag left the shop bursting its seams with two stretched and primed canvasses, a travel easel, paints, brushes and linseed oil.

The taxi transported them back to the Cruise Terminal via a different quicker route but with the same scenic background spoilt briefly by the sight of a roadside McDonald's. With all the beautiful fresh fruit, vegetables and fish in Bali some deluded people still wanted burgers in a bun.

The taxi stopped at a roadside stall, his cousin's, amazing taxi drivers the world over all seem to have cousins with shops, she was selling locally grown fruit and vegetables.

Pete (James) and Collette tasted some, the succulent flesh of a spiky red rambutan, and the sweet creamy centre of a smelly durian, so powerfully horrible that it is banned from hotels and aeroplanes, they left them but still took with them delicious pineapples stripped of the outside seed which they ate holding the leaves like lollipops.

"Have you seen enough of me for one day?" asked Pete (James) when they were back onboard the Cruise ship.

"Not at all," she replied. "I will buy you dinner tonight," she added.

"And I will gladly accept, 8 o'clock, wine bar."

At the door to Collette's cabin Pete (James) handed her back the beach bag that he'd toted from the taxi to ship and kissed her cheeks.

"Until 8," he said as the door was closing behind her.

Chapter 45

It was ridiculously early in the morning in New Jersey, 5 o'clock to be precise, but still Emmanuel Strauss replied by return to Pete (James) e-mail.

'Collette Bernard is on the hook,' Pete (James) had said.

'Good, I'm on standby, waiting to deliver your next communications, just blip as and when,' was the reply.

One more, 'Okay' e-mail and Pete (James) closed his tablet and put it on charge, it was a vital tool in the deception of Collette Bernard.

Collette and Pete (James) were lucky to find a table and seats in the well-attended wine bar.

Collette was her usual elegant self, stylish and chic in flared white trousers and floral overshirt.

She sipped her Chianti Classico and opened the conversation reverting to Pete (James) African mineral finds.

"I remember you said, not gold, or silver, or oil, but are you able to tell me what you did find?"

"No, no gold or silver, and most of the world's oil is accounted for below the sea."

He paused for effect, as if he was considering his next words, "Of course I can tell you, I don't think you're going to share the secret."

"Of course I'm not," she replied with disdain.

"To be technical, the reports say Bernite, or Peacock ore as it's sometimes called, the colours I suppose, and Chalcopyrite, both minerals with high copper content, and there are huge quantities of both."

"That's good?" she queried innocently.

"It is if I can put my name on it."

"Tell me more," she requested, her curiosity seriously piqued.

Pete (James) had prepared a basic script and held it in his memory banks, he pulled it to the fore.

"Africa, pretty much the whole of Africa, is rich in all sorts of minerals, it's a case of finding them in sufficient quantities and in places they can be practically and economically extracted and exported."

He paused for a swig from his bottle of Sam Adams and continued.

"Over the years I researched many areas of Africa using data obtained from many sources, from this info I have carried out field tests on the most likely prospects."

"A couple of wasted years, and now, bingo, copper, and lots of it."

Another swig of his beer, not so much to slake his thirst, but to judge Collette's reaction.

She was sat forward in her seat awaiting Pete's (James's) next words, a very good sign.

Pete (James) was on a roll, acting and telling lies were his forte´, his God-given memory was surely not intended for this purpose, but Pete (James) accepted his gifts and used them for his purposes.

"I was hopeful of a couple of sites in Zimbabwe," he continued, "But they were no good, copper, but not economical to extract."

"But this one?" interrupted Collette questioningly.

"Oh yes, this is the one, it's in an accessible location, and there's the ways and means to transport it for export."

"I'm pretty sure that the mineral field extends far beyond the area that I surveyed but I'll be happy with my few acres."

"Acres, what are acres?"

"Sorry, British measurement, 1 acre equals just over 4000 sq. metres."

"Ah!" she replied as if she could visualise metre measurement.

"My research led me to this farm, a stock farm in Angola, that just happens to be on the market, as a farm of course, but hopefully I will buy it for what's under the soil not what's on top."

"I suppose the farmer is unaware of the copper?" she asked as if she already knew the answer.

Pete (James) confirmed, "Absolutely, the surveys were all carried out at night, very cloak and dagger, very expensive, but it looks like it's paid off."

Previously Collette had only had one pre-dinner glass of wine but rapt as she was with Pete (James) account she emptied her glass and suggested another.

Pete (James) obliged, replenishing his beer at the same time.

He resumed where he'd left off, "I hired the equipment for seismic tests and then a core drilling rig and took samples around the perimeter of the farm, and hence the reports."

Another pause, another drink.

"It was all done at night, hiding away during the day, working at night, the German farmer had no idea we were there."

"And you found copper, and it's accessible, and economical to export?"

"All yes," replied Pete (James) with an elated smile.

Pete (James) had done his homework, and done it well, he had created a plausible history of the farm and its owner, all intended to enhance the mythical find.

He went on, "The farm, the site of the copper ore, as I said, is for sale, nearly 10,000 Acres, 15 sq. miles, nearly 40 sq. kilometres, $300,000 is the asking price, I think I'm good for that from my Trust Fund, thanks to good old dad."

He stopped briefly for another drink.

"Did I say where the farm and the copper is?" he asked.

"Yes you did, Angola, you said."

"That's right North East Angola, between Lucapa and Saurimo toward the border of Zambia and the Democratic Republic of Congo, I'd never heard of either of them before," he added.

She frowned, "I'm not good at Geography, never have been, I've heard of the countries but not the towns."

"Flat scrub land, only good for hardy stock, the Ex-Pat. German that owns the farm, Gunther Hoffmann has been there since 2002, he's 68 years old, widowed, no family, and wants to retire, so now I'm going to provide his retirement fund."

He supplemented his fable with additional supporting creative history.

"I researched Herr Hoffmann, it was his father, also Gunther, that bought the farm in 1958, then in 1961 when the Angolan War of Independence began, he sold the stock and did a runner to Brazil."

"Civil War raged in that part of the world until 2002, and that's when Gunther, the son returned to restock and flourish, the old man died in Brazil."

"I'm not so sure that Hoffmann was their original name, Gunther Hoffmann Senior's earlier history is a bit clouded, I suspect, but couldn't prove, that he left Germany in a hurry before the end of WW2, so maybe…"

"You think, perhaps, Nazi?"

"Quite possible, so I'm looking forward to cheating a Nazi son out of millions."

"I wish you well," she said. "What do you do now?"

"I've already started, I'll tell you over dinner," he replied emptying his Sam Adams' bottle.

Chapter 46

The backdrop of the Atrium band and the many voices of the wine bar was replaced with the refined strains of Andreas Bocelli singing arias in his native tongue.

It was Collette's treat, she had chosen the restaurant, the Italian Caravaggio.

She'd reserved a table for two in the corner giving them a vantage point to observe the other diners while offering privacy of conversation.

The Caravaggio was typical of high-class Italian restaurants, the décor was mock Roman, artificial columns, murals and Romanesque sculptures, yellow and terracotta colours and pristine white tablecloths.

A plethora of miniature lights dominated the matt black ceiling giving the impression of dining beneath the stars, all in all a romantic scene was set, but romance was not on Pete's (James) mind, business was, and if romance was required to finalize the business, then so be it, it would be no hardship with the beautiful Collette, but her money in his bank was the priority.

Mario, yet another Italian waiter called Mario, it must be a mandatory name, served the Chianti and left them to study the menu.

"Before you continue about your copper, I would like a favour," Collette began.

"I'm good at favours, if it's possible, it's yours," Pete (James) replied.

"Would you sit for me, let me paint you?"

"You mean a portrait, a portrait of me?"

"Not exactly, paint you, yes, a portrait of a kind, would you pose naked, in the bluff, is that what you say?"

"Close, in the buff is the word, naked, no clothes at all?"

"You can wear a hat if you want?" she said smiling.

"I presume this would not be on deck?" he joshed.

"Of course not, my cabin, but do not get any ideas."

"I don't know what you mean," he said suggestively.

"Will you?" she asked.

"Why not, tomorrow, while we're at sea?"

"Tomorrow and the day after, both days at sea."

Pete (James) quickly mulled it over in his head, *"More time together, more time to sell the con, and posing nude, no problem."*

"Consider that a date, two dates, two sittings, but you provide food and drink."

"I think that could be arranged," she agreed immediately before the return of the waiter.

They ordered, Collette following her normal trend of light meals, a Caesar salad starter and grilled tuna steak with new potatoes while Pete (James) followed a more substantial high-calorie route, Minestrone soup (a must in an Italian restaurant) and Veal marsala with broccoli spears and baby carrots.

"You were telling me about the farm, the German and the copper," said Collette.

"So I was," replied Pete (James) picturing the script and the point he'd reached.

"Where was I, oh yes, Gunther Hoffmann, the junior, still runs the farm, but his health is not so good, his wife died two years ago, he has no children, and he wants to retire, so the farm is on the market, $300,000, worth it as a farm, worth millions more for the ore."

"I'm 99.99% sure that the ore field extends much further than just the farm so the end value is anybody's guess, multi-millions, billions, who knows, but I'll be happy to make a million, maybe two or three by selling the farm to a multi-national copper corporation, with the test results there should be no problem ."

"I've instructed my solicitor, I think you say advocate, to offer the full amount, $300,000, now I just wait."

In truth, Pete (James) had sent an e-mail instruction to buy, to, Mitchell and Ayhurst, Solicitors, 21st Floor, 22 Leadenhall Street, London EC3V 4AB marked for the attention of Andrew Winterbottom.

But, of course, it hadn't really gone to the fictitious Mr Winterbottom at the totally fabricated solicitors, it had been despatched to the ever-attentive Manny Strauss who was expecting its arrival.

This e-mail and the reply (when it arrived) would be shown to Collette to further convince her that Pete (James) and his dealings were genuine, while sitting as an artist's model, that would be a good time.

Pete (James) weaved the conversation away from the copper and the farm, and his financial dealings, enough had been said at this time, a waiting period, he had found, whetted the appetite more, enhanced the interest and made the subject, Collette Bernard, in this instance, more susceptible.

"So the supplies you bought in Ubud are being put to use tomorrow," said Pete (James) sampling the very good Chianti.

"If you're a good boy and sit still."

"Will it take long?"

"As long as it takes," she replied.

"Should I bring sandwiches," he said mischievously.

"If you like, you can, but maybe we can use room service," the intended joke had gone over her head.

Throughout the meal the conversation meandered through many subjects, everything from artists to zoos (well not quite) excluding politics and religion of course.

It was a good meal, with good wine, good conversation, and best of all good company.

They parted at Collette's cabin door with the kissing of cheeks and a friendly 'Good night'.

In his bed, Pete (James) thought of Collette, she liked him, she liked him a lot, that he could tell, but sex didn't seem to figure in their relationship.

Was he losing it, or what?

No matter, sex was normally a by-product of conning money from women, this might be a first, a relationship without the physicality, *"That's okay as long as the cash goes in my bank,"* he surmised.

Pete (James) checked his e-mails, nothing in the in-box, he electronically conversed with the insomniac Manny keeping him informed of the Collette situation and planning the next moves.

Sleep came easy, nothing worried Pete.

Chapter 47

The gymnasium was seriously well attended, maybe it was because it was a sea day, with nowhere else to go.

Men outnumbered women at least four to one, and the majority of these were fit-looking under-thirties.

Pete (James) slumped forward regaining his natural breathing pattern as the rowing machine flywheel slowed to a stop.

He looked around, the usual suspects were there including Joey, the Aussie and the two hairless Neanderthals.

Pete (James) sniggered as the thought occurred that maybe more of the young exercising males had attempted to satisfy the insatiable appetite of the two promiscuous Kouris sisters, *"They were welcome,"* he concluded.

Collette had already eaten her meagre rations when Pete (James) joined her in the dining room.

Immediately the attentive waiter was at hand to take his breakfast order, a not so healthy full English.

Collette had again acquired a table for two, she leant forward and whispered, "A reply, have you received a reply?"

Not only had she taken the hook, she was running with it, "Brilliant," he thought.

"You mean about the land purchase?"

"Of course, what else?" she said eagerly.

"No, not yet, the trading hours in London, South Africa and Angola are the same, so hopefully I should hear some time today," of course he knew that to be the case, it was already organised with Manny.

Pete's (James's) breakfast arrived, "I'll see you soon, my room when you're ready," she said.

The waiter moved her chair to allow her to rise, he frowned as he overheard her comment and gave Pete (James) a wry smile.

The wry smile changed to an "I know where you're going" leer as Pete (James) said "G'morning," and followed shortly after.

Collette opened the door to Pete (James), she looked very Bohemian with a broad mustard-coloured bandanna surrounding her blonde hair, a Chinese-pattern, knee-length dressing gown and the white Cruise Line slippers completed her casual look.

The cigarette holder that would have been carried by most women of the Bohemian era was replaced by a slim paintbrush.

She ushered him in.

Collette had already adapted the cabin into a temporary studio, she had set up her easel on the balcony to one side of the open sliding door.

The balcony table held her equipment, from somewhere, probably the cabin steward, she had acquired two large jam jars, one held her brushes, the other her linseed oil, her tubes of paint were in a line ready for use.

She'd placed the desk chair by the bedside pointing in her direction, this would be for Pete (James).

"All ready to go," he commented as he set his tablet on the dressing table open, switched on and ready to receive the pre-planned e-mails.

"When you are," she replied making minor adjustments to her equipment and picking up her empty palette ready to begin.

Pete (James) casually stripped off his tee-shirt, shorts and sandals.

"The boxers as well please," said Collette.

He stepped out of the boxers without any sign of embarrassment and sat on the chair.

"No, not sitting," she said.

He stood awaiting further direction.

She joined him, "Stand to one side of the chair, put one foot on the chair and rest your elbow on your knee, and look forward to me."

He did as was bid, "Rest your chin on your hand."

Collette stepped back and assessed the pose, she looked him up and down, "Very nice," she commended.

Whether that assessment was for a whole, or a part, Pete (James) was unable to ascertain.

"Hold that pose," Collette requested returning to her painting position.

Collette removed her dressing gown, she wore a bikini, a pale yellow self-patterned bikini, she had retained her modelling figure well, she was a very attractive woman, "I thought you might feel more comfortable if I was naked as well, but it was too much, a bikini is far enough."

"Spoilsport," Pete (James) jokingly replied.

She squeezed several colours on to her palette and began to paint.

Apart from when Collette stepped to one side of her easel and canvass, all that Pete (James) could see of her was her spiky hair and her bare legs.

There was no conversation.

It wasn't the first time that Pete (James) had posed naked, not by a long way, as a University student he'd augmented his grant and escort earnings by posing from time to time for the local Art Society, he began to reminisce.

There had been a woman, wasn't there always in Pete's life, a member of the Art Society, who had requested and received private sittings.

Inevitably the sittings became more than just painting sessions, he pictured the scenes.

The thoughts transferred the information unwittingly to his nether regions, unintentionally blood flowed to his flaccid penis, flaccid it wasn't for long.

It had a mind of its own and it grew bigger and bigger, it did not go un-noticed.

"You seem to have something on your mind," said Collette putting down her palette and brush and walking toward him.

She kissed him lightly on the lips and gently took his erection in her hand, it grew some more.

Tacitly she stroked and unhurriedly masturbated him looking into his eyes enjoying his pleasure.

His hand found her small firm breast, she smiled.

She continued expertly tenderly squeezing and caressing drawing him nearer to orgasm.

He attempted to enter her bikini, but she stopped him with a firm "No!"

Surprise showed on his face, but he did as enjoined, her steel-blue eyes said thanks as she continued to pleasure him.

Pete (James) was expert in orgasmic control but Collette was an apparent expert in sexual gratification, he accelerated to a climactic finale ejaculating volitionally.

Collette slowly released his quickly diminishing erection and made her way to the bathroom.

Nothing was said.

Moments later she was back. "You may wish to shower," she suggested but Pete (James) was already on his way.

He had both hot and cold showers and emerged refreshed.

He returned to pose vowing not to let his mind wander again.

Collette was busy applying paint to the canvass out of Pete's (James's) sight.

She spoke shakily. "It isn't that I don't want sex with you," she began. "But…" she paused, "It's not possible…" she paused again. "I-I had a medical condition a few years ago, I had to have an operation…" another pause, Pete (James) could tell she was close to tears. "I'm okay, fully fit, but full sex is not possible."

No more was forthcoming. "I'm sorry, I didn't know," he said and actually meaning it.

"You weren't to know," she hesitated. "I hope it won't affect our relationship, in such a short time I…" she faltered.

Pete (James) joined her on the balcony, he held her in his arms, kissed her gently on the lips. "It's okay," he whispered. "It's okay," he repeated.

Collette sobbed, tears ran down her face, he held her until the crying subsided.

He glanced at the canvass and attempted humour, "Is that me or an acrobatic frog?" he said.

"It's not finished," she replied digging him in the ribs and forcing a smile.

"Thank God for that," said Pete (James) holding her at arm's length, "You okay?" he whispered.

She produced a tissue and dabbed her eyes and cheeks. "I'm fine," she lied.

Pete (James) had not anticipated this situation, far from it, but in no way would it affect his plans, friendship, love and sentiment played no part in Pete's world.

"Back to your place slave," she said forcing back her emotions and replacing them with frivolity.

"As you will, mistress," he replied returning to the chair and the 'Thinker' attitude.

Pete (James) modelled, Collette painted, and the sound of the sea replaced all conversation.

Pete (James) allowed his mind to wander again, primarily to the in-hand con, anything but sex.

Pete's (James's) tablet had long since gone into sleep mode but an e-mail alert drew both Pete (James) and Collette's attention, it was what Pete (James) had been waiting for.

Pete (James) pressed keys and the e-mail appeared on the screen.

The e-mail purported to be from Andrew Winterbottom of Mitchell and Ayhurst, it was of course from Manny Strauss, it read, "James, your offer of $300k has been accepted by Gunther Hoffmann. it is being processed as we speak. Speed is of the utmost importance if you wish to purchase this land. The conveyancing is in the hands of his lawyers, LTDA & Associates, Luanda. I look forward to your reply asap. Regards Andrew."

Collette was by his side, they read it together.

"Great," said Pete (James), "I'll instruct him to start the buying process immediately and I'll arrange the money."

It felt odd to Pete (James) to be sat in front of a computer completely naked with a scantily clad woman by his side, but what the hell, his plans were taking shape, next phase was the trickiest stage, capturing some of Collette's money.

Whilst Collette looked on Pete (James) sent two e-mails, the first a reply Andrew Winterbottom urging him to proceed as fast as possible.

The second was to Spore, Hammond and Jardin, Solicitors, 79 Guild-hall Street, Bury St Edmunds, it read: F.O.A. James Goodwin Trust Fund – Joseph Jardin. Please release to Andrew Winterbottom of Mitchell and Ayhurst, Solicitors, 21st Floor, 22 Leadenhall Street, London EC3V 4AB the sum of $300,000 (Three hundred thousand dollars) for the purchase of valuable land in Angola. I have advised Andrew that you will contact him for bank exchange details. Your urgent attention is requested. Should you wish to converse with me you have my mobile number or reply to this e-mail. The land is rich in minerals and will, not maybe, make a very, very good profit. Regards James Goodwin.

"Good for you," said Collette, "I hope you make millions."

"So do I," Pete (James) replied.

"I think we've done enough for this morning, a good time to take a break, shall I send for some lunch, or shall we go to the buffet," asked Collette.

"Let's go top side, eat alfresco and take some sun, I'll leave the tablet, I don't expect an immediate response."

"Okay, let's do just that," she replied slipping on the white dressing gown.

Pete (James) quickly dressed.

The whole of the Lido level was awash with fellow passengers taking advantage of the hot sunny day, tables and chairs on the open deck were as rare as rocking horse manure, they were compelled to eat inside.

They managed to acquire what was probably the only unoccupied table for two in the whole of the restaurant.

Pete (James) occupied one of the chairs while Collette collected her lunch and then vice versa.

Conversation through the light meal was spasmodic and of no consequence until they were taking coffee, "I'm sorry about the little outburst," said Collette matter-of-factly without any hint of emotion, "But it's the first time I have had to deal directly with the situation."

Pete (James) for the first time for a long while didn't know what to say, "It's okay," was what came out, "You don't need to say any more," he added.

"But –"

"No, it's okay, it's fine, I still want to be with you, it's not everything," said Pete (James) producing another performance as good as any of Richard Burtons.

It was certainly good enough to convince Collette, she smiled graciously, leaned across the table and squeezed his hand.

"Back to the salt mine," suggested Pete (James).

Pete (James) tapped the tablet screen, it sprang to life.

There had been no further communications.

One by one Pete (James) discarded an item of clothing while humming the famous 'Stripper' tune from the 1960s while Collette waited patiently behind her canvass smiling disdainfully.

With the occasional break for Pete (James) a muscle stretch, Collette worked diligently on the canvass through the afternoon.

Pete's (James's) tablet indicated a message, he looked at his watch 3.30. Right on cue.

He pulled on his shorts as Collette, her curious self, stopped mid brush stroke and joined him at the desk.

There were two more e-mails, it was not coincidental, Manny had sent them one after the other, to be read in the right order.

The first read as if from Andrew Winterbottom, offer of $300k accepted. All land searches complete. Everything in order. Arrange money transfer to Merchants Bank. Sort code. 06-12-31 Account No. 87452771 as soon as. Regards Andrew.

Collette wrapped her arms around Pete's (James's) neck, "Brilliant," she said kissing his cheek leant over his bare shoulder.

Pete (James) tapped the screen and brought the other e-mail in view.

This one professed to be from Joseph Jardin of Spore, Hammond and Jardin and was headed James Goodwin Trust Fund, James, it said, 'The terms of the Trust are such that apart from your monthly allowance, the maximum single amount withdrawal in any single fiscal year is £100,000. Please advise if you wish to make this withdrawal. Yours Joseph Jardin.'

Neither Collette nor Pete (James) spoke, they stared at the e-mail.

When Pete (James) did speak, it was a single expletive "Bollocks," he didn't apologise.

Silence reigned.

Collette broke the silence. "What will you do?" she asked with concern.

"Nothing I can do, that's my total funds, there is no more, it won't happen," he said dejectedly.

The e-mail continued to fill the screen, Pete (James) sighed loudly, this was the moment, would she, would she enter the net, more silence.

"I have the money," she said. "Tell them to buy."

"But it's $200,000, you can't. It's a lot of money, you hardly know me," he knew he couldn't just accept her money without some resistance, that might be a giveaway.

"Yes, I can, I'm a rich woman, if you want we can write some sort of loan agreement, something like that," she insisted.

"But it might be some time before I could sell and repay you."

"No matter, do it, I'll arrange the money," she said resolutely.

Pete (James) made to think.

"We'll be partners, 50/50, you own half, you get half the re-sale value, there's more than enough for both of us."

"If that's what you want, I would just loan you it you know."

"No, we'll be partners, Goodwin and Bernard, Bernard and Goodwin if you like."

"Either, it doesn't matter," she said.

"Right," Pete (James) said firmly, "We do this properly, all legal like, we will have a contract. I'll reply to Andrew Winterbottom immediately and then to the Trustees."

"Sure, do what you think best, if I can use your tablet, I will arrange the money transfer to wherever you want."

"Not until we have the contract," stressed Pete (James).

He typed a reply to Andrew Winterbottom (Manny): 'Andrew, slight change of plan. $300k. buy to go ahead, but in order to fund I now have a partner, Collette Bernard, by return please send a suitably worded contract document for both signatures to the effect that for an investment of $200k we will be 50/50 partners in any profits from the resale of the land. Regards James.'

Joseph Jardin of Spore, Hammond and Jardin (also Manny) was advised to send the £100k. to Andrew Winterbottom forthwith.

These sent Pete (James) rose and took Collette in his arms and kissed her on the lips.

"Thank you partner," he whispered.

"Partner," she repeated returning the kiss.

Pete (James) made to view the painting but was denied by Collette who threw a towel over it hiding it from him completely.

Pete's (James's) modelling was done for the day the Land transaction had proved to distract Collette from any further painting, Pete (James) was not pleased, he was ecstatic, the finale was close, Collette's $200k (to match his supposed input of £100k) would soon be his.

Using her mobile phone and Pete's (James's) tablet Collette organised the transfer of the $200k to the Merchants Bank.

Pete (James) despatched another e-mail to Andrew Winterbottom (Manny) to confirm Collette's money transfer and to expect his £100k. from Joseph Jardin.

Within the hour Andrew Winterbottom replied confirming receipt of instructions and monies, the land transaction was progressing to completion.

In addition Andrew (Manny) enclosed a Contract in legal gobbledegook for both Collette and Pete (James) to sign to confirm their bogus partnership.

Pete (James) had planned for this moment, from his faithful duffel he drew his portable A6 paper size printer, he linked it to his tablet and print-ed two copies.

In turn they signed and dated them, a copy each.

"Now we are Partners," said Pete (James) knowing full well that the contract wasn't worth the paper it was written on, who was James Goodwin, any search would be fruitless, Peter Holmes, complete with all evidence and .$200k would be long gone, hopefully never to be found by Collette Bernard, the police, or any Private Investigator she may employ.

Peter Holmes's plan had worked, Collette's money would soon, if not already, nestle in his 'Retirement Fund'.

Now he wanted away, away as quickly as possible, back to London, back to his books and Marianne.

His escape route was planned, the hapless Collette would need to be kept amused for a few days more, he mustn't give her any cause for concern, the deception must be maintained until they returned to Singapore.

Briefly the thought of jumping ship at the next port of call occurred to him, but was just as quickly dismissed, escape from a 120,000-tonne floating hotel through an unknown country without an organised itinerary was fraught with problems.

Patience was the order of the day.

Chapter 48

Pete (James) returned to his own cabin.

$200k travelled quickly electronically from James Goodwin's account to Peter Holmes' offshore stash, all pre-arranged on the proviso that all went well, and it had.

It didn't worry him that Collette had seen names and numbers on the screen of his tablet, all had been fictional, and on her own admission, Collette did not possess a good memory.

The tablet and its contents rested with him, but soon it would be history, a thing of the past, all evidence of, James Goodwin, Peter Holmes and the fraudulent relief of $200k from Collette Bernard would be obliterated.

He contacted Manny Strauss. "Mission accomplished," he wrote.

"Well done, my bill is in the post," he replied.

Pete (James) stripped, laid on the bed and slept the sleep of the innocent.

He awoke with a slight pain in his penis and testicles. Overuse, he thought flippantly as he touched himself gingerly.

Gently, he held his penis, it was tender to his touch, he looked for bruises or abrasions, had it been rubbing in the confines of his boxers, there was nothing to be seen, but the pain persisted. *Maybe it's nothing, it'll go away,* he thought.

The pain subsided. *See, it was nothing,* he told himself.

Pete (James) showered, changed and made his way to the Wine Bar, he carried his tablet with him.

It was early, not yet dark outside, he had the pick of the seats, he chose one in a corner, a good vantage point to watch the cruising world go by.

As requested, the waiter brought him a beer, a Singha Special Brew.

He set his tablet on the table and booted it up ready to continue the Angolan land saga on Collette's arrival.

In the meantime he surfed the web to find out what was happening at home in the world of sport.

Collette arrived, gone was the passé daytime Bohemian look to be replaced by the fashionable look of today's Paris or Milan, or that was the impression of Pete (James) and the others that watched her glide across the floor to greet him.

She had obviously visited the hair salon as her blond hair was no longer spiky, it now had a softer look it was brushed generally downward but across forehead creating the hint of a parting and a fringe over her left eye, a far more sophisticated look than random spikes, Pete (James) was impressed.

She wore small gold sleeper earrings and her makeup had, he was sure, been professionally applied in the Salon, she looked even more beautiful than she had before.

The dress she wore was again, no doubt, tailor-made in the workshop of one of the leading fashion designers' houses, it was sheer elegance, knee-length of self-pleated cashmere coloured chiffon that crossed from bust to waist held closed with a large diamond-shaped diamanté broach, the broad sheer shoulder straps carried the same diamanté pattern.

Apart from the stud earrings the only jewellery she wore was a gold bracelet and her normal finger rings.

The shoes that finished the ensemble were high-heeled sandals the same colour as the dress and had probably originated from Jimmy Choo or some other high-end emporium.

Pete (James) was the envy of every hot-blooded male in the wine bar and she was the envy of every woman.

She looked stunning, yet again.

Although Pete (James) had already successfully separated Collette from her money he still had to entertain her for a few more days, a necessary task he would have preferred to be without, but there are worse things in the world than having the company of a beautiful woman in opulent surroundings.

Pete (James) walked slowly and cautiously to the bar, the pain in his nether region had not abated, in fact, he was more uncomfortable, pain, he had thought, was all in the mind and could be easily overcome, but now he was beginning to change that view.

With her regular Chianti in her hand, she referred to the open tablet, "Everything okay," she asked politely.

"Yeh, I'm not expecting any problems, but I brought it anyway," he replied.

"Here's to a successful partnership," Pete (James) reiterated raising his bottle to clink Collette's glass.

"Of course," she replied.

Pete (James) continued, "When we get back to Singapore," he began, "I am going straight to Luanda to collect deeds for the farm and all the contractual mumbo jumbo that Angolan law may entail."

It was a lie, of course, he had no intention of going to Africa, it didn't figure on his agenda in any way, "When I've finished there, it should only take a couple of days or so, I'll come and join you wherever you are, that's if you want me to," he added.

"Of course I do," she replied.

She opened her clutch bag; cashmere coloured with diamanté relief and took out a small diary.

She turned the pages, "Milan, I'll be in Milan, back to Paris, and then on to Milan, a show and some photographic work."

"So I'll meet you there, where will you be staying?"

She referred to the diary again, "The Palazzo Parigi."

He created a new tablet file and typed it in, "While I have this open give me your mobile number."

She located the phone pressed a button and read him the number, "Don't forget to add 33 for France," she added.

"And this is my number," said Pete (James) giving her the number of the defunct phone he'd dumped in Barbados, he gambled that she wouldn't use it while they were on the cruise, after that, he couldn't care less.

"Dinner or a show?" asked Pete (James).

"I'm not so hungry, how about a show and a light supper?" she suggested.

"Fine," he agreed.

The show was good, very entertaining, the small cast of singers and dancers travelled the world of musicals from Abba to Zorba, almost 2 hours free of Pete's (James's) lies.

It wasn't that he enjoyed lying but it was a necessary part of any confidence trick and he did do it well.

There was time after the show to eat in one of the several waiter service dining rooms or restaurants, but they chose to snack from the buffet and eat alfresco on the Lido deck under the clear star-filled sky.

Pete (James) opened the tablet, there was an unopened message, "Transaction complete, all documents available for despatch or collection from LTDA, Luanda, Congratulations, Andrew."

The "Congratulations" was a sardonic addition of Manny's.

"There we go partner," said Pete (James) offering his hand for a partnership shake.

A kiss was added before Pete (James) replied, "Thanks for everything, I will personally collect documents from Luanda, be there in 8 days' time. James."

The show and Collette's company had distracted Pete's (James's) attention from pain in his genitals, it returned with a vengeance, he felt nauseous, for the first time for a long time he wanted to be alone but didn't want to disquiet Collette by curtailing the evening together.

His concern was alleviated, "Do you mind an early night?" Collette asked.

"No, not at all," he was more than pleased to say.

"Until tomorrow, breakfast," said Collette one hand on her door handle.

"And posing and painting after?"

"Of course," she replied kissing him good night.

The pain was extreme as he peed, even when he'd stopped the burning sensation continued. He inspected his penis again: was it his imagination or was it truly swollen? He thought the latter.

In bed, in the foetal position, the pain subsided, but not altogether, he had a fitful night's sleep.

Chapter 49

He was awake and out of bed earlier than normal, the pain had eased slightly only to return with a vengeance as he had his morning constitutional.

"Is it a water infection, something I've eaten or drunk? It's like an acid burn," he thought. "I*'ve not had anything different to normal,"* he answered himself.

His visit to the gymnasium, the rowing machine and jog were cancelled for the day.

On the way to breakfast he called at the Ship's general goods shop, he bought some painkillers telling himself that his little problem was temporary and would soon go away.

"Enjoy your morning exercise," asked Collette.

"Yeh, good," he lied carefully taken his chair.

"I'm having fruit juice and muesli as usual, you having your high cholesterol English?"

"Not this morning," he replied, "I'll have the same as you."

"A new diet regime," she suggested sarcastically.

"No, not really," he replied straight-faced, "I'm just not hungry," which on this occasion was true, the pain was affecting his appetite as well as is bodily functions.

Before stripping for another naked posing session he used Collette's bathroom, he gulped down two of the painkillers before he used the loo.

He wanted to stop, the burn was worse than before, but stop he couldn't, he clenched his teeth grimacing until he'd finished, the burn disappeared but the pain did not.

He took his place, foot on chair, elbow on knee, head in hand, his genitals in full view.

The previous day this naked pose and not bothered him one iota, but now he felt uncomfortable, not just the pain, it was as if, he couldn't put it into words, vulnerable, no that wasn't it, exposed, yes he was, but that wasn't it, it was more than that.

He smiled through his personal adversity, "Collette mustn't know," he was embarrassed, to say the least.

He did think, *"If the pain is still there this afternoon, I must see the Doc., I don't want to but needs must."*

Collette brushed and scraped in silence, her once pristine white robe gradually becoming multi-coloured as more and more paint found its way on to it.

Pete (James) held his pose with great difficulty the genital pain worsening, each time Collette's head appeared so did his smile replacing the grimace of continual discomfort.

He tried to dismiss the pain by thinking of his past, his teenage years, they'd been good, dawn till dusk sport be it summer cricket or winter soccer and rugby; a good set of mates and a ball, what more could young lads want?

It worked until inevitably the thought of teenage girls and early sexual exploits came to mind, the pain reappeared.

At last the words he had been longing for came, "You can relax, I'm just adding the finishing touches," said Collette.

Pete (James) dashed to the bathroom, he felt unclean.

The shower helped, but not much.

A seriously sharp pain shot from his penis to his abdomen, an alien discharge seeped from his meatus through his foreskin, *"Shit, what the hell, the doc., and as soon as possible."*

He dressed and joined Collette, he hid his discomfort, she had no idea of his pain.

"What do you think?" she asked inviting him to look at his portrait.

"Mmmm," said Pete (James) uncommittedly, in his eyes it was hardly a recognisable portrait, it was a confused mass of misshapen colour, gone was the dancing frog, but what had taken its place was debatable.

"Mmmm," he repeated.

"You don't like it?" said Collette.

"To be honest, no," he admitted.

He was telling the truth, in one way he really did think it was awful, but he liked it in another way, no one, not even his mother, would recognise him from this so-called portrait, that was why he did like it.

Pete (James) had made a distinct effort to avoid Collette having a photograph of him and he was delighted that the painting still left him anonymous.

"Well I like it," stressed Collette.

She took the canvass from the easel and set it to one side to dry.

She bundled her equipment together on the table and wiped her hands on her dressing gown, two multi-coloured palm prints were left as a gift to the laundry.

It was lunchtime but Pete (James) felt little like eating, he was feeling positively unwell, something completely alien to his normally super-healthy self.

He needed to see the doctor, but without Collette's knowledge.

"I have some work I must do," he lied, "Would you excuse me for the afternoon, and I'll wine and dine you tonight."

"No problem, you look after our investments," she replied, "Meet you in the Wine bar as usual," she added.

Pete (James) kissed her on the cheek, "Sorry I don't like your painting, but I'm sure you would prefer I be honest," he said glibly.

"I do," she replied returning the kiss.

Pete (James) walked from Collette's cabin as upright as he could, avoiding any signs of his discomfort. There was much he needed to keep from her, this was one more thing.

Chapter 50

The sign on the door read "Ship's Doctor – Harry S. Moon. M.D."

Pete (James) knocked tentatively.

"Come in," he only just heard.

Dr Moon was a diminutive man, slim, with a head of short grey hair, he sported a similar coloured small moustache under a bulbous ruddy nose that supported circular gold-rimmed glasses.

He wore a tropical all-white uniform, shoes, trousers and shirt with epaulettes of three gold stripes signifying Doctor.

"How can I help you?" he asked in a light-coloured antipodean voice.

"A problem downstairs, doc," he replied.

"I see, sit down and tell me about it."

Dr Moon sat behind a modern teak desk upon which sat a monitor, keyboard and mug of pens, Pete (James) sat on one of the two chairs facing him.

Pete (James) described the pain, the burning sensation when he peed and the discharge.

"Your name and cabin number, Mr err?" he asked matter-of-factly.

"James Goodwin, Suite 377," he replied.

Dr Moon tapped a few keys and peered at the screen.

"James Goodwin, Bury St Edmunds, England," he read.

"That's me," replied Pete (James) attempting flippancy.

"Right then, Mr Goodwin, let's have a look at you."

As Pete (James) dropped his shorts and boxers, the doctor donned surgical gloves.

Dr Moon knelt at Pete's (James's) feet, he examined his penis, first with his eyes and then by touch, he squeezed gently, he didn't need to ask "If that hurt". Pete's (James's) grimace and sharp intake of breath told him it did.

"You are well endowed," commented Dr Moon. "Is this normal or is it swollen," he asked.

"It's is swollen a little," Pete (James) replied.

"Mmmm," mused the doctor. "You may dress," he said returning to his desk chair.

"You look in good physical shape Mr Goodwin, any other problems?"

"No just the pecker, what do you reckon, water infection?"

"I don't think so Mr Goodwin," he paused, "You're a man of the world Mr Goodwin, been around I reckon."

"I guess so," was the curt reply.

"Might I guess you have in the none too distant past, been…Eh! Eh!" he coughed, "Been straying from your normal partner."

"What are you saying?" asked a now very concerned Pete (James).

"Mr Goodwin I have to tell you that you most certainly have an STD, a sexually transmitted disease, which exact one I am not sure, the symptoms are pretty much the same for several strains, it could be Gonorrhoea but only further tests will tell, and I'm afraid we do not have those facilities here."

"Shit, sorry Doc," Pete (James) cursed, "And there's naïve me thinking the young lady would be clean."

"I see," commented Dr Moon knowingly.

"Would you bloody believe it, first time I've ever paid for it, and I finish up with clap."

"Sorry mate, shit happens," said the no doubt worldly doctor.

"What's the treatment Doc?" solicited Pete (James).

"Penicillin used to be the answer, but not anymore, I have a broad-spectrum antibiotic called Doxycycline that we use for a number of bacterial infections that should do for now until we can establish the definitive strain."

Dr Moon once again tapped a few more keys.

"We're in K.L., Kuala Lumpur tomorrow, I'll send you to see an old friend of mine who has practised there for years, you okay for that."

"Most certainly," replied Pete (James).

Dr Moon scribbled a name, address and telephone number on a page of a note pad and handed it over, "I'll ring him to expect you, we dock at 8, shall we say 11 o'clock."

"That will be fine."

Dr Moon rose and disappeared through a door behind him.

He reappeared moments later carrying a syringe and a small phial.

He set them on the desk.

"Where would you like it?" he said as he filled the syringe from the small phial.

"Wherever?" replied Pete (James) who had a natural fear of needles but was reluctant to show it to the little doctor.

Dr Moon reached high to inject the fluid into Pete's (James's) upper arm, Pete (James) looked away.

The doctor returned to his chair and began typing.

"Would you care to tell me where you might have acquired your little problem," he said.

"Little problem you call, bloody painful, I call it," replied Pete (James).

"I suppose you're right," acceded the Doctor.

"Singapore," added Pete (James), "Monday just gone, a place called the Music Club, a girl called Puteri."

"Thank you, I'll make some discreet phone calls to people I know in Singapore, see if we can stop an epidemic."

"Peturi won't get arrested, will she, I know she gave me a dose, probably didn't know she was infected, wouldn't like to think I got her thrown into prison."

"Don't worry, that won't happen," replied Dr Moon as he entered the information. "Sorry Mr Goodwin, but here's the bit where I hurt your pocket, could I please have your cruise card?"

Pete (James) had expected this and produced his card.

"$200 I'm afraid," said Dr Moon entering the card into a handheld machine.

He handed the slip to Pete (James) who added his signature.

"Come back and see me on Tuesday after you've seen Dr Carney," said Dr Moon as he ushered Pete (James) out into the corridor.

Chapter 51

"Fuck," said Pete (James) to himself as he walked slowly and painfully back to his cabin, *"Bastard Peturi,"* he thought not being quite so generous as he was when talking to the doctor.

He showered again, he definitely felt unclean, maybe the antibiotic had kicked in, the pain had subsided a little, but had far from gone.

He had planned to accompany Collette wherever she wanted to go in the greater Kuala Lumpur area the following day, he would need to make some excuse so he could make the Dr Carney appointment, he thought on it, business, some sort of fictitious business meeting, that would have to do.

"She must have the most extensive travelling wardrobe in the world," thought Pete (James) as Collette arrived in another designer outfit.

On this occasion, she wore a red two-piece suit, a slim blazer jacket and tapering trousers.

To complete the outfit she wore a black camisole top and black strappy high-heeled shoes.

Yet again she was the envy of most women as they monetarily assessed her outfit in the coin of whichever realm they were from.

As per usual Collette's aperitif was a Chianti Classical while Pete (James) stuck to his daily dose of Singha beer.

Pete's (James's) problem of how he would make the secret doctor's appointment disappeared when Collette announced that she had a planned photoshoot in the Shangri-La Hotel.

She did ask if Pete (James) would like to join her, but of course he declined.

"What will you do with yourself?" she asked.

"Oh, I don't know, Petronas Towers maybe, shopping maybe not, I'll find something I'm sure."

"I'm sure you will," she agreed.

They decided to dine in the main Dining room and share a table with others.

The Head Waiter showed them to a large table where they were joined by three other couples.

An elderly married couple celebrating their Golden Wedding Anniversary who hailed from Adelaide sat to Collette's immediate right, while to Pete's (James's) left were two recently married 30 + men from Wales.

Across the table it was almost a case of Deja vu for Pete (James) the third couple comprised a large brash American and his pretty demure wife, once again he did all the talking while she fluttered her eyes at the uninterested Pete (James).

Pete (James) spent an uncomfortable two hours sat on what started off as a comfortable chair but finished being like a bed of nails, it was only the good food and the interesting conversation that went some way to helping him forget the constant dull pain.

He wasn't overly upset when their coffee cups had been drained and they meandered to the Explorers Bar, albeit gingerly.

The brandies that they sipped stood at the bar listening to the dulcet tones of the duo turned out to be nightcaps, for which Pete (James) was thankful.

Since Collette's sexual rebuff Pete (James) had found it difficult to know how to be amorous with her without appearing overly aggressive or on the other hand less caring.

At her cabin door he kissed her lightly on the lips, she responded likewise.

"Bon nuit," he said.

"Adieu," she replied.

With great relief Pete (James) stripped to his boxers and climbed into bed.

Normally he slept in the buff but the thought of possibly marking the sheets decided him against.

Chapter 52

The rowing machine and the jog around the ship were kicked into touch, as was breakfast. Never before had he felt so down; no energy and the constant pain were something alien to the normally fit and healthy Peter Holmes.

Apart from measles as a kid and the odd sniffle he'd ailed nothing, nothing more than an occasional sporting bruise, he'd been lucky, until now.

The Cruise Terminal for Kuala Lumpur is actually situated in Port Klang which is 30 Km. from downtown K.L., and not the prettiest place Pete (James) had ever been, but then port areas rarely are beautiful.

The majority of disembarking passengers gathered to join Cruse organised tours, Pete (James) bypassed them and made straight for the taxi rank.

He handed the slip of paper with Dr Carney's address to the driver of the taxi first in line.

He read it and nodded, "Okay boss, $25."

Pete (James) nodded acceptance and clambered in, it was a comfortable Hyundai of some description.

The journey through towns and villages with the sporadic verdant spaces took about an hour. Another day Pete (James) would have taken great interest in these new surroundings, but not today, he was quiet and introvert, something completely alien to the usually outgoing Pete, but then he'd never ailed before.

Pete (James) was lost in the maze of highways, avenues and streets of downtown Kuala Lumpur, but the driver never wavered, he knew exactly where he was going.

The taxi turned into a busy narrow street and came to a stop in a space between another taxi and a flat back lorry.

Pete (James) stepped on to the litter-strewn pavement.

He was confronted by a three-storey building that would have been innocuous had it not been painted a garish red.

Between an Oriental restaurant and a camera shop was a single large heavy wooden door.

On the wall was fixed a brass plaque engraved "Bill Carney. M.D and a string of other qualifications."

The stairs to the first floor were uncarpeted and well worn, the ceiling and walls were painted plaster that badly required some TLC.

The landing was carpeted albeit threadbare, there were three doors along its short length.

Pete (James) entered the "Reception" signed first door.

The difference between the stairs and landing and the Doctor's reception area was as chalk and cheese.

The reception area oozed opulence, the painted walls were covered with original paintings, the floor carpeted in a burgundy thick pile carpet and the furniture, including the receptionist's desk, was modern metal and plastic.

"You're the 11 o'clock?" asked the pretty Malay.

"I guess so," replied Pete (James).

She used the desk-mounted intercom to announce his presence.

Almost immediately an internal door opened.

"Jimmy, Jimmy Goodwin, the bloke from Harry Moon, I'm Bill Carney, come on in," bellowed the doctor.

Dr Carney was exactly the opposite end of the physical spectrum to Dr Moon, Bill Carney was at least 6' 8" tall and minimum of 18 stones, he had broad shoulders and, no doubt at one time, a narrow waist, now it had thickened and bore a middle-age paunch.

He vigorously shook hands, his huge hand engulfing Pete's (James's), who until now thought he had big hands.

Doctor Bill Carney had laughing grey eyes with a canopy of bushy eyebrows, his nose was aquiline with a slight kink, the result, no doubt of a sport-related break.

His chin was square and clean-shaven, and his permanent smile revealed a perfect set of white teeth.

His mop of unruly dark greying hair and large handlebar moustache dominated his face.

Pete (James) had never seen a more resplendent specimen. Merv Hughes, the Australian fast bowler of past years, was famous for his moustache but his was tiny in comparison.

Over an open-necked blue shirt he wore a white short-sleeve button-down medical lab coat jacket with a Jacquard kangaroo on one breast pocket and the words "What's up Doc" on the other.

A stethoscope hung from his neck like a mayoral chain confirming his professional status.

Pete (James) took the offered chair opposite Dr Carney, his large imposing desk separating the two.

Pete (James) noted the military arranged desktop, a keyboard sat in the middle with a monitor to its left leaving an unobstructed view to the patient, to the right of the keyboard was a note pad and a miniature billy-can of pens and pencils, the rest was clear polished top.

"Harry tells me you've been dipping your donger into an infected mutt."

"I wouldn't have put it that way, but that's about the strength of it," replied Pete (James).

"Okay, so let's have a Captain Cook."

Pete (James) once again dropped his trousers and boxers, Dr Carney squeezed his enormous hands into surgical gloves.

The size of his hands belied his touch, gently and almost painlessly he examined Pete (James) penis.

Doctor Bill Carney was forthright and said what he thought, "You've got a beauty of a wanger there, Jimmy my boy, pity it's poorly."

Dr Carney's carefree approach put Pete (James) at ease, although the pain was still there, the earlier embarrassment had gone.

"Before you put that monster away, I need to take a sample, I'll be as gentle as I can."

Like Dr Moon the previous day, Dr Carney entered another room, Peter (James) could see shelves of medical equipment as the doctor disappeared from view.

The syringe he held on his reappearance had a needle a foot long, it wasn't, but that's what Pete (James) eyes were telling his brain.

"Don't look," advised Dr Carney, a comment that was superfluous to requirements as Pete (James) looked anywhere except downwards.

Pete (James) didn't need telling that the needle was being carefully inserted into his urethral orifice, the small hole through which water and semen passes.

He clenched his teeth as he felt the additional pain.

"Okay," said Dr Carney as he returned to the small room with the syringe.

"Nearly done," he said on his return, "Just need to check your blood pressure and take a blood sample, don't worry that's from your arm this time."

"That's good," he commented reading the gauge of his sphyg "140/90," he said, "Apart from your dick you seem as healthy as an ox."

"Thanks," replied Pete (James).

"Don't worry Jimmy, we'll have you back to shagging mode in next to no time," he lied.

"Pleased to hear it, what now?"

"You go twiddle your thumbs for three hours while I get these samples off to the lab."

Pete (James) checked the fingers of his right hand as he passed through the reception area and into the dismal staircase, they were all there, *that would be the last handshake with Dr Carney,* he promised himself.

Three hours to kill in an unknown city, where to go, what to do.

The same taxi that was there when he entered Dr Carney's building was still there, the driver lounged against the bonnet drinking a coke.

"Ride, boss," the driver ventured.

"Why not," thought Pete, "How about a tour of the city, three hours and back to here."

"Sure thing, boss, $60 American, yes."

"Why not," replied Pete (James) climbing in.

"Where you want to go?" asked the driver as he pulled away from the kerb.

"Oh, I don't know, all the places you take tourists, just park up for photos."

"Okay boss, will do."

A whistle-stop tour of the major Kuala Lumpur attractions included the Petronas Towers, Bukit Bintang Shopping Complex, KL Tower, The National Mosque as well as the old Railway Station and the usual tourist hotspots.

Exactly, to the minute, three hours later, Pete (James) counted out $70 into the hand of the well-satisfied driver.

Pete (James) avoided the crushing grip of Dr Carney.

He once again sat uncomfortably awaiting the Doctor's prognosis.

"Well Jimmy," he began, "It's definitely Gonorrhoea, and nothing else, so here's what we do."

"What do you mean, nothing else?" queried Pete (James).

"Sometimes Chlamydia and Syphilis go hand in glove with Gonorrhoea, but not in this case."

"Thank God for small mercies," said Pete (James).

"When do you get back to Pomme, you are going back to the UK aren't you?"

"Yes, directly after the cruise, from Singapore," lied (Pete (James) knowing full well he had planned a devious route home to avoid future detection.

"Okay, I'm giving you the beginnings of a course of treatment, I'm going to give you a single injection of Ceftriaxone now, this hopefully will do the trick but go and see your doctor the moment you get home, you okay with that?."

"Sounds good to me, will the pain subside straight away?"

"Afraid not, if you must, take Paracetamol."

For the third time in the day a needlepoint entered Pete's (James's) body, thankfully his arm.

"No rooting until the dose is well gone," chuckled Doc Carney.

"Not bloody likely," replied Pete (James).

"Right, that just leaves the most painful bit, at least for you," said the doctor.

He continued, smiling below his hairy lips, "Make a noise like $300 US."

"One expensive jump," commented Pete (James) parting with six $50 dollar bills.

"That'll teach you to be more careful where you put it in future," said the doctor philosophically, "I'll give Harry Moon a ring or an e-mail," he added.

Pete (James) waved the doctor goodbye avoiding the vice-like grip.

The tour taxi driver was waiting in precisely the same spot as Pete (James) had left him.

He'd anticipated Pete (James) needed another ride, and he wasn't wrong.

"$40 US if you get me to the cruise ship at Port Klang in under an hour."

"No problem boss," he replied jumping behind the wheel, finding first gear and accelerating down the busy street narrowly missing a handcart of fresh vegetables.

The driver earned his $40 easily.

It was mid-afternoon, back on board, and Pete (James) suddenly realised he hadn't eaten since the previous night, the pain had subsided, whether psychological or not he didn't care, and now he was hungry.

It was a toss-up: English afternoon tea, which on American ships wasn't truly English, or the Lido deck buffet.

The buffet won.

Chapter 53

The vast majority of passengers had obviously taken shore excursions as there were several poolside sunbeds vacant.

Pete (James) collected his current book, as for the first time in a while he had time to catch up with Isaac Bell, Van Dorn's top detective.

He stretched out fully clothed under the hot sun and settled down to read.

From the corner of his eye he detected movement.

It was the younger of the two Kouris sisters, Stella, she smiled sweetly in his direction but did not speak.

"Fuck you," thought Pete and then laughed out loud, *"You and your bitch of a sister are in for a shock, I hope,"* he mused.

He laughed some more when he thought that the same dose could now be germinating in their genitals and of several more passengers, including Aussie Joey, Doc Moon was going to be busy.

Stella Kouris looked in his direction he could see in her face, she wondered why he was laughing, *she'd find out soon enough.*

Furnished with the usual Chianti and Singha in the Wine Bar, Collette and Pete (James) shared details of their day in Kuala Lumpur.

Pete (James) described the various places he'd seen on his taxi tour omitting to mention his visit to see Dr Carney.

The sumptuous Shangri-La, as Collette described it, had hosted a celebrity list of the world's top models, including herself for a group photoshoot.

She had been a veteran alongside new names as young as 18 and although she didn't say, she must have replaced several thousands of the dollars that she didn't know she'd lost to Pete.

They had plenty to talk about throughout the evening, dinner spent together at their own table and later in the Explorers Lounge.

It was there that the Kouris sisters were once again in the company of young men, *"More for possible venereal problems,"* surmised Pete (James) but was disinclined to give any warning.

Their relationship had blossomed into one of companionship, love maybe on her part but false on his, a sharing of intellects, it had everything but sex, they were almost like an old married couple where sex had become a thing of the past.

As he was, at this time, incapable of safe sex it was just as well that the lovely Collette was disinclined for some reason unknown to Pete (James).

Chapter 54

The following three days, the last of the cruise were spent, apart from the nights, in each other's company.

For two days, wherever Collette went, so did her sketch pad.

The tour of Penang was dominated by temples, reclining, seated and upright, large and larger, they appeared everywhere, at each stop, a sketch and a host of photographs, Pete (James) tagged along amazing her with snippets of information he'd gleaned from who knows where.

Phuket had its share of temples too, but the tour that they bought included elephant trekking through a rubber plantation, sketching was suspended while bumping along at the back of the Mahout.

There were some interesting sights in the city of Phuket, not least the ladyboys that paraded in and around the gaudy bars, discreet photos were taken by both Collette and Pete (James) and not so discreetly by the brash American of a couple of nights previous, his overt and loud enthusiasm lead to a near fracas, Pete (James) intervened bravely and averted any possible violence.

His genitals, that up to this point had been relatively pain-free suddenly reminded him that all was still not well, it was the sight of these prostitutes, albeit male, that reignited the ache.

They moved on quickly, to yet another temple.

The routine of the evenings was maintained, the Wine Bar, a meal, a show and/or the Explorers Lounge, both Collette and Pete (James) continued to sleep alone.

Several times Pete (James) saw the smiling faces of the Kouris sisters, they looked fit and well, the STD had not as yet materialised in their vital parts, *"But soon it would,"* or so he hoped.

The last full day of the cruise was at sea and like the previous four days Pete (James) gave his usual physical exercise a miss.

Once again, he met Collette for breakfast, not saying, but giving her the impression that he'd just left the gymnasium.

After breakfast Collette set up her easel with a new blank canvass in an alcove on the deck overlooking one of the swimming pools.

Pete (James) searched and found two vacant chairs which he claimed and carried to the alcove.

It was another cloud-free hot sunny day, the pool area was awash with scantily clad bodies, many of which would have been better kept under wraps.

Pete (James) read of the adventures of Isaac Bell as Collette painted.

From time to time he glanced at the canvass, *"Can you tell what it is yet?"* came to mind, *"No,"* was the simple answer, he made no comment.

The whole morning and afternoon, apart from a short lunch break, was spent in the alcove.

Pete (James) devoured several chapters but was no nearer to determining who the villain might be.

The sun was well on its way to the horizon when Collette announced she'd finished.

"And your opinion is?" she asked.

"Yeh, it's good," he did, in fact, like the blaze of colours, but had no idea what it was supposed to be.

"You do?" she asked with doubt, "Tell me what you see?" she added.

Pete (James) held his chin as he studied the canvass, she hadn't worked from a sketch or a photo he'd noted, *"Must be the scene on the deck below,"* he guessed, he ran with that.

"The pool and the bodies surrounding it," he said positively, with a good imagination it might well be that.

She seemed pleased, "Glad you like it."

Pete (James) portered the easel, the canvass and her equipment back to Collette's cabin.

"The last night, shall we dine Steak or Italian?" asked Pete (James).

"Italian please," not surprisingly replied Collette.

"I'll arrange that, Wine Bar 7.30."

"Fine," she said.

They kissed and parted.

Collette had saved the best until last from a couture point of view.

Louis Vuitton, Christian Dior or one of the top designers her dress was, Primark, Matalan or even Marks and Spencer's it was not.

It was a full-length evening gown self-patterned black, strapless and figure-hugging with a large bow on her right hip.

Her long neck was accentuated with a triangular-shaped necklace of black stones.

She had again visited the hairdresser as her blonde hair had been re-modelled into a curly wayward look, she belied her age by a considerable margin.

Little had been said over the last few days about the Angolan land deal and their partnership.

Pete (James) felt that some reassuring words were overdue, "I've heard from Andrew Winterbottom, you remember my solicitor, the documents are on the way," he prevaricated.

"Great," she replied accepting his word without question.

"When we meet in Milan, it all should be a done deal, and we'll discuss our next move, that okay partner."

"Sure is, pardner," she replied as best she could in a not-even-close John Wayne accent.

"I know I've got details in my tablet but remind me where and when," said Pete (James).

Collette's clutch bag on this occasion was made of the same material as her dress with a small bow echoing that at her waist.

She found the same small diary as before and opened it at the relevant page.

"We're back in Singapore on the first, Paris 3rd and 4th, Milan 5th until the 10th," she read.

"That should work," replied Pete (James) while thinking "Who cares I'll be miles away."

He continued, "From Singapore to Luanda, say two days there, that takes me to say the 4th. I can definitely be in Milan for the 6th, maybe even the 5th."

"That would be good," answered Collette.

"Palazzo Parigi, the 6th then."

"I'm going to be away early," he said truthfully, "I'll go straight to the airport and fly to Angola by the quickest route available," he lied.

"So it's our last night together until Milan."

"Another drink and a fine meal seem to be in order, the Caravaggio if we can get a table."

"That shouldn't be a problem," said Pete (James), "If I was the Head Waiter I'd throw somebody out to find you a table,"

"Smoothie," she replied but the compliment made its mark, for once he wasn't lying.

The evening finished with a lingering kiss at Collette's cabin door.

"Milan, soon, very soon," said Pete (James).

"Not soon enough," she replied.

Another lingering kiss and she was gone.

As in Barbados, Pete had held onto his luggage, he undressed packed the last remaining clothes, emptied the safe and set out his gear for the following day's quick departure.

He made his way to sleep totting up the contents of his offshore retirement fund as an insomniac would count sheep, another $200k took the total above the million mark.

He was soon sound asleep, a sleep of the innocent, although he was far from it.

Chapter 55

James Goodwin (Peter Holmes) cleared passport and security of the Cruise Terminal and made a beeline for the adjacent Harbour Front Centre and the first public amenities he saw.

Interred in a cubicle he opened his professional make-up kit and used the contents to become someone else.

Before leaving the UK, Pete had made a visit to his forger and acquired another passport.

For this passport he had changed his appearance considerably, the photograph looked intentionally like a different person.

The name in the passport was Louis Francis Johns from Manchester, apart from those that lived in the neighbouring counties, Lancashire and Yorkshire, no one seemed able to differentiate between the two dialects, thus he could adopt his normal brogue.

His date of birth had become October 13, 1946, and the photograph reflected his new age.

In less than ten minutes he emerged, he looked like a 69-year-old, he wore a grey/white wig, an expensive one, long and slightly unruly, not unlike Manny's in New Jersey.

He'd applied cosmetics as directed by his old friend the professional makeup artist to make his skin look sallow, crow's feet around the eyes and a wrinkled neck completed the look.

It was a complete transformation.

Peter Holmes, now Louis Francis Johns was not particularly looking forward to the protracted journey home on his planned devious route, but the alternative of flying out was obvious and fraught with the possibility of recognition and, worse still, apprehension.

Through the shopping centre he dashed in time to board the 10.50 ferry to Pulau Batam, Batam Island.

Santosa Island, the playground of Singapore, disappeared in spray as the fast ferry crossed the Singapore Strait.

The 20km, 50-minute journey was bumpy but not unpleasant, the fast boat carried about twenty other passengers a mixture of backpackers and locals, no one noticed the elderly gentleman sat quietly at the back surrounded by his luggage and engrossed in his book.

Louis (Pete) stooped and walked gingerly in order to deny his true height and appear the age printed in his forged passport.

The Batam Ferry Terminal was a modern concrete structure with western style facilities.

Louis (Pete) used the disabled toilet facilities to revert to his normal self.

With all the traces of the elderly Louis Francis John washed down the hand basin he became Ben Jolliff, as in the Caribbean.

He stowed the now redundant Louis Johns passport and pocketed the Ben Jolliff one.

A Blue Bird taxi stood at the front of the rank, Pete (now Ben) commandeered it for his journey to the Hang Nadim Batan Airport.

Twenty five minutes later he paid the driver and entered the airport, the time was almost 12:30.

Ben (Pete) entered the long airy single-storey reception area and viewed the departure board.

Lion Air had flights leaving for Jakarta at 13:25 and 19:05 he strode directly to their desk.

With luggage it was a close call to make the 13:25, he decided not to try.

Citilink Indonesia had a flight at 14:15, he paid cash for this flight and checked in immediately.

He made his way through security to the main departure to find food and drink.

It was midday, there were few other travellers, that was fine by him, it was easier to maintain his anonymity, he would have been amazed, nay, shocked, if anyone here recognised him.

With a Bintang beer in one hand and an Indonesian omelette, that had been labelled as a Martabak in front of him, he had a leisurely lunch.

The Martabak, which turned out to include chocolate on beef was not quite to his taste, but it disappeared.

Installed in his favourite rear seat of the Airbus 320 as it climbed rapidly into the clouds Ben (Pete) relaxed for the first time since leaving the cruise ship, he closed his eyes.

The Citilink Flight No. 843 landed on time, 15.55., in Jakarta.

Jakarta Airport, or to give it its full title, Soekarno-Hatta International Airport, comprises 3 Terminals, T1 and T2 reflect the local Indonesian architecture but T3 opened only a few years ago is Western modern.

Pete, using his Ben Jolliff passport arrived at Terminal 1.

Consulting the departure board it was clear that all the major airlines left from T2, he made is way there post haste, the clock showed 16.50.

The board showed a Qatar flight leaving at 17.45 via Doha, that was pushing it a bit.

Turkish Airlines had a flight via Istanbul departing 20.35.

He enquired at the Turkish Airlines counter, not only had they seats available, but his favourite seat at the back was free, he paid cash in US dollars, he was still alias Ben Jolliff.

The three hours to boarding time dragged, Jakarta. Like most International Airports is not short of places to eat, but as one would expect most outlets serve oriental style food and drink, a curry dish and a beer kept Pete (Ben) going.

His occasional visits to the boys' room were, he was pleased to note, gradually getting less painful, but still he cursed the beautiful Puteri for the unwanted gift.

Pete (Ben) had company on the flight, a young Italian returning from a friends' wedding in Bali slumped in the adjacent seat.

The smell of stale wine and the constant loud snoring made for an unpleasant few hours.

Pete (Ben) slept intermittently, at least the combined effect of the Doxycycline and the Paracetamol appeared to have taken effect, he was almost pain-free but still uncomfortable and that he thought could be psychological.

The further away from Collette he travelled, the more he thought about her, she was a nice person, beautiful and intelligent, he'd liked her a lot.

Did he feel any remorse separating her from 200k? No, maybe a little, but no more than that.

Once she realised, he wasn't going to meet her in Milan, would she conclude she'd been duped?

"She would in time," he decided, "How much time was debatable."

"Would she send the dogs after him," she wasn't at all like the demure and more gullible Helen Schmidt, "Yes," he concluded, "Sure she would."

Would those dogs, experts in following a scent, pick up his, he'd made every effort to cover those tracks, he dearly hoped he`d done it well enough.

It was dark when he landed in Istanbul and light when he left, the transit from one flight to the other passed without incident.

Chapter 56

In comparison to the long haul from Jakarta to Istanbul, the flight to Rome seemed like a short hop. A clear blue morning sky greeted him as he stepped out of Leonardo da Vinci Airport.

He thought as he passed along the arrivals corridor, *"I've cleared well over $180k after expenses on this last venture, why not a couple of days in the spectacular Holy City."*

"You speak English," he asked the taxi driver as they left the rank.

"Si," was the brisk brief reply.

"Then take me to a five-star city centre hotel and make it a good one."

"Si signor," the driver replied immediately punching a number into his mobile.

He spoke quickly and was back in full two-handed control as they met might of the Rome traffic.

Pete was impressed with the external façade of the Grand Hotel Palace and even more impressed with the reception area.

He was expected, the taxi driver's phone call, he registered in his true name, James Goodwin, Louis Francis Johns and Ben Jolliff had all served their purpose and would now leave this mortal coil forever, he was back to being himself, Peter Holmes.

The cost for two nights including breakfast, he was advised, was 650 Euros.

He generously tipped the porter that had carried his luggage into his double room.

Pete's jaw dropped; he'd become used to three stars plus accommodation but this was his introduction to five stars.

"Wow," he gasped looking around.

The room was Art deco in design and furnishings, lots of white and pastel shades, "Sumptuous," Pete described it to himself.

"A few more clients like Helen Schmidt and Collette Barnard and this is the life for me," he thought.

There ensued two full days of must-do tourist sights, the Vatican, Colosseum, Trevi Fountain and the rest, plus one enforced visit.

Dr Carney had told Pete to see his G.P. the moment he got home.

He should have been in London two days previously but there he was, still in Rome.

He could hardly walk into a hospital, clinic or doctors and say, "Hello, I have gonorrhoea, can you give me a jab of Ceftriaxone."

He needed to see a doctor, a dodgy doctor, not one that was useless, but one that operated slightly outside of the law, one that didn't keep records and readily forgot a face.

This kind of doctor was not to be found in the yellow pages, he needed to page the oracle in the shape of Manny Strauss who he knew had contacts everywhere; if he couldn't find a suitable suspect, no one could.

In less than an hour of sending an e-mail, Pete had the name and address of a discreet doctor.

The taxi dropped him outside a typical city centre four-story apartment block of classical 19th Century Roman design.

Adjacent to the large wooded door was a modern door entry panel with 16 push buttons, Pete depressed the one-labelled Sig. Fattore.

A deep voice answered "Si," Pete gave his name as John Smith, he was expected, "Enter please," said the voice.

Pete heard the click of the door release mechanism and pushed the door open.

Signore Fattore stood on the first-floor landing looking down into the all-marble reception hall, "Come please," he said in Italian style broken English.

Signore Fattore's door opened onto a luxuriously decorated and furnished lounge. *For a dodgy doc, this guy's doing okay,* thought Pete.

Pete was brief, "I've contracted a dose," he began, "I had a shot of Ceftriaxone a week ago, I was advised to see another doctor now."

"Okay let me take a look," said Fattore.

The name suited the man, he was short and fat, very fat, he struggled to kneel before Pete to carry out his examination.

Never before, but now twice inside a week a man handled his penis, Fattore's gloved fat hand gently explored his genitals, there was some pain that demanded a grimace but not a scream.

"Without samples it is difficult to say how the remedy is progressing," he said rising to his feet wheezing.

"Best if you have another shot of Ceftriaxone," he determined as Pete dressed.

"Okay," replied Pete.

"Takes a seat, make yourself comfortable, I won't be long."

Fattore left Pete to lounge on the very comfortable settee.

Pete had dropped asleep; he awoke with a start when Fattore returned an hour later.

Pete soon found out how Fattore afforded the lavish apartment, a prostitute shag cost him a further 300 Euros.

The Rome Yellow Pages did give Pete the name and address of a Scrap Merchant.

He used his tablet one last time to locate the place and how to get there using public transport.

From the open gate of the Scrap Yard he could see the machine he had hoped they possessed.

Casually he strolled past the makeshift cabin office and the huge piles of defunct cars.

The huge jaws of the hydraulic metal press were slowly closing as he nonchalantly tossed the redundant tablet into the morass of doomed metal.

All material evidence of the so-called Angolan land deal, the bogus copper reports and everything associated with Collette Bernard were gone.

He exited the scrap yard with a carefree swagger, no one saw him enter no one saw him go.

Pete's dalliance in Rome had added greatly to the expenses of his Oriental cruise adventure but there was plenty in the bank.

Chapter 57

After his extensive and circuitous travels the short flight to London took no longer than the train to Leeds. He was home, back in the "Smoke" as his dad called it.

Pete waited a couple of days before visiting his G.P.

Another kit inspection accompanied this time by the taking of a sample.

The N.H.S. Laboratory in its inimitable fashion took three days to return the results, three more added to the week or so without sex, without any pain Pete felt the need.

He was given the all-clear, there were no signs of the infection.

He phoned Marianne.

There was no response, no ring tone, just an electronic hum.

He waited a while and tried again.

No joy, maybe she'd changed her phone, strange he would have expected her to let him know.

Two more attempts convinced him that that was the case.

He phoned her on her house landline, with any luck it would be she that answered.

He was out of luck, it was her ageing husband, "Can I speak to Marianne, it's her hairdresser," he lied.

"She's not here," replied her irate husband.

"Do you know when she'll be back?" asked Pete warily.

"No, I bloody don't, she's gone, taken her clothes, and a fair slice of my bank account," he shouted, and the line died with a resounding bang as the receiver slammed down.

She's finally done a runner, she's been threatening to for a long time, thought Pete, *But she's not been in touch, that's strange.*

Almost three weeks worth of junk mail had accumulated in his letter-box on his return.

He'd done nothing with it except pile on the coffee table for looking at later, three days it had sat there, with great reluctance he gave it his attention.

There was nothing of consequence except a letter he recognised as being from HSBC.

It was a monthly statement of his working day to day current account.

He noted the bottom figure, as usual skimming over the individual transactions.

It read £550.67. A little lower than normal, but, no problem, it was time to transfer a thousand or so from his offshore retirement fund.

Pete's everyday PC that he used for gaming and net surfing sat on his desktop but his Toshiba laptop containing all his personal and working information he kept hidden.

It was contained in a sling he'd installed under the bottom shelf of the TV cabinet.

It was completely concealed and as far as he was aware no one knew it existed.

He recovered it and booted it up entering his password.

"To be safe I'll move £2000," he thought as he accessed his offshore account.

"What the fuck," he exclaimed.

The balance figure jumped out at him because there was no figure only a zero.

He repeated, *"What the fuck"* whilst flicking the cursor to Recent Transactions.

£1,233,157.89 had been paid out four days previously to another account, an account he didn't recognise, it certainly wasn't one of his.

"Not possible, not fucking possible."

He read it again, £1.2 million disappeared.

"A big fucking mistake, a computer fucking error that never fucking happens."

He sat staring at the screen.

He was about to contact the bank, but something, intuition, whatever, told him to look at his e-mails.

There it was, from him to the bank, instruction to move the money.

There followed several more between the bank and "himself" following the necessary procedures complete with the necessary passwords.

"It's not possible, it can't fucking happen, how's it happened, a zero, a big fucking zero."

He did phone the bank, they were not helpful, they had all the necessary documentation to say that it was him Peter Holmes that had authorised the payment.

When he asked about the account to which his money had been sent, they gave him an emphatic refusal, information they were not at liberty to give.

He threw the telephone across the room, it hit the wall and fell in pieces to the floor, it didn't help.

He slumped into his TV chair. His head ached; he felt sick.

"No this is not fucking happening."

"Think," he told himself, *"Think, it just can't fucking vanish, somebody…"*

"Somebody accessed the laptop."

"That same somebody knew where to find it and put it back."

"The security codes, how did he know them?"

He pondered, but not for long.

"It wasn't a he, it was a she, a computer whizz, a first in Computer Programming, a key to the flat, knowledge of the laptop's location, Marianne, the bastard."

The laptop bleeped to announce the arrival of an e-mail.

It read, 'Hi Pete, Enjoyed our years of shagging, but I'm going to enjoy your dosh more. Love, Marianne.'